The Little Death

A Paradise Ours Novel
Susan Beth Cole

Cover Art and Design by Meowlayn

Scene Break Illustration by Jen Wolpoff

A Six Ten Wolf Press Book

ISBN 9781966452003 (paperback)

First edition 2025

To anyone who has ever been told they were going to Hell because of what they do or do not believe.

And to those who believe we are destined for eternal damnation? Be careful what you wish for.

Content Note

Beware!

Spoilers below!

The Little Death is a dark, paranormal, erotic romance centered around a polyamorous couple who are strongly committed to one another but like to share. Expect MF, FF, FFF, MFM, some light sword crossing, and an orgy. Kink, BDSM, impact play, two separate scenes involving plant bondage, dubious consent, and consensual non-consent. The book starts with some light attempted murder/kidnapping via drowning.

The FMC encounters a human serial killer who ignores her safe word during what starts as a consensual MF scene and attempts to murder her. He also kidnaps and sexually assaults one side character off page. He has other victims who did not survive, but there are no graphic details.

One reference to a family dying due to illness.

Oh, right. God is a narcissistic asshole, and demons are the good guys, mostly. There is demon possession of a minor, but it is resolved, and she will be okay!

One

MINA CADERE LEANED AGAINST the railing of the large yacht, cooling in the shade of the upper deck, hoping to keep her phone in signal range. "I feel like such an asshole. Mom spent so much money on this singles cruise, and I know I'm just completely disappointing her."

There were more people out and about than she had observed the previous two afternoons, many of them likewise on their cell phones.

The cruise, limited to a group of eighty or so, all clients of the same matchmaker with whom Mina's mother, Sandra, had hired for both herself and her daughter, promised to connect Bay Area singles regardless of age, background, or socioeconomic status—provided you could afford the service to begin with. Sandra had been single the ten years since her husband's death, and she claimed she was sick of it. But it was obvious that what Mina's mother was actually sick of was seeing her eldest daughter alone and approaching her mid-thirties.

"You can't force it," Mina's sister, Dahlia, said, her voice mostly clear through their less-than-perfect network connection. "And Mom knows how flipping picky you are."

Mina watched the waves crash against the side of the yacht. Despite the chill in the air, she still felt hot from the crowded ballroom where she had spent the last hour attempting to salsa, but she shook off the notion that the water would somehow be refreshing instead of bitterly cold.

"That's why she brought me here. Forty of the most eligible bachelors San Francisco has to offer, and I still can't stand a single one of them," Mina said.

Mina's mother had been after her to settle down and have children since the minute she had crossed the stage at her college graduation. Honestly, Mina knew that Sandra had been disappointed her eldest daughter hadn't found someone special in college, although she did her best to keep it to herself. Mina would turn thirty-four this year, and though she wasn't too concerned about her biological clock, Sandra clearly heard its slowing tick-tick-tick.

Anytime the topic of another failed first date, a fun one-night stand, or a guy who had had some potential ghosting Mina after the third date arose, Sandra would visibly die a little. Dahlia and Mina would share a look, and a small bit of Mina would fall prey to that tiny monster named guilt. Guilt that she was different enough that she had never been anyone's ideal mate. Guilt that her standards were too high and she refused to settle. Guilt that her mother was growing older and running out of years to spend with any future grandchildren.

Sandra, a compassionate and emotionally intelligent woman, must have read it all over her daughter's face, so she brought up her concerns sparingly. The space Sandra instinctively gave her daughter allowed Mina to finally admit that she was ready to try something drastic. Something like a matchmaker.

Not that it had done much good. She was here now, elbow deep in marriageable bachelors—*supposedly* marriageable bachelors, but there wasn't a single one here with whom she would really even consider a drunken hookup, much less an actual date. With talking. Or, worse, exposing vulnerabilities.

No one who would accept her for her darker desires.

No one who enticed her to explore those desires.

It would be so nice to meet someone who just got her instantly. What a fucking fantasy. She sighed heavily, shaking her head.

"But not everyone is your age, right?"

"There's a mix of ages, but the matchmaker says that age is just a number when it comes to love, and I guess she would know." Mina shrugged, rolling her eyes.

"Okay," Dahlia said, "but Mom's also probably glad for some quality time with you. You've been working so much lately that we've all hardly seen you."

"I guess that's true," Mina said.

Recently, her hospital administration job had taken up a lot of her time. Between software changes, a sudden yet understandable push in pandemic preparedness by the health department, and the usual hospital drama, Mina had been working close to eighty hours a week. Even living with her mother, sister, and niece, Mina had not found time for them, often eating dinner at the office and arriving home long after her niece's bedtime. She rarely had time for herself and none at all for her art.

Mina ached a little at the thought of all her neglected paintings. It had been an age since she had last set foot in that small section of garage, partitioned off as her art studio when she moved back with her family several years ago.

"Stop being so hard on yourself and relax, Big Sis," Dahlia said.

"It would have been nice to spend the long weekend with all three of you. I miss Tabby. Are you two enjoying your mother-daughter time?" Mina bit her lip to keep that pang of sadness at bay. She'd helped raise Tabitha, staying up late for feedings when Dahlia took night classes, soothing Tabby back to sleep when she was teething. Mina had been there when Tabitha took her first steps. For years they had a weekend ritual of watching morning cartoons over milk and cereal while Dahlia did homework or, after graduation, worked on whatever paperwork she could bring home from the office. Mina would do anything for her niece. That girl held more of her heart than anyone else on the planet.

"It's been really nice," Dahlia said. "We're going to go shopping later today. She's outgrown all her jeans again."

Mina pressed herself into the railing to make space as a large group of people moved past her.

The upper rail dug into her abdomen. She felt pressure at her waist and more on her calf before the world tilted wrong side up and she found herself on the opposite side of the railing. Her scream filled her ears as gravity pulled her down.

The surface of the ocean met her like hard, cold earth. Her lungs seized in pain at the impact, and Mina made unsuccessful attempts to draw in air. Panic surrounded her as she flailed to grab purchase of anything but water.

When her body finally responded to her desperate pleading to inhale, there was no air to be had. Only water. But she couldn't stop herself from pulling it in anyway. She tried to find the surface. If she could only get there. But it was no use.

She'd lost which way was up in her confusion. And her body was preoccupied with trying and failing to eject the water in her lungs.

The cold seeped into her bones, making it hard to move, to fight.

Her vision narrowed to a pinprick before everything went dark.

⁓⟨᧬⟩⁓

When she came to, the cold had been replaced with an intense heat. She covered her face with her hands to block out the bright, red light that came at her from all sides, her eyes slow to adjust. The rocky earth beneath her warmed her back uncomfortably. The air was heavy with sulfur, and Mina coughed.

"What the fucking Hell?" Mina asked, standing on shaky legs. She felt her body. No broken bones, thank goodness, and, aside from the sulfur, there appeared to be only air in her lungs. Which didn't make any sense given her last memory. Where was she? If she had to hazard a guess, she would say that she really was in Hell.

The heat radiating from below her was oppressive. Although heat distortion prevented her from making out a lot of details, the rocky, barren landscape stretched as far as she could see, except where towering mountains blocked her view. Above her, there was no blue sky, only shadowy reds that flickered against something opaque and ragged—just more rock.

The thought that she was now in Hell, however, was too preposterous to hold on to for long. Instead, she conjured any other explanation, no matter how far-fetched, to explain her new surroundings. Perhaps this was an elaborate set for a game show, and if she kept searching she would find some hidden cameras and a C-list celebrity.

Maybe this was a trendy, new nightclub. One whose proprietor didn't understand that a theme could be taken too far.

Wherever she was, it was deserted. She couldn't hear screaming, and there were no pitchforks lying around. She marked that in the Not-In-Hell column she had started in her mind and took two tiny steps toward a ravine where lava flowed. Kicking in a loose rock, she gasped as the lava bubbled up around it. Well, the lava was real. She added that tidbit to the In-Hell column.

Mina forced herself to take several calming breaths, doing her best to ignore how the hot air burned her lungs. Okay, so most likely she was in Hell. So what? That was no reason to freak out. She would handle this the same way she handled any crisis, by taking it one item at a time, not jumping to conclusions, and only reacting to what she knew empirically to be true. She could wait to freak the fuck out until she had confirmation.

It would be just her luck to be murdered on a singles cruise and end up in the underworld. She'd never been overly religious, much to her mother's chagrin. Even so, thinking back on her life, she couldn't come up with any action so horrible as to earn her eternal damnation.

"Hi there."

Mina startled, shifting to her left to find a tall man with dirty blond hair and green eyes. The light seemed to shimmer around him as he moved. When he got closer, the intense heat and sulfuric smell dulled perceptibly. He stopped a foot away from her, and Mina could see that his eyes were speckled with gold and amber. His skin looked slightly reddish, but Mina thought it was just reflecting the surroundings. With a strong jaw, broad shoulders, and powerful legs, he was without a doubt the most gorgeous man Mina had ever seen. He wore black jeans that hugged his hips and thighs and a simple t-shirt. Definitely not dressed like a demon.

She blushed as she found herself gawking. He either didn't notice or was too polite to point it out.

Mina gasped when he braced her face between his hands and peered at her, her body stiffening in his hold. But then she felt the almost microscopic brush of his thumb against her cheekbone, and the tension slowly slipped away.

"Oh, Mina, you're in shock," he said.

How did he know her name?

"It's okay. We'll take you someplace cooler and get you water." He dropped his hands and stepped back.

The adrenaline that had been keeping Mina upright and rational ran out at that moment, and she started shaking. Her legs gave out, and she would have tumbled over if he hadn't been there to keep her upright.

"It's okay, Mina, love. I've got you," the man said before scooping her off the ground and into his arms. Reflexively, she wrapped one arm around his shoulder and rested her head against his chest.

She focused on her labored breathing and tried to stay present. It was a losing battle. She bounced gently against him as he made his way through the seemingly never-ending hellscape.

He carried her down a long corridor, around a corner, and into a cave. The heat and light receded the farther they traveled from the ravines full of lava, and Mina calmed.

As far as caves went, it was a nice space, with a black leather couch, a coffee table, and a large four-poster bed. There was even a little kitchenette to their left as they entered and a large partition that Mina guessed hid a bathroom. Mismatched throw rugs covered the ground.

Mina looked up and gasped. Glittering stars, planets, and galaxies cluttered the ceiling. They seemed to dance and move, rotating about as gravity pulled them along their foretold courses.

This cave was cooler than the surrounding cave system. It couldn't be more than sixty-eight degrees. Did that mean they were closer to the center of Hell? Mina tried to remember back to her Western Lit class. Didn't Dante find the center of Hell to be a block of ice? Clearly the guy didn't know his geology, but maybe he got the metaphysical aspects right.

The man set Mina on the couch before crouching on the floor in front of her. He placed his hands on her thighs and stared at her intently. She couldn't help squirming just a little under those large, powerful hands warming the flesh beneath her thin dress.

The pounding of her heart beat in her eardrums. She had *never* experienced this level of attraction. Usually, encountering someone this sexy triggered the construction of some serious emotional borders. It had always been easier to assume they were an asshole than to expect them to give her a second glance. But this man was staring at her like he had never desired anything else.

The thought was as arousing as it was terrifying.

The tension between them built until Mina couldn't take it any longer. "Can you please explain to me what is going on?" she asked.

"Oh, Mina," he said, "I have finally found you."

She stopped breathing at his words.

"You are the love of my eternal life. The only reason I keep going day after day in this horrible place." He paused for a moment as if he expected her to respond, but when she only stared back at him without blinking, his face adopted a contemplative look.

"Oh," he said, as the tension in his face eased, "I am Luci."As if that explained everything.

Two

MINA SCRUBBED AT HER face with her hands as she tried to make sense of what he had just said, but when she peered up at him again she was just as lost as ever. "Urm, what?"

"Let me get you a glass of water. You are starting to get that look in your eye again." He patted her knee then stood up and moved into the kitchen.

I am Luci.

Luci? As in Lucifer? No way. There was no way. And all the things he had just said—absolutely unbelievable. Who tells someone they just met that they are the love of their life? Best case scenario, he was terribly mistaken. Worst case, he was trying to manipulate her.

Men had said similar things to her in the past. They were never up to any good. She didn't believe in love at first sight, true love, or soulmates.

But here was the kicker. For some unfathomable reason, this time felt different. She found herself believing this beautiful man. *No,* she amended, *you just want to believe him.*

"Luci? That's not by any chance short for Lucifer, is it?" she asked when he placed an ice cold glass of water into her hand.

"Uh-huh! That's me!" he said with the most adorably lop-sided grin.

Oh, God. Was the Devil supposed to be this cute and likable? "What the actual Hell?"

Luci guffawed and then tucked a stray strand of auburn hair behind her ear. "You're just as beautiful as I remember."

"I'm sorry. Can you please start acting like we aren't long-lost lovers, especially since we just met, and start answering my questions?" Mina glanced around the room. She was having trouble sorting through her thoughts while looking at him. He was too damn distracting. It was completely unfair how attractive he was.

"What questions?"

"All of them. Literally every single question. And I don't mean literally in the way that everyone always says literally when they actually mean figuratively. I mean literally in the sense of every single question that has ever been asked and ever will be asked."

"Okay, well, let's see." He pursed his lips in thought. "I think I'll just answer the questions that are relevant to our situation, at least to begin with. If that's alright?" He paused, waiting for her nod to continue.

"I met you a long, long time ago. I think it's been between twelve and fifteen lifetimes for you. A thousand earth years. For me it's been, well, a really long time. I don't experience time the way a mortal does, and the Hell realms wreak even more havoc on my perception of time, but I'm rambling."

He took a moment to catch his breath, his hand reaching up to cup Mina's cheek in his palm. Mina was shocked to find herself leaning into him. His smirk deepened. Mina gulped at the throbbing in her core.

"You live. I find you on Earth. We spend beautiful, wonderful time together here—as much time as I can manage to squirrel away for us. But eventually you decide that you want to go back to your family. I send you back, and then you live out your life happily, die, and the cycle starts all over."

"I think I'm going to need some time to process all that." She shivered, her skin breaking out in goosebumps as she brought one hand to her forehead. Her other hand shook as she lifted the glass to her lips and took a long drink before setting it on the coffee table.

"You don't believe me. It's that mortal brain of yours. It can't process the eternity of your soul," Luci said as he stood up, kissing the top of her head on the way.

"How?" Mina asked. "Is that why I feel this way around you?" Mina couldn't keep her eyes off of Luci's muscular chest, inches in front of her. His green t-shirt clung to him, and, as he reached to the top of an armoire beside the couch to grab her a blanket, his shirt pulled up to reveal the perfectly defined ridges of his abs. It took everything she had to keep from reaching out to brush her fingers across his skin.

Luci wrapped the blanket around her. "You are cold and, I think, still in shock."

She knew he was right. Her brain was going in circles just trying to keep up, and yet she had to bite the inside of her cheek to keep from yawning. So she grasped on to what she could. She had not asked to be found or taken from Earth. Who would ask to be brought to Hell?

"You brought me here against my will," Mina said, throwing the blanket off her shoulders. "Despite what I'm feeling, I know that that isn't okay. You kidnapped me."

"Well, that's not strictly true," Luci said. He sat down next to her and pulled the blanket back up, tucking it around her. "When we first met, the connection was instant, at least on my part. Somehow, I won you over. That was one of the few times you stayed with me. And when you were dying, because God couldn't be bothered to give you a longer lifespan, you made me promise that I would find you and bring you back to me."

"God?" Mina asked.

"Yeah," Luci said. "Every once in a while, God used to get the bright idea to share his master plan with some humble and pious mortal. You were the third and last he ever showed all of his creation to."

"Why was I the last one?"

"Probably because you ripped him a new one."

"I did?"

"Yep. Something about how torture and awfulness only begets more torture and awfulness, and if He really wanted His creations to strive to be worthy of Him, He might try compassion and love instead."

"Huh," Mina said. "Well, yeah. Shoving someone in Hell to rot for the rest of time is pretty barbaric. Especially if you supposedly love them."

"You helped me reintroduce reincarnation. Now the only people who come here have issues to work out. Once they do, they rejoin the cycle."

"You say 'only,' but that's still mostly everyone, right?"

Luci's eyes lit up, and he nodded.

"I'm sorry. This is really hard to wrap my head around. I'm not even sure I believe there is a God or a Hell. You seem pretty real, but that doesn't mean you're the devil."

Luci chuckled, patting her arm. "That's okay. Take your time. I know this is a lot."

"Am I dead?" Mina asked. The thought should have terrified her, but instead the life she had left behind felt like a distant memory. Like a dream that is easy to remember first thing in the morning but only lingers as the knowledge that a dream had been had, that it left a profound impact at the time, and not a single detail can be recalled. Just a muddy framework.

"Oh, no. You aren't. Not yet. Not technically. Sorry, I was the one who pushed you over that railing." He gave her another lopsided grin then rushed to add, "But I am jumping in after you very soon."

Mina gave him an exasperated look and nudged his shoulder with her own. She remembered the pressure on her calf and her waist. The thought of him grabbing her and flinging her over the railing had her pulse racing, but not for the reasons she would have expected.

"Time works differently here than it does there. We have lots before you have to make a decision."

"We have time?" Mina asked. She had an idea, a very bad idea. But it refused to let her ignore it. Every time she pushed it away, it circled back with a greater intensity.

Luci nodded, a smirk tugging at the corner of his mouth drawing Mina's attention to his supple, kissable lips. His last emote had been playful, but this one was purely seductive. He wiggled his eyebrows so slightly that Mina questioned whether she had imagined it.

"You are definitely charming," Mina said, and then she kissed him. She told herself that she was kissing him because she needed to know if what he was saying was true and not because the thought of not kissing him any longer was likely to drive her completely out of her ever-loving mind.

Luci grunted and pulled her onto his lap so she was straddling him, the blanket left discarded on the couch beside them. The skirt of her dress bunched up around her hips, sticking slightly to the drying sweat on her skin. He gripped her butt in one hand and slipped the other behind her hair to cup the back of her neck. As Mina parted her lips, he wasted no time slinking his tongue into her mouth.

Mina gasped playfully and pulled her mouth from his. "What a scandal! Your tongue—it isn't forked!" Putting that tiny amount of space between them allowed her a moment of clarity, just enough to realize how irrational she was being. She had just met this man—no, this demon, if what he said was true.

"I can fork it for you if you'd like," Luci said. "But if I remember correctly, you like it when I save that for later." He bent to kiss up the side of her neck to her ear. She was lost again to her urges, and she ground against his growing hardness.

She needed to get control of herself. In the back of her mind, she knew that. Maybe she should stop calling him Luci? A nickname implied a level of familiarity, and although the brush of his lips against her skin felt like coming home, it shouldn't.

Lucifer. This was Lucifer. Satan. The devil. Underneath her. His ragged breath against her throat left her with little doubt that he craved her. The pressure of his hand on the base of her skull was almost reverential.

Holy fuck. Lucifer, the morning star, the light bringer, the devil incarnate, wanted her. Claimed he loved her.

Her reaction to that notion gushed from her, pasting her underwear to every curve of her labia and rendering the cloth useless.

So, that backfired. Talking. Talking was a good distraction, right? Pressing her palms to his chest, she leaned back. After a deep breath, she counted to three.

"You seriously have me at a disadvantage. If, big if, I choose to believe you. Your story is a little far-fetched. I'd have to seriously power-up my already overactive imagination to even consider it. For all I know, you say this to all the girls, and you'll have your way with me and throw me into a pit of never-ending Hellfire."

He thrust against her, the texture of his jeans scraping against her soaked panties, and she blushed at the moan that escaped her parted lips.

"I would never do that! Never to you, anyway." Luci said before burying his face into her cleavage. She pushed her arms against her sides and thrust her chest out at him. Her nipples were hard and pebbled through the bodice of her sundress. Luci roughly bit one.

"Gah! That hurts!"

"You love it," Luci mumbled into her skin.

Equal parts surprised and thrilled that he was right, Mina said, "It seriously creeps me out that you know that."

"Does it also creep you out that I know that the thought of being thrown into Hellfire gets you more than a little wet?"

Some look must have crossed her face because he added, "Stop feeling fucked up about it. You are perfect."

"What?!" Mina asked, pushing back so that she was only just barely perched on his knees.

Luci shrugged. "Am I wrong?"

"Fuck," Mina said, shaking her head. "Okay, mister know-it-all, if you really know me so well, why don't you prove it?"

Three

"CHALLENGING THE DEVIL? OH, you are in for it now."

Luci pushed Mina onto her back and leaned over her. He grabbed her wrists in one large hand and held them above her head. As he stared down at her, she could feel him taking in every detail—how her breathing had hitched when he had grabbed hold of her, the way she was biting her bottom lip, and how the top of her dress was straining against her chest.

"Leave your hands there," he ordered as he released her wrists. He dragged his hand up the length of her arm, his touch never straying as his fingers skated across her ticklish armpit, along her collarbone, and to her throat, where he gripped her firmly. Her eyelids lowered as she lifted her chin to grant him better access, and he smirked at her.

He continued to hold her with one hand while he hitched up the hem of her dress, shoved a hand into her panties, and rubbed his middle finger against her slit.

Mina's fingers twitched, but she didn't give into the urge to touch him in return. She knew in that moment that she would gladly give herself to him, would do anything he asked so long as she could continue to feel like she belonged to him. A flash of fear registered briefly, but the pleasure Luci gave quickly overcame it.

"You are soaked," Luci said, "already." His eyes were so dilated that the green had all but disappeared. He removed his hand from her throat and wrapped her legs around his waist.

Luci stood, gripping Mina's ass in one hand and her back in the other so she rose with him. She flung her arms around his neck.

After almost tripping over the coffee table, Luci stumbled clumsily to the bed.

"So smooth," Mina laughed. But the thought that she'd somehow unbalanced his equilibrium made her core tighten.

"Just you wait," Luci said as he threw Mina onto the bed. She squeaked. "Now, I'm going to need you to remove your clothes."

Mina looked down at her pink sundress and sandals. "Okay," she said, shrugging playfully before flicking her shoes onto the floor and climbing up onto her knees. She grabbed the bottom of her dress and slowly pulled it up, slipping it over her toned thighs, her flat stomach, and her bra-clad breasts. Then she flung it at him. Luci caught it and chucked it to the couch.

"Are you sure you want me to remove all my clothes? I mean, you don't want to see my boring body. Someone like you could have anyone they wanted," Mina said. She wiggled her shoulders at him and tried not to giggle.

"Right? And yet for some reason you're all I can think about," Luci said as he joined Mina on the bed. "For the last million-plus years, there's been nothing on my mind but you."

"That's a pretty intense thing to say to a girl you just met." Mina barely had time to unhook her bra before Luci was on her. He tugged the bra from her arms and flung it blindly behind him. It landed in the kitchen sink.

"Allow me," Luci said as he scooted down the bed and tucked his fingers into the sides of her lemon-patterned panties. Brushing his lips against her belly button before kissing a trail to her left hip, he freed her from her last stitch of clothing.

Luci traveled from her thigh to her knee before moving his way in between her legs, inching closer to her apex. Tickling her with his breath. Tormenting her with his listlessness.

"Mmm, you smell good," Luci said as he buried his nose against her clit, surprising a squeal out of Mina. She ran her hands through his hair and massaged his scalp, eliciting a purr from him. His tongue flicked out briefly against her, and she arched into him.

"Yeah," Luci said with a frown. He sat up and devoured her with his eyes. "This isn't really working for me."

"Oh, no. Here's the part where you throw me into Hellfire."

"Nope. It's worse than that," Luci said, snapping his fingers before Mina even had the chance to gulp.

Lengths of silky rope wrapped themselves around her wrists and tugged them toward the headboard, more similarly tying and spreading her ankles.

"That's better. A blank canvas to work on."

Mina wiggled in the bonds, and Luci, narrowing his eyes at her, snapped his fingers again and the bonds tightened.

"That's cheating. You're using superpowers," Mina said. She couldn't struggle one bit, but she wasn't uncomfortable either.

"They aren't superpowers. It's just me," Luci said. He tilted his head to the side, studying her intensely. "Tell me if you start to lose feeling, if you get stiff, or if anything becomes too much."

"I will."

"Promise?"

"Promise." She nodded and struggled to hold back the smile that threatened to reveal just how well he was doing.

Luci fell on her once more, grabbing her breasts and gently kneading them before pinching her nipples. He tugged gently, trapping her left nipple in his mouth as he moved his hand down to her vulva. His fingers rubbed against her lips as he ground his palm into her clit. One moist digit slipped inside her briefly, only to retreat and tease her entrance. Mina strained against her bonds, but they held her immobile.

"Oh, God," she moaned.

Luci let go of her nipple and chuckled, "Not even a little bit." He moved up her body and kissed her mouth.

"Sorry," Mina said, biting her bottom lip as he slid his finger into her again.

"Next time, I'll make you pay," Luci said, working his finger in and out of her, curling it slightly on the exit so he hit her spongy g-spot.

"Oh, God," Mina moaned again without thinking.

"And I warned you and everything," Luci said as he forcefully added two more fingers, shoving them into her. She stretched to accommodate them, but not without a little pain. A pain she found only enhanced the pleasure. He pumped away at her with abandon, all the while watching her intently.

"Oh, Luci!" Mina balled her hands into fists, curling her toes until her feet ached.

"That's better." But he did not relent. Not even when a pitiful sound erupted from her.

"You ready to come?" Luci asked.

"Mmhmm."

"Then come, my little slut." Luci pressed against her internal bundle of nerves and ground his thumb against her clit. She exploded, but his fingers kept thrusting, and he teased her entrance with a fourth.

"Think you can handle another digit?" he asked.

She whimpered at the thought and shook her head.

"Later then," he promised. "I want to see you come again." He picked up the pace, slamming into her as deeply as possible. She could feel him trying to spread his fingers out, but her channel was too tight. With the pressure mounting once more, she knew she couldn't keep from coming for long. But she wanted it to last forever.

He moved down her body again and wrapped his lips around her clit, alternating between sucking and flicking his tongue against it. Although she could feel herself right at the edge, she tried to hold off.

"Stop being selfish, Mina, and give me what I want," Luci demanded before biting her clit hard. She screamed and unraveled, thinking she would injure herself the way she bucked. But she didn't care. Couldn't. Not when he was making her feel like the force of a galaxy springing into existence.

As she came back down, Luci flicked his wrist and her bonds evaporated. He scooped her up, rolling over so that she was on top of him, her head pressed to his chest.

"That was amazing," Mina said.

"Convinced I was telling the truth? Ready to stay with me forever?" Luci asked as he stroked her hair.

Mina believed him. *She fucking believed him.* And all it had taken were two orgasms? Granted, the two best orgasms she'd ever had, but still.

It wasn't just the way he could play her body like a fiddle. It was how attentive he had been. How he checked in with her. Gave her a way out. He had suggested that he knew her on a cosmic level and then proved himself correct by acknowledging that she still knew herself better.

"I'm convinced, but don't ask me that other question yet. I haven't orgasmed that hard since, well, ever, and it is definitely clouding my judgment."

The pleasure must have killed some very important brain cells, because she truly believed this creature to be her soulmate. His touch alone woke up parts of her that had long been dormant. All those things about herself that she had always been scared to share—he not only knew about them but adored each and every one.

"Oh, you have definitely come that hard," Luci said. "You just don't remember."

Mina propped her chin on his chest so she could look up at him. "Any chance I'll get those memories back?"

"Eh, you could always do a past life regression. No guarantees the results would be accurate," Luci said. "But some might come back to you. It has happened before. It's a lot of memories, though, so you wouldn't want them all back at once."

"Do you think maybe I just inherently know what you like?" Mina asked as she unfastened his jeans.

"I think you'll happily find that what I like is you," Luci said, stripping off his shirt.

Four

Oh, boy. He was doing it again, saying those things she so desperately wanted to hear. Any reservations she had about their situation were quickly dissolving into nothing. So, this is what it felt like to be a fool for someone.

"You have got to stop it with that stuff. My cheeks hurt from blushing," Mina said as she wiggled his jeans off his body. "Oh! Commando! You are the devil, aren't you?"

"What can I say?" Luci shrugged.

"But no tail? You don't completely come as advertised." She winked at him before grabbing the base of his cock in her hand. He was big, substantial even, but not so big that she was running to the other side of Hell or worrying that he wouldn't fit. She climbed between his legs and relished the feel of his velvety, hard length against her cheek before nuzzling her nose into his balls and inhaling. She pulled back abruptly and gasped.

"I don't smell that bad, do I?" Luci asked.

"I could come from that smell alone," Mina said before going in for more. He smelled musky, like undiluted want. But did he taste as good as he smelled? Without delay, she flicked her tongue against him.

Eyes closing in bliss, savoring his unique blend of skin and salt, she licked her way from his testicles up to his shaft then circled her tongue around the head. Her eyes drifted up to Luci's to find him resting his head against the pillows with his eyes closed.

Mina took a deep breath before plunging her mouth down over Luci's cock. Bobbing up and down on it, she didn't rush as she worked to engulf more and more of him into her until the head of his penis bumped against her throat, setting off her gag reflex. Chills swept down her spine, and goosebumps popped up over her arms.

When she pulled off of his cock for a brief moment to catch her breath, Luci's gaze seared her with desire. She had never felt more sexy, even drooling all over him and her diaphragm still protesting.

She had only given a handful of blow jobs. Mostly to ex-boyfriends with whom she had only shared a small piece of her sexual self and never any of her deep desires. Never before had she wanted so desperately to please a man as she wanted to please this demon. It made her brave and ambitious. The thought of taking him as deep as she could was too good to resist, despite her limited experience.

Hesitating only a little, Mina slipped her lips around his hard length again. This time, though, she anticipated gagging. She pushed past it and found her nose pressed against his groin, her tongue flat along the underside of his cock. Pride swelled in her chest, and the urge to bring Luci to the brink overwhelmed all others.

Luci groaned and cupped the back of Mina's head. She reached up and slid her hand across his, pressing her fingertips against him and willing him to take charge. His fingers slid into her hair, gripping it in a tight hold and using it to control her pace. Mina moved one hand down to cup his balls while the other caressed its way up his hip and waist, ending on his stomach.

Luci tightened his hold on Mina's hair and pumped her mouth furiously onto him. When she wasn't gagging, she was moaning. Her drool pooled on the bed under them. It did not take long before Luci finally pumped his ejaculate into the back of her throat, just as Mina's jaw started to go numb. She happily gulped him down and licked him clean before he pulled her off his cock and tugged her back up the bed.

"Mmm," Mina said, exploring the contours of his chest with her hand and nuzzling into his neck. "I liked that way more than I should have."

"No, no guilt here over what you like," Luci said, kissing the top of her head.

"I'm kind of shocked how much I liked letting you use me like that," Mina said.

"First of all, you were completely in control. Secondly, you're in a safe space. Hell is a safe space, and so am I. Besides, what happens in Hell stays in Hell."

"Does it though? It's hard for me to imagine demons being all that concerned about keeping secrets," Mina said as she left a trail of tiny kisses across his chest.

"Well, you should, because they keep all the secrets. And it's your fault that they do. There's that whole client ther-apist-confidentiality thing going on now." Luci's fingertips danced across the flesh on Mina's upper back.

"What do you mean?" Mina asked.

"We don't torture people anymore, unless they would find it beneficial. Now we spend a lot of time reviewing life choices and coaching people through learning healthy behaviors."

"And that works?"

"For a lot of people, yes. And for everyone else, it basically amounts to the same as torture." Luci's hand rested lazily on her upper arm, tracing gentle circles.

"All the demons were okay with making this switch?" Mina asked.

"Nope. Not even close. There are a bunch of demons moping to this day. The worst of the bunch do what they can to escape Hell and cause all kinds of mayhem on Earth."

"Escape from Hell? Could you do that?" Mina asked.

"Not very often. It takes a lot of energy and willpower. There are ways to summon me, but don't you even think about it being an option. It's a very dangerous thing to try and hard to control. You never know who you might end up getting," Luci said.

When they made eye contact across the expanse of his muscular chest, he growled at her in a low rumble. Clearly he did not want to continue this line of discussion and could read the defiance on her face.

Mina ignored his warning and tickled her way down Luci's stomach to his hip. "I'm starting to think you might be worth the danger."

Luci snapped up her hand and rolled her so she was on her back and underneath him, his eyes flashing with intensity. "If you feel that way, then choose to stay. Be here with me. Be my Persephone."

"I know I only just met you, but the thought of spending eternity with you—well, nothing has ever sounded nicer," Mina said, pushing up on her elbows and pressing her lips to Luci's. As their mouths met, Luci immediately opened for her, letting her swoop her tongue in and play against his. He bit down lightly, just enough to elicit a gasp of surprise.

Mina wrapped her arms around him, enjoying the feel of his smooth back, while he tugged her bottom lip between his teeth. His fingers dug into the flesh of her breast. He flicked her left nipple and pinched it, rolling it between his fingers. After tugging him closer and wrapping her legs around him, she thrust her hips against his.

Mina moaned and turned her head away, "Luci."

Luci continued to kiss her cheek, her neck, her ear, sucking her earlobe into his mouth.

"Seriously, Luci," Mina protested.

"Hm?" Luci asked, kissing down to her collarbone.

"No one has ever made me feel this way. You are intoxicating. How am I supposed to make a rational decision in this state of mind?" Mina asked.

"Sorry. I can't answer your question right now. I'm a little busy," Luci said as he kissed his way down to her right breast, flicking his tongue out against her nipple.

"Luci, I'm serious."

Luci looked up at her with a crooked smile. "I know. But you have time, and I would like to enjoy this with the hopes that maybe you'll stay. Just a little longer before we both have reality crash down on us, please?"

Mina nodded. "More kisses, please."

Luci obliged, sweet at first, and Mina felt all of his love in it. She couldn't really make sense of it yet, but she was starting to feel like she didn't need to. It all felt so real. As Luci intensified the kiss, his hand made its way to Mina's clit. He rubbed it in circles, then dipped his middle finger into her.

"More," Mina mumbled into his mouth, bringing her hand in between them so she could stroke his beautiful cock. It grew larger and harder in her hand. Luci hunched over her so he could continue to kiss her as he nudged the head of his penis at her opening.

"Yes." Mina's moan was muffled by the ongoing kiss. Luci slid into her agonizingly slowly, and once he was in, he stopped. He didn't move for another half a minute while he lazily kissed her. Not until she was whimpering underneath him, digging her fingernails into his back in frustration.

Mina yanked away from his kiss with a pouty grunt. "I thought you said that you didn't torture people anymore."

"I would break every rule for you," Luci said as he played with her clit, his gaze never once wandering, devouring her as if he could copy her into his mind and keep her forever. "But you and I both know that you are one of those people who crave it."

"Fuck me, Luci," Mina said. "Please."

"All you had to do was ask, Mina," Luci said as he started to drive into her. She lifted her hips in response. Luci ground against her clit and angled his pelvis so that his cock rocked against her g-spot. Before she knew it, Mina was crashing into her orgasm and falling apart at the seams. She clenched down on Luci's length, and soon he was coming, too.

"That was over too fast." Mina frowned. "Reality setting in." She buried her face against his chest.

"I'm not out of you yet," Luci said. "Who says it's over?" He started to move again. "We haven't even got to the real kinky stuff yet."

Mina whimpered as Luci picked up the pace. He grabbed her ankles, prompting her to bend her knees, and pushed up until her knees were above her shoulders. "Are you ready?" he asked, waiting for her to nod before pounding into her.

The angle was exquisite, hitting her in all the right places, reaching new depths. Only her grip on him kept her grounded.

He snapped his fingers, and silky ropes secured her ankles to her thighs, snaking behind her knees then around the headboard, but leaving her hands free, before tying themselves off.

The heat of his breath found her pebbled nipple while his fingers pinched and tugged at her clit.

Mina's toes curled as her pleasure built, and sparks ignited along her spine. Luci inherently knew the exact amount of pressure to employ to send her speeding toward the edge and didn't relent.

The orgasm that hit Mina was devastating and seemingly never ending. It rolled on as Luci slammed into her, twisting both her clit and biting her nipple in unison. His supernatural stamina and strength seemed endless as he moved over her.

"You're nothing but my dirty girl," he whispered in her ear. "You will be mine forever. I already own a piece of your soul." His teeth marked her neck. It would bruise, but Luci didn't break the skin. He left a trail of bites from her neck to her collarbone before biting down on her opposite nipple.

Her orgasm crescendoed again. "Yes," she moaned. "Make me yours. Take all that you want from me."

"Do you want to feel my devil tail in your ass, my filthy little human?" Luci growled. "I bet you do."

Mina opened her mouth to answer, but found that he had gagged her with another silk rope. She knew he didn't have a tail, so how could he offer one? Then she saw it hovering over his back. It was bright red with a bulbous tip that reminded her of her favorite butt plug. It wasn't very large but had her shaking and salivating all the same.

Luci pulled out of Mina, and the loss lashed at her. His smirk wasn't playful. It was predatory and possessive. His tail dipped into her pussy, fucking deeply into her, nudging at her cervix, before retreating. His cock once more took up residence inside her.

He stopped all movement as his tail moved between their legs and nudged at her anus.

"If you need me to stop at any time, tap three times anywhere on my body," Luci instructed. Mina panted around the silk rope and nodded.

Luci pushed forward with his tail slowly, backing off only to return again, until it popped through her tight ring. Because the lubrication was sufficient, because he'd been slow but persistent, she felt no pain. Only a bit of pressure, then pure ecstasy. Her screams of pleasure filled the gag as his tail tip continued pressing forward until it was lodged fully inside of her.

He pounded away at her from both ends. Her toes flexed, and her eyes rolled back as she came yet again. The last thing she registered before passing out in bliss was the feeling of his cum gushing into her.

When she came to, only a few moments had passed. She was no longer gagged, but Luci had moved between her spread legs and was lapping up their combined juices. His forked tongue flicked out against her clit, and her bottom lip quivered, her eyes filling with tears.

"So intense," she mumbled but did not request that he stop. She wanted to see how far he could take her.

Luci shrugged and gave her a few more laps until her tears spilled over. When she came again, every one of her muscles contracted, and she shook uncontrollably. The pain was intense, but it only twined with the pleasure, heightening it to new peaks. Her molecules unraveled and flew apart. There would be nothing left of her but what he made her feel.

He chuckled as he licked his face clean and sat up. Her bonds disappeared.

Mina turned on her side, curling in on herself. She focused on her breathing as she willed her atoms back into formation. Luci's warmth enveloped her as he spooned her, using an edge of silk rope to clean her face of tears.

"Was that too much?" he whispered, sounding like a scared child worried he might lose the privileges to his favorite toy.

"Yes," Mina said, "but it was also perfect."

Luci made a contented sound and buried his nose in her hair.

Moments of comfortable silence passed with only the steady rise and fall of Luci's chest against her back to calm her.

"So, how much time did you say we have?" Mina asked.

"Anything longer than three days is risky."

"Yep. Still more unanswered questions."

"It depends on whether you'd like to be dead for a minute or five," Luci said. "We should really keep it to no more than three minutes if you decide to go back. I wouldn't want you to suffer any brain damage."

"And three minutes Earth time is equivalent to three days Hell time?"

"Yep, pretty much."

"Three days," Mina said, her mind whirling to compute the implications on Luci's lifespan and failing miserably. "So we could get some shut eye? Together?"

"Mmhmm," Luci said as he buried his face against her neck. He worked a leg between hers and then a black-as-night feathered wing draped over her, surrounding her in warmth better than any blanket. It filled her completely.

"I know this feeling," Mina said. It was the same every night. Right before sleep claimed her, she would feel someone engulf her in warmth, whisper how perfect she was or how much they loved her, and help her drift to sleep. It was so fleeting that she always assumed she imagined it. That it was just some trick she had learned early on to help herself fall asleep.

"I know you do," Luci said. "I'm with you every night. When you are in between consciousness and sleep, I can visit you. And I always do."

"I thought I was just self-soothing," Mina said.

"It's always been me. Nothing or no one can keep us from those few stolen seconds," Luci said.

"You have wings," Mina reached up and traced the boning of his wing with her fingers, and Luci's breath hitched.

"Fallen angel, remember?" Luci kissed her neck. "Now get some sleep so I can ravage you when we wake up."

"But you didn't have wings before. Or a tail."

"I have many forms." Luci pressed his lips to her shoulder. "Hush." He brushed her hair behind her ear and rubbed her temple.

And Mina couldn't keep her eyes open a moment longer.

Five

MINA WOKE WITH A start, a heavy weight on her chest. Where was Luci? A frantic millisecond later, she relaxed. Luci was the weight.

He had nestled into her breasts, using them like pillows. His wings and tail had disappeared, and she wondered if they had ever been real or just another magic trick. The thought only left her feeling more discombobulated. She couldn't tell reality from fiction, and she didn't even know the time.

"Luci! Did we oversleep?" Mina asked as she tried to push down the panic.

Luci looked up at her, his face the picture of calm. "No. Of course not. Eight hours on the dot."

"So we have two and a half days left?" Mina asked, clutching him to her.

"About that. But I take it from this reaction that you've already decided to go back."

Thoughts of holding tiny, newborn Tabitha sprung into her mind. If she stayed in Hell, she would never see her grow up. And her sister. Dahlia was her best friend. They'd raised a child together, coordinating college classes and work schedules in those early years. They'd gotten close through those struggles. And, sure, her mother was aging, but she had at least two decades left in her, years that Mina would miss. She couldn't, wouldn't, be the one to cut that time short.

"I have to, Luci. You're asking me to leave my mom, my sister, and my niece. I can't abandon them," Mina said, her eyes pleading.

Luci only frowned.

"But the thought of leaving you, it's giving me panic attacks."

He kissed her chest. "No panic attacks. Remember, I'm with you even when I'm not."

"But what if it isn't enough? After all this."

"I just need to overload you so much that you get sick of me. Then you won't have any qualms about leaving," Luci said. He cupped her face and rested his forehead against hers. "The very last thing I want is for you to feel conflicted. I will support your decision. For these few stolen days, it's always worth it."

He was sweet to say so, but his wasn't the only opinion that mattered. There were a litany of reasons why she couldn't just enjoy a weekend with him and be satisfied. No one she met in the future could ever possibly replace him. They wouldn't even come close. That meant a lifetime of the loneliness he had only just helped her shake off. The thought hit the pit of her stomach like a brick.

But he had mentioned demons escaping Hell. If it were her only hope, she didn't care about the perils.

"Tell me how I can bring you to my world," Mina demanded.

"I told you that it's too dangerous," Luci said.

"And I told you that *you're* worth it," Mina said.

"You don't know that, Mina. It's difficult to summon a regular demon, and I'm Satan."

"What's the worst that can happen if I summon someone else? Can't they just pass the summons along to you?" Mina ran her fingers through his blond hair, scratching his scalp lightly with her fingernails. His purr as he pressed closer to her settled some of her growing anxiety.

"A few can and might, but there are rules about summoning a demon. It takes energy from them, and they expect something in trade. None of them can harm you. I told you I own a piece of your soul, remember? Well, you own a piece of mine. And while that grants you a certain level of protection, it doesn't grant you a free pass." He traced his fingers up and down her side lazily.

"What would they do?" Mina asked as Luci's fingertips lightly tickled across her tummy.

"Spread your legs," Luci whispered in her ear, and she complied.

"Luci, what would they do?"

He raised up on one elbow so he could more easily see her. "Tease you, fuck you, humiliate you." Luci lightly slapped her vulva with a cupped hand. Mina gasped at the sting that shot tingles to her toes. "Some of them may choose to harm those around you, since they can't harm you directly." He flicked lightly at her nipples, and they grew into stiff peaks.

"What?" Mina asked, her eyes large, her breaths coming faster. "You would let them?"

"I would have to, Mina. Like I said, there are rules," Luci said. "Also, I never mind sharing you." He slapped her vulva again, and she growled.

"Can you prepare me for what they might do to me?"

He gripped her hip, vibrating his hand and pulling her full attention to him. "You are seriously considering this." He studied her face like he was seeing something new in her.

Mina swallowed then nodded.

"We only have two and a half days."

"So, kink me up now, and then tell me about all the ways for me to bring you into my world," Mina said.

"I am agreeing to the kinking. I am not agreeing to that second bit," Luci said, climbing out of bed and reaching a hand out to Mina. She took it, and he didn't just pull her off the bed but plopped her over his shoulder.

"Eek! Where are we going?" Mina asked.

"To my torture chamber," Luci said nonchalantly as he delivered a strong, open-palmed smack to her ass. "And there's a spank in it for you for every additional question you pose."

"Aha! I already posed all the questions in the universe, remember? So I've technically asked them all already."

The sound of the next slap registered before the sting. "Keep it up and I'll be playing the drums on these gorgeous globes."

"You think you got the rhythm for that?" Mina goaded.

Luci's hand came down twice more, once on each cheek, as he carried her past the partition and into a marble bathroom. He opened a door built into the cavern wall on the far end of the room, carried her through it, and dumped her unceremoniously down on a table.

The back of her knuckles brushed a metal hinge. A small gap ran the width of the top.

Before Luci slipped a blindfold over her eyes, Mina got a quick glimpse of the room, but there wasn't much to see. Other than the table, the room was bare.

After placing a gentle kiss against her temple, Luci pushed her flat. Rough rope coiled around her limbs and pulled them taut, denying her the ability to so much as wiggle.

"I've got you exactly where I want you," Luci cackled. For a moment, Mina panicked. Maybe this was all just a game to him and she only a conquest. Maybe this was how he got his kicks.

But then she remembered him draped over her the night before, and the way his warmth made her feel like she had come home. And despite all of the uncertainty, or maybe because of it, moisture had gathered between her legs at that cackle. He had said he knew what she liked, and he was delivering on that promise.

His hot breath hit her ear before he said softly, "Tell me if any of this becomes too much."

She heard a buzzing sound and then felt the hum of a vibrator on her clit. All of her muscles tensed. Luci rubbed the toy up and down her slit before pressing it against her pussy. It wasn't very large and slid comfortably inside her.

The bonds connecting Mina's lower limbs to the table slackened, and her ankles were lifted into the air. There must have been a hook in the ceiling, because the ropes grew taught again, pulling her legs straight and up.

Three clicks sounded, and Mina's equilibrium faltered. She thought she was falling as the half of the table beneath her hips and ass suddenly dropped away, the hinge allowing it to fold down.

The cold air of the cave brushed against her bottom, and she felt completely exposed. He had access to not just both of her entrances but also her sensitive butt cheeks.

The blindfold, the rapid change in position, the sudden disappearance of half the table left her disoriented and on edge. It only heightened her anticipation.

Luci's lips on her labia both thrilled and grounded her. She knew he planned to push her, to let her plummet through pleasure, but that he'd be there at the bottom of that hellish pit to catch her.

Luci sucked on her clit before tracing her lips with his tongue on his way to her tight rosebud. He circled it with his tongue, doing his best to lubricate it with his saliva.

"Luci," Mina gasped.

"Trust me."

"I do," Mina said. And Luci slipped the tip of his smallest digit into her. He must have lubed it too, as it went in smoothly. The vibrations of the fake phallus inside her reverberated through his finger. She wanted more. His pinky was smaller than the tip of his tail had been, but he still gave her a moment to adjust to the feeling before working it in and out of her. Mina quivered.

This was different than the previous night when he had fucked her ass with abandon. And it was eliciting a different reaction. She wanted him to take her hard again, but she could be patient. Especially if waiting meant he could make her feel this good.

Luci swapped his pinky for his middle finger, pushing it farther into her and picking up his pace. Bending down to suck her clit between his lips, he bit her gently then flicked his tongue against her nub.

Mina whined, so close to coming. But she needed something. Luci's chuckle rumbled against Mina's clit before he pulled back.

"What do you need?" Luci asked.

"More," Mina said. "I don't know what, but more."

"Don't worry. I know exactly the thing. You just have to convince me to give it to you."

"Convince you?"

"Not with your words," Luci said as he placed a fabric gag into her mouth and secured it around her head.

Mina attempted to protest but only produced muffled consonants. Luci chuckled as he removed his middle finger, inserting his thumb in its place. Mina gasped and then mumbled more unintelligible words into her gag.

"I don't think you quite grasp the concept of the gag, my love," Luci said. He brushed a rogue strand of hair from her forehead as he began to pump his thumb in and out of her. "I'm going to fuck your brains out in a minute," Luci whispered into her ear, and she exploded. Luci didn't stop fucking her ass with his thumb. Not even when she started begging or when the blindfold dampened with tears. She came again.

At the top of her climax, Luci removed his thumb and inserted a medium-sized butt plug. He pulled out the vibrator and placed it against her clit. Mina felt the head of Luci's cock teasing her vaginal opening. He ran it between her labia before slipping inside of her wet sheath.

"You are so tight," Luci growled. "So wet."

Their intoxicating smell filled the room. Mina breathed in deeply through her nose. A moment of calm fell over them as he ran a finger along her jaw.

When his fingertip retreated, Luci plundered her. The top part of the table must have been bolted to the floor. She couldn't imagine that the piece of furniture would otherwise stay put against the onslaught of his rhythm. Even with the force of each thrust, he kept the vibrations perfectly placed against her clit. His balls slammed into the base of Mina's butt plug, jostling it inside of her.

Mina came with a fury. Her toes curled, and she screamed so loud that the gag might as well not have been there. Her vaginal muscles clamped and spasmed around Luci's cock, and he shot his load into her, grunting with each twitch.

Luci stopped moving, but Mina couldn't keep from shaking. Goosebumps covered her arms and legs. Luci didn't waste a moment before freeing her and pulling out her gag. He scooped her up into his arms and carried her to the bathroom.

With a wave of his hand, the large bathtub filled with warm water and the jets spurted to life. Luci climbed into the bathtub with Mina. He clutched her to his chest as she clung to him. Mina rested her head on Luci's shoulder, the warmth from the bath engulfing them.

"You asleep?" Luci murmured into Mina's hair.

"I must be. There's no way this is real."

"Not real, huh?"

"Ouch! Did you just pinch me?" Mina sat up so she could shoot Luci an indignant look.

"Still think this is a dream?"

"No," Mina pouted. "Maybe a nightmare."

"Let me make it up to you." The shelves around the bathtub held a plethora of soaps, bath salts, shampoos, and conditioners. Luci unscrewed the cap on an unmarked bottle and dumped some in the tub. The room filled with a flowery scent, and the bath water took on a pink hue.

"Bubble bath?" Mina asked. She scooped up the bubbles that were forming around them and blew them at Luci.

"Yeah, but maybe you can't handle it. You're getting them all over the place," Luci said before growling and grabbing Mina's wrist in one of his hands. He leaned over and kissed her hard.

Mina moaned into the kiss before pushing Luci away. "You have to stop that. My body needs a break."

"Oh, yeah," Luci said. "I knew that. That's why the relaxing bubble bath and candles. I can't think clearly around you."

"Candles? What candles? There are no candles."

"There aren't?" Luci did a quick scan of the room. "Well crap. There were supposed to be." With a shrug and a snap of his fingers, Luci conjured candles on every open surface, and the overhead lights snapped off. The shadows cast by the flames flickered across the ceiling and walls.

After crawling on top of Luci and snuggling against him, Mina rested her head on his shoulder. "You are definitely entertaining," she said before kissing his neck. His skin was smooth and firm against her lips, so she kissed him a second time.

He tapped his fingers against the base of the butt plug still snug in her ass.

"I said stop," Mina said, but she was laughing, already ready for more. He smacked her butt cheek hard and bubbles flew out of the bathtub.

"I really can't wait to fuck this ass," Luci said.

She nuzzled against him for a minute, enjoying the quiet. The only sound was that of the water dripping from Luci's hand as he stroked her hair.

"Luci?"

"Hm?"

"Earlier, you said you didn't mind sharing me. Who have you shared me with?"

"Are you sure you want to know?" He started pulling at the base of the plug, obviously trying to turn her on so she'd definitely say yes.

"I wouldn't have asked if I didn't want to know." She found his nipples with her thumbs, rubbing them in circles.

"Humans, demons. Especially demons with big, knobby cocks." He was fucking her with the bulbous toy now, and she pushed up onto her knees to give him better access.

"I really love watching another girl go down on you or fucking your tight cunt with her fist."

Mina gasped. "Luci!" But she smiled.

"What? I asked you if you were sure you wanted to know." He shrugged. "Turn around, please. I want your ass in my face."

She obliged him, wiggling her hindquarters as she rested her head and arms on the far edge of the tub. He grabbed her globes and sunk his fingertips into her flesh before pulling back one hand and bringing it down with a resounding thwack.

"Ouch!" she yelped. He rubbed the sting away.

"That didn't hurt that much," he said and kissed the offended cheek.

"Do it again," she requested, jiggling her butt for him.

"I can deny you nothing, my love," he said, smacking her other side. She vocalized once more, but he paid her no mind before swatting her right buttocks. The spanks fell in a regular rhythm, and in about five minutes Mina's moans filled the air and her legs threatened to give out. Even though she hurt, the warmth was tantalizing. She rested the full weight of her head on her arms, drifting into that blissful space where she could just be.

"You are dripping," Luci said, swooping in with his tongue for a taste. He stopped his light punishment and rubbed her down, pouring on an ointment that took away the edge and left her tingly.

"I'm going to move you up to the next size," Luci said as he began to twist her butt plug. Tugging on it, he slowly took it from her, fucking it back into her and then pulling it back a few times. Finally, he tugged it free and set it on the side of the bathtub.

He must have conjured the next one from thin air, a trick Mina was learning to anticipate. She could feel herself opening for the larger plug as Luci teased her with its tip. But he quickly put it aside and instead inserted a syringe full of body-temperature lube and pushed down on the stopper. Mina shivered with anticipation while Luci applied more lube to her opening with his fingers.

The juxtaposition of the cooler lubricant with the warm hand prints decorating her bottom and the heat from the bathwater left Mina dizzy.

Once she had been adequately prepared, Luci began to push the toy into her ass. He went slowly, giving her plenty of time to adjust until it settled comfortably inside her with only the base exposed.

"One more of those, and I think you'll be ready for me," Luci said as he grabbed her around the thighs and pulled her back, turning her, so she was resting against him once more, her head tucked under his chin.

"More?" She asked.

"In a little bit. After you rest."

"More!" she demanded.

"Maybe once you have regained your ability to speak more than monosyllabically."

"Hmph." She nuzzled against him. She was getting pretty sleepy. But her mind protested her exhaustion. They had only just woken up. They should have had hours more until she needed sleep.

"I love you, Mina." Luci rubbed gentle circles on her back.

Her eyelids were indeed getting heavier. She tried to speak the words, to tell him how she felt in return, but they flitted away as soon as her thoughts formed. Until all she felt was the contentedness of being in his arms, and sleep could no longer be put off.

Six

CONSCIOUSNESS RETURNED GRADUALLY. As frustrated as she had been to lose out on time with her demon, she couldn't bring herself to rouse. He held her still, and she was afraid to break this spell. She had never felt so safe.

She could never compare anything to the love of her family. It was precious. Life-affirming. Home.

But this was different. It was so focused. And thrilling. If her familial love made her thankful every day for the life she had, this new love with her ancient soulmate ignited something in her. A spark that would kindle her entire future. For better or worse.

As the steady rise and fall of Luci's chest threatened to pull Mina back into slumber, a memory started to surface.

She had lived in a small hut with her mother and teenage sister lifetimes ago. The year prior, their father had gone off to raid across the sea and had yet to come home. It was just the three of them, but they were managing.

They lived outside the village because the villagers still did not fully trust the healing that Mina's mother had learned from her mother, despite the fact that the family was devoted to the Christian faith. The old gods had been abandoned, if not completely forgotten.

It could get lonely, just the three of them. Mina had been so thankful that they at least still had each other.

At night, Mina and her younger sister would sit outside and stare at the stars, wondering if their father was, at that moment, also star gazing, using them to guide him home.

Mina prayed every day for his safe return, but she feared that her prayers would go unanswered. As if in oblation, Mina and her family provided shelter and sustenance to anyone who stumbled upon their meager home, regardless of their affiliations or occupations. Even though she knew her family's good deeds were unlikely to bring her father back, she took heart in knowing that at least she was sending other wayward fathers back to their loved ones.

It also provided another, unintended benefit. Her family's reputation grew beyond their village. Word quickly spread that to harm them would lead to retaliation by such a large host of warriors that it essentially amounted to suicide.

One sunny day, the oldest man she had ever seen appeared on their doorstep. His hair was bright white, and he was hunched over with nothing more than a sturdy branch for a cane. In the rare moments, when he spoke, his voice cracked.

She gave him food, water, and a clean, dry pair of socks her mother had recently darned. When the sun dipped below the horizon, Mina offered him her mattress in the loft. Sleep often eluded her when they had guests anyway, so she spent her evening in the warm summer air outside, gazing at the stars.

In the morning, the man who descended the ladder, popping down several rungs at once and landing gracefully on his feet, was almost unrecognizable. No longer hunched, he appeared to have grown almost a foot in height. His voice was clear and strong, and even some of his wrinkles had disappeared.

Mina tried to hide her surprise but failed. "Grandfather," she addressed him with a title befitting someone of his age, "you are much recovered. Please, tell me your secret."

"I have many secrets, my child," he responded. "To which do you refer?"

"When you arrived yesterday, you were, forgive my frankness, haggard and decrepit. And now you are as spry as my kid sister. Surely my aid alone wouldn't result in such a recovery."

"If I explain this secret to you, will you promise to come with me?" he asked.

Mina gulped. She had always carefully avoided any situation that would lead to a marriage proposal, and it was hardly appropriate for her to take off with a man she'd just met with whom she shared no familial relation and without being made his wife first.

"No harm will come to your honor. Did you not just call me Grandfather?" he asked.

Mina nodded.

"Then you'll come with me?" he asked.

Mina nodded again, although she wasn't sure why she was saying yes. In that moment it just seemed like he needed her to assent ever so much, and she hated to disappoint him. She'd be kicking herself in a minute, though, when he revealed his secret to be nothing other than drinking a flagon of olive oil daily.

"I am both old and young," he said as he reached out for her hand, "because I am no man at all but the creator of all things."

Well, she definitely hadn't expected him to go and say a thing like that. What were her options? To laugh at the man or take his hand and see where that path led. She refused to let a guest feel uncomfortable. Besides, she believed him. Enough of her did, anyway.

Mina placed her hand in his. There was a flash, and they were on the move, hopping from one place to another so quickly that Mina had no time to take it all in or process the fact that this man had not been lying or delusional. He was actually God.

God showed her the world around them, the moon, stars, other worlds—all lifeless and barren. He showed her Heaven full of its fluffy clouds and singing angels. Although it was mostly empty of human souls, the souls there looked blissful enough, if not a little lonely.

Back on Earth, God sat them down on top of a mountain range. He kissed Mina's hand and smiled sadly.

"Has our time together come to an end already?" Mina asked. She looked around for something familiar on the horizon so she could find her way back home should God decide to leave her here.

"Not just yet, little one," He said. "I just need to prepare you for the next portion of our tour. I plan to show you Hell, where evil men and sinners will spend eternity. You will see many awful things there. Things that a girl like you shouldn't even have to guess at. But it is part of my creation, and I would like you to see it all."

'I've seen the horrors of men, of war." Mina said, thinking back to the many times she had patched up wounds from swords, spears, and the other crude weapons that mankind fashioned.

"Yes," God said, patting the top of her hand, "I suppose you have."

There was another flash and hellfire sprung up around them. Mina made a startled sound, taking a step closer to God, who placed a reassuring hand on her shoulder.

"You are safe with me, child. Do not fear. Your heart is true, and your actions godly. Your flesh will never be subjected to the horrors of this place."

She spun around. Everywhere there were people strung up and demons whipping them, burning them, peeling back the flesh from their muscles and tendons. Mina gagged.

"What did they do in their lives to deserve this?" Mina asked.

"These are adulterers and whores," God replied.

Mina didn't want to imagine being forced by circumstance into a life of selling her body, only to come to Hell and be subjected to this torture forever. Suddenly, God provided no comfort. If she thought she could have yanked her hand out of his reach without bringing attention to herself, she would have.

Each new area he showed her was the same. The punishments changed. The sins too: pride, lust, simply not believing in God or Christ, or believing but in the wrong way. It all meant endless pain. Mina watched it all in a daze, concentrating on keeping the contents of her stomach in place.

He pulled Mina along to yet another group tied to chairs around a table. The table was full of food, but the people could not reach it. Every once in a while, someone would manage to wiggle free of their bonds, but when they brought the food to their mouths it melted into molten flame and scorched them. Those desperate enough scooped the bubbling lava into their mouths and burned themselves to cinders, only to reappear moments later strapped down once more.

"These were the gluttons, who were never happy with what they were given," God said. "Always reaching for more."

"They were ambitious?" She thought of her father off in far away lands struggling to provide his family with a better life. Is this all that waited for him? Or was he here already? Had this been his reward for loving them? She thought briefly about asking God but decided that she wasn't ready for a definitive answer.

"I suppose you could call it that," God shrugged.

Mina dug her heels in and gaped at him. God turned back when He found that he couldn't easily tug her along.

"Is something wrong?" God asked.

"They will go on like this for eternity?" Mina asked.

"Yes," God said. "As is my grand and perfect design."

"Grand and perfect?" Mina barked, a bit more sharply than was wise. Her temper rose, rivaling the hellfire around them in its heat.

All the good she had tried to do her fellow man. She knew every single one of them were sinners. They had murdered, raped, and pillaged. Many of them clung to the old gods or mindlessly slipped into old habits. She had hoped that her kindness would be catching, but if this was all that awaited them—no. She wouldn't allow it. "More like barbaric and disgusting."

"What?" God asked, His eyes widening.

Mina didn't realize it at first, but she was gaining an audience. The demons stationed around them had turned to watch her. One in particular, who stood transfixed on an outcropping of rock above her, exuded so much power that he could only be Satan. He was too far away to make out any of his features.

She didn't let the attention deter her.

"These are your children, are they not?" Mina asked, pulling her hand out of God's grasp and clutching it to her chest. "You love them, and yet you would let them suffer this way for all eternity? No hope of redemption?"

"They could have redeemed themselves during life." God shrugged. "They have disappointed me."

"Is that so? Tell me, how many human lives have you lived? How many times have you had to make the decision between feeding your family and not going to war? Where is your compassion? The world you have created for us is beautiful, but it is also harsh and unforgiving. The will to survive is stronger than I think you credit. You have set us up for failure, sir. As evidenced by how few of us succeed."

She threw her hands down to her sides in exasperation.

A tall, blond, green-eyed man—the demon from the out-cropping—approached, hands up and arms spread as if he was ready to physically break them apart. "Hello, God. It's good to see you." His voice was like honey, but there was an undercurrent of bitterness that Mina barely caught. He was lying. "Who is this enchanting creature you have brought to my domain?" He dropped his hands as he took a half step between the two.

His eyes danced along Mina, taking in every inch of her. He must have liked what he saw, because he gifted her with a genuinely warm smile.

God begrudgingly acknowledged the man. "Hello, Lucifer. This is Mina the kindhearted. Mina the ever-giving. Mina the opinionated." God rolled His eyes.

"Mina," Lucifer said, bowing his head to her. He scooped up her hand and pressed his lips to her knuckles. "Mina the beautiful."

"She's a filthy human, Lucifer," God said. "Stop toying with her."

"Don't quote me now." Lucifer bowed low to Mina. "I am Lucifer, Prince of all Seven Realms of Hell."

Mina found herself curtsying in return, and she immediately felt silly. Lucifer caught her blush and grinned knowingly at her.

God grumbled under His breath. "You are interrupting, Lucifer. Mina was just presuming to tell me how my grand design is flawed."

"I just—" Mina started, but she shook her head, unsure of how to explain this awful feeling in her gut.

"It is okay, my child," God said. "Please speak from the heart."

"This feels wrong. People do the best that they can. They aren't perfect. Far from it. But maybe with more chances, with the time to see where they went wrong, they might make better choices. They might honor you the way you are meant to be honored."

"Hmph," God said, crossing His arms and stomping His foot like a child. "I'm the creator of all. I am infallible—"

"If you are infallible, then why does my heart ache at the sight of this place?" Mina interrupted, gesturing to those in pain around her.

"Excuse me?" God said, eyes wild. "Well, if that's how you feel about it, you can just stay down here until you see the wisdom in my design."

"What?" Mina asked. "My family—"

"I don't care," God said. "Lucifer, you just got another soul."

"Her? She doesn't belong down here, God, and you know it," Lucifer said.

"Now *you* are questioning me?" God made Himself impossibly big, puffing out His chest and turning His full attention to Lucifer.

"Yes, but don't act too shocked. Questioning you is what I do," Lucifer snarled.

"Then show her the error of your ways," God said before He disappeared.

Seven

"HE LEFT ME?" MINA had asked in a daze. Shivering, she had felt tears threatening behind her eyes. She would never see her sister grow up, never find out if her father was still alive, never again get to tell her mother that she loved her. And they would have no idea where she had gone. She hadn't even had the chance to say goodbye.

"Oh, hells," Lucifer said. "Come with me." He hooked her arm with his and pulled her down a long corridor and into a chilly cave. It was bare with the exception of a pile of hay in one corner. There were no locks or doors even, but Mina couldn't help but feel that he had brought her to a jail cell.

"What are you going to do to me?" Mina asked.

"Nothing," Lucifer said, looking shocked that she would assume he had designs on her. "You aren't dead, so you aren't technically under my domain. And even if you were, God still has a claim on you. You just pissed him off. He'll be back, so long as he remembers that you still exist when he calms down."

"Then why did you bring me here?"

"Did you want to be surrounded by all those horrors? I can take you back there if you wish. You are by no means bound to stay."

She'd heard about Lucifer. Satan. The angel who had chosen to fall from grace rather than serve in God's kingdom. Because of his loathing for all of humanity, he had led Eve astray.

She knew as soon as she heard his name that he wasn't to be trusted. That's why she was so surprised when she finally understood that he was trying to help her.

"Oh." She slumped onto the cave floor. All the fight had left her. How embarrassing. The Prince of Darkness felt sorry for her.

Lucifer grumbled before sitting down across from her, his legs stretched out and crossed at the ankle. With both palms firmly on the ground, he braced himself. "You are a perplexing creature," he said.

"Am I? What exactly do you find so perplexing?"

"Well, you are human, and even so I think I quite like you."

"You don't like me. You just met me. Don't be absurd."

"Little Miss Mina thinks she knows everything," Lucifer chuckled.

"No," Mina responded, her eyes finding his. She noticed the gold and amber speckled in them and almost lost her train of thought. "I just know that this place feels wrong. It's hopelessness and despair. And the waste of an eternity."

Lucifer wasn't smiling any longer. He moved to his knees and scooted closer, staring intently into her blue eyes. "Well, you know that much," he agreed. She saw sadness in his eyes, and before she could stop herself she reached out and clasped his hand.

"What did he do to you?" she asked him.

He stared down at her hand. "He betrayed me. He forced me out, and this place is all I was left with. But even here I do his bidding." He shook his head as if in disbelief. "You feel like hope, though, for the first time."

"Surely not the first time," Mina said.

Lucifer only stared at her, and Mina wondered if he was worried she would cease to exist if he looked away.

"He betrayed you when he created us?"

"I thought so until about five minutes ago. But you don't feel like betrayal. Why is that?"

Mina shrugged and rubbed her thumb over the back of his hand.

"He made his angels perfect, and yet we were not enough."

They sat in silence for a moment, each contemplating their fates in the easy quiet between them until Mina asked, "Will you show me your realm?"

"Why would you want that?" Lucifer asked.

"You say that I feel like hope. I cannot help from this cave."

"I will," Lucifer said, "but first you must tell me everything about you."

"I offer to help you, and you want to make a deal?"

"Eh, it's in my nature," Lucifer said, a crooked grin on his face.

Mina shook her head. "You don't have to make a deal with me to learn more about me. All you need to do is ask."

She told him about her humble home, her mother's terrible sense of humor, the songs her father sang to her when she was a child. She told him about the men she helped, and the horrors she had seen. With each new tidbit, Lucifer moved a little closer to her.

"In the summers my sister and I always stay up late in the grassy fields outside our cottage to stargaze. I taught her many names for the clusters of stars, and we named some of our own." She glanced at Lucifer's arm where it was slung across her shoulders and allowed herself the small comfort.

"That sounds lovely. Not much stargazing down here, I'm afraid," Lucifer said as he squeezed her arm.

"It always helps us feel closer to my father, knowing that he is using the same stars to guide his way."

Lucifer laid down on the cold ground, tugging Mina back with him so her head rested against his chest. With his free hand, he reached toward the ceiling and snapped his fingers. Little stars burst into being on the cavern ceiling. Beautiful clusters, planets, and galaxies danced as they settled into place.

"Lucifer," Mina gasped.

"I'm sure it doesn't match the sky at home."

"It's lovely, and ours to share." She sat up and beamed at him. She was astonished at how quickly she was becoming accustomed to the idea of eternity with him. Clearly it had been a traumatic day, and she was clinging to what safety she could.

But then Lucifer smiled back at her, a genuine smile with no flirtation or swagger in it, and Mina forgot about her objections. Unending eons with a friend like him felt nothing like damnation.

"Tell me more," Lucifer said as he sat up and propped his elbow on a knee.

So she did. She told him about her people. How the chieftain had heard the word of God before she had been born. How her father had converted to win the heart of her mother. How he still had trouble adhering to a new belief system and the fights that fueled.

When her throat had gone raw and she was sick of the sound of her own voice, Lucifer had curled around her, his chin resting on the top of her head, one arm clasped in front of her with his hand resting on her arm, the other hand lightly tickling her hip.

It had felt natural in the moment, but with nothing between them but silence, propriety rushed back at her, and she stiffened. At once, Lucifer disengaged and stood up.

No sooner had Lucifer held his hand out to help Mina stand than God reappeared. "There you are!" He said. Mina let herself believe for a half second that He had returned for her. She dusted off her dress and looked at Him hopefully, Luci's hand temporarily forgotten.

"I almost forgot. I renounce my claim on Mina. She is yours to do with as you like, but do punish her. Maybe once she has received a taste of what total damnation feels like, she'll come to her senses."

In a flash, God was gone again.

Eight

MINA HAD TUCKED HER legs under her chin and grasped them to her, trying to make herself as small as possible. She had just been abandoned by God and left defenseless in the face of pure evil.

Lucifer knelt before her and put a reassuring hand on her knee, but his face was anything but. There was a gleam in his eye that made her feel like a cornered rabbit. "I am going to have to torture you a little bit, Mina. But I promise to make it as enjoyable as possible."

Mina stared at him in shock, trying to wrap her head around the fact that the individual who had just sat and listened to her entire life story also couldn't help but get excited at the thought of hurting her. He had been so gentle only moments ago. Had she really misread him so terribly?

"I won't lie to you, Mina. What God just did is nothing short of a gift. The second I saw you, I knew I wanted to poke and prod at you just to see all the little noises you'd make."

"You wouldn't," Mina said. "A moment ago you were trying to help me."

"I'm still trying to help you, you beautiful creature. If I'm not the one to torture you, one of my lackeys will do it. And if they do it, it means real pain." He then flashed her a cocky grin. "My way's fun."

No. This couldn't be. She could not stop herself from shaking.

"We'll start slow," he said as he grabbed her by her arms and pulled her up so she was standing in front of him. Her legs almost gave out. "Do you think you can trust me?"

Mina hesitated for only a moment before she breathed out, "Yes."

He kissed her, and Mina gave in almost immediately to the soft pressure of his lips. He wrapped his arms around her, and she melted into him. It was a good thing he was holding her against him, because, as he pulled her bottom lip between his teeth and bit down ever so gently, her knees did what they had been threatening since God's reappearance and gave out. Lucifer quickly lent his support and kept her standing.

A gasp allowed Lucifer the opportunity to delve into her mouth. His tongue flirted with hers. He tasted like vanilla and sunlight, like a warm spring day after a night of heavy rains.

Lucifer scooped her up into his arms and carried her deeper into the cave system, his lips never leaving hers as his tongue explored her mouth. She was drowning in this kiss and drinking him in like he was oxygen.

Tentatively, she moved her hands up to tug his hair, to cup his cheek, or to grasp the back of his neck. She couldn't make up her mind where she wanted to touch him.

Lucifer set her down on something hard, grabbing her hips to swing her around to face him so he could stand between her legs.

"How to start?" he asked her, brushing the hair from her face.

"Can't we just continue?" Mina asked. She felt so deprived from the loss of his mouth that she surprised herself by kissing him. It was barely more than a peck, but yesterday she would have never dreamed of being so forward.

Lucifer laughed. "I guess there's plenty of time. Wrap your legs and arms around me."

Mina happily did as she was asked, and Lucifer tucked his hands under her bottom, pulling her against him. He immediately pushed into her mouth. Moaning his name, she arched into him as he moved against her.

With each thrust, he coaxed her into following his retreating tongue with her own until he successfully led her into his mouth. She toured the new territory with glee. His muscle pulsated against hers in time with the rhythm of his hips, and Mina quivered against him.

Something was building within her, a desire—no, an all-consuming need. It was overwhelming, and Mina clawed for more of it before the intensity became too terrifying.

Out of breath, Mina pushed away, scrambling back as far as she could without falling off the table. "What are you doing to me?" Her breath came fast and shallow.

Guilt welled inside her. It was too good, this thing she was feeling. She could almost make out the sounds of her fellow man, and she knew how many were in pain a few cave passages away. And, oh no, her family. What would they think? She had just disappeared.

"Have you never done this before?" Lucifer asked.

"No." Mina swallowed.

"Makes sense. God likes His virgins."

"Ew." Mina crossed her arms across her chest. She was suddenly cold and way too exposed.

"We can slow down if you want," Lucifer said. He watched her for a moment, reading the reaction on her face since she offered no verbal response.

"Or we can speed up. You were letting yourself get lost in me before your conscience woke up. I can help you leave it behind again." Lucifer grabbed the hem of her dress and flung it toward her, exposing her legs. After removing her right shoe, he traced lazy circles starting at the delicate arch of her foot up her calf and then to her knee. Mina could bring herself to do nothing but stare at him in fascination.

She had been feeling like the whole world was spinning around her, like she had had too much to drink, and the table she was sitting on would dump her over any minute. But his touch gave her something to focus on. It grounded her at the same time that it pulled what she was feeling, this growing urge to give herself to him, to the forefront of her mind. She couldn't ignore it now. And she wouldn't deny it.

Chills ran through her as he removed her left shoe and repeated the dance of his fingers along her left leg.

"Yes," she said, "yes."

Lucifer beamed at her, a warm glow filling his eyes and catching her up in it too. He grasped her ankles and tugged her back down to him. When she was wrapped around him again, he slid his hand up her leg and tickled her thigh with his fingertips.

"I want to play a game," he said, "with only very light torture. Have you ever orgasmed?" He tangled his free hand in her hair.

"I don't know. I don't know what that is."

"Do you ever touch yourself?"

She shrugged, unsure what he meant.

"Perhaps at night while your family is asleep?" He thrust against her core and she gasped. "At your center?" He ground into her a bit, hitting something that sent a jolt of pleasure and longing into her scalp and her toes simultaneously.

She shook her head.

"Well, this isn't going to be a very fair game for you, but after the first round or two, you'll do just fine." Lucifer tugged on Mina's hair firmly until he had exposed her throat. Kissing her neck first to warm her up a bit, Lucifer left a trail of light hickeys from her collarbone to her jaw. At first she fidgeted. Then she squirmed. By the fourth love bite, she had kicked him at least once. But he only smirked as he traced his finger to the inside of her thigh.

There were no undergarments under her dress, except a thin underdress, giving Lucifer easy access to her sex. Right where she throbbed most. He pressed the pad of his fingers to that same spot and rubbed in circles.

"I'm going to give you pleasure. When you feel yourself about to break with it, I want you to tell me. I'm going to deny you that release at least a couple of times. It will feel like torture in the moment, but I promise the payoff will be worth it."

"And if I," Mina managed between gasps, "can't?"

"Then your adorable little butt is going to get spanked." Lucifer bent to her neck again, leaving another love bite. Mina wiggled wildly beneath him. The rumble of his growl flicked lightning down her spine.

"I'm going to have to tie you down next time," he murmured against her ear.

"You would do that?" Mina gasped, scraping her fingers along his back, his black tunic rough against her skin.

"In a heartbeat," he said.

The thought of being tethered to the table beneath her, unable to move or protect herself, had Mina trembling. He could do anything he wanted to her if she was tied, and there would be no way for her to stop it. She had never been that powerless before, and the thought of being in his complete control had her quivering. The rush was too much, and her nerve endings exploded.

"Luci!" was all she managed before she came undone against his fingers, drenching her skirts and the table beneath her. He held her as she settled back into herself but still maintained the friction against her clit. He wanted her to ride it for as long as she could.

"Did you call me Luci?" he asked, after her breathing had mostly returned to normal.

Mina blushed. "I'm sorry. It's all I could get out before my mind went numb." She buried her face in his chest, as if she could hide from her foolishness. Had her body always been capable of this? It was hard to reconcile it with the meager experiences she had had during her life thus far. The joy of a home cooked meal or a warm fire on a cold night was nothing in comparison.

"I love it," he said. "Promise never to call me anything else."

"I almost promise," Mina said. "But I'm not willing to throw away the opportunity to call you Satan from time to time. Or My Dark Prince. Or maybe Morning Star."

"Fair enough." He pressed a kiss to the top of her head. "Now on your feet. It's time for your punishment."

Nine

LUCI HAD GENTLY LIFTED Mina from the table and set her on the ground. "Turn around and bend over the table, please."

Her knees had only shook a little as she did as he asked. It helped to know what he had planned, even if she did not know how rough he would be. Up until this point, he had been nothing but gentle with her, and she hoped that he would continue in that manner.

"Reach your arms out and grip the edges of the table." Again, Mina followed instructions. "I'm going to start the spanking now. The first few will be over your clothing, but I won't allow any protection from the last couple."

Mina barely had time to process what he had said before he began but, startled at most, found that she quite liked the way her ass began to warm beneath his hand. It hurt a little, but that funny feeling was returning—like butterflies fluttering away in her stomach and making their eager way down between her legs.

Lucifer pulled up her dress, flipping the wool over her head so that she was blinded. After tucking her undergarment around her waist, he didn't touch her for a long minute. What he was doing, she didn't know, but the anticipation of what he was about to do only heightened.

His foot nudged against hers. "Spread your legs, please, Mina," he said.

She whimpered when she complied, knowing that she was exposing even more of herself to him. Still he did not touch her—no reassuring brush of her hip, no hard swat to her bottom.

An anticipatory tremble had just begun in her lower limbs when Mina finally felt Lucifer's hands grasp the globes of her bottom. He tugged them apart and she heard him groan. "You're beautiful," he whispered before he released her.

Mina heard the hard smack of his palm against her bare flesh before she felt it.

This time it stung, but that only brought on the warming sensation faster. She was sure she felt fresh moisture dripping down one thigh. Lucifer brought one last smack, this time between her legs, spiking both pain and pleasure into Mina's vulva. She almost came apart again but was able to stop it.

"Luci, the breaking is coming back."

His laugh was the thing of nightmares. It echoed through the cavern, and Mina was sure that if she turned around to look at him she'd find a red devil with horns, pointed teeth, and a spiked tail. The only indication that he was the same Luci who had not yet hurt her, not really, was the way he rubbed her smarting ass gently.

"Is it terribly wicked that I'm so close already?" she asked, her voice catching a bit with the fear that she might disappoint him.

"I suppose some might say so. Personally, I find it delightful, especially in light of the way I got you there. It does, however, change the game a bit." He slipped a finger inside of her vagina, his thumb resting lightly against her sensitive center, and Mina squeaked.

"No one has ever touched you here, have they?" Lucifer asked.

"No, never," Mina gasped.

He pressed the pad of his thumb into that cataclysmic spot. "Do you know what this is called?"

She shook her head but realized he couldn't see her underneath her skirts. "No."

"This is your clitoris. A lot of your pleasure is centered around it. But not all of it." He wiggled the digit inside her until he brushed against another mass of nerves. "This is your g-spot." He increased his pressure. "Do you like the way that feels?"

"Yes," she gasped.

He tugged her skirts back down. She thought he might let her back off the table, but he started pulling at the strings that laced her dress instead, untying them with a single hand and his teeth, pulling them through their worn leather loops as he continued to work her most sensitive areas in tandem.

"Would you like to feel more?" he asked as he kissed the small of her back.

"Please," Mina said. "I want anything you are willing to give."

"Then stand up and take off your dress," Lucifer demanded as he stepped away from her, his absent hand leaving her empty.

She stood and tugged her dress from her shoulders, turning toward him on instinct. He nodded at the underdress, and she unclipped the fastener. Her clothing formed a pool at her feet.

Although she wanted to, Mina did not cover her breasts. Luci took in her medium-sized breasts tipped with pink nipples and licked his bottom lip.

"Angel bodies don't look as perfect," he said. He flicked his wrist and her discarded clothing was gone. "Now, back as you were."

Once Mina had bent herself back over the table, Lucifer picked up where he left off. As he swatted her rear end, he slipped two fingers into her wet passage, feeling for her g-spot and pressing down on it.

His hand fell on her ass faster and harder; he added a third finger to her velvety passage, and she panted, "I'm about to!" Lucifer pulled his hand from her wet tunnel but continued to smack her ass, this time even harder. It stung.

Again and again he brought his hand down until she was screaming with each strike. He thrust all three fingers back inside her, bringing her close to another climax, while rubbing her smarting cheeks with his hand. "It's happening again," Mina moaned, and Lucifer removed his hand.

He leaned over her and asked, "Can I fuck you?"

Mina groaned. She knew enough of the world and had seen enough male bodies to know what he was asking. Lucifer didn't wait for her response before he was behind her again, leaving gentle kisses on her red behind. He kissed down to her clit and flicked his tongue against it, slipping his fingers inside her once more. She almost slipped over the edge before she caught herself and told him.

"Please, Mina, beg me to fuck you," he said before slipping his tongue into her. This time she didn't need to say anything as she approached a climax. He instinctively knew and pulled away from her.

"Oh, Luci, please f-fuck me." She stumbled over the profane word before her speech devolved into muddled begging.

Lucifer pulled Mina upright and into a tight embrace. He kissed her hair, her temple, her cheek, her neck. Lifting her up into his arms, he carried her out of the separate cavern and back into the larger space they'd left.

Its appearance had changed almost completely. The hay was gone, and a simple bed stood in its place. The walls of the cave were draped in fancy curtains, and the cold floor had been covered with warmly colored rugs. Their stars, however, still sparkled above them.

Lucifer deposited Mina onto the bed, following her down until he was on top of her. The sheets were silken beneath Mina's naked skin, and she gasped when she saw that Lucifer was also naked. His beautiful cock stood at attention before her. She couldn't resist the urge to wrap her hand around it. He was silkier than the sheets and so hard.

Lucifer tugged her hand from his cock and held her wrists over her head with a single hand. Flat on her back, Mina let Lucifer push her feet apart. He was between her exposed thighs in an instant, the head of his penis pushing at her opening.

"Are you sure?" he asked.

She nodded.

"You are certain that you want Satan—the master of all that is dark, evil, and villainous—to fuck this sweet, innocent, virgin cunt?"

"Yes," Mina said, ensuring their eyes met and held. She hoped he could read the desire and desperation in her eyes. His crude language had only added to it. This creature she had just met already possessed all of her. If he asked her to sign over her soul to him, she would have gladly agreed.

He kissed her, and she felt all of her desperation and desire reflected in it. Then he was nudging his way inside of her, and she felt the walls of her vagina give way to him. She had expected it to hurt, but, aside from a temporary sting that ended before it had really begun and the oddness of feeling so stretched, there wasn't much discomfort.

Once he was fully seated, he made small movements that hit her in all the right places. Soon that denied climax was threatening a comeback with a vengeance. Mina gasped as she felt herself start to twitch around him.

"Come on me, Mina," Lucifer demanded, and she exploded, seeing the stars above them even as her eyes rolled back.

His thrusts grew more forceful. He grunted as her velvet sleeve continued to contract around him. Soon he was coming too, filling her with demon seed.

Mina didn't register any pain until it was over. She glanced down and noticed the inconsequential bit of blood on the sheet below them as Lucifer rolled off of her and wrapped his arms around her in a tight embrace. She ached in multiple places, and she shifted to her side so that her butt was no longer pressed into the bed.

"I'll apply some ointment in a bit," Lucifer said as he pressed a kiss to the top of her head. She nuzzled into his chest hair and laughed as it tickled her cheek. "God better not come back for you now, because He's going to find that I am unwilling to give you up."

The sobs took Mina by surprise, and Lucifer too, judging by the pained expression on his face as he hovered over her. The distraction he had so kindly provided was gone, and the reality of her situation set in. She was happy to be in his arms too, and she didn't want to leave him either. But how could she just abandon her family?

"What's wrong?" Lucifer said as he sat up in the bed, pulling Mina into his lap so he could cradle her in his arm. "Are you regretting what we just did?"

Her heart caught in her throat. She looked up at him and cupped his cheek in her hand. "I will never regret any of what you just did to me. But my mother and my sister must be worried sick. I hate that I never even got to say goodbye. And they'll never know what happened. That I'm alive. That I have found someone who might possibly—" she trailed off, afraid to complete the thought. If she said it aloud, it was the same as wishing for it. And wishes were fickle things, often proved impossible the moment they flickered into being.

"Who might possibly what? Might possibly care for you?" Lucifer had asked.

"Do you?"

Lucifer had laughed. "It appears I do. We will find a way. Either a way to send you back or at least a way for you to say goodbye."

Now, back in the modern bathroom, Mina pulled herself from her doze and stared at Luci. She was still snuggled against him in the bath of miraculously warm water. But the candles had burned down a bit, so she knew that some time had passed.

"Luci, I remember meeting you. I remember the first time we made love. How quickly our feelings for each other had formed. You didn't tell me that God abandoned me here."

Luci sighed heavily. "In the past, you have not taken well to hearing that God is an asshole. I've found that it is easier for you to remember that fact on your own. I'm sorry if I was less than truthful."

"I want to remember it all. Every time you've ever touched me."

Luci laughed and tucked a piece of hair behind her ear. "You would go mad with all those memories. Too many to fit in a single mortal mind. Let's just make more memories."

Mina couldn't help but smile and nod at him, a blush creeping up on her cheeks.

"Now, I need that butt in the air again. It's time for the next size up."

Ten

WRAPPED IN ONLY A towel, Mina stood on the plush rug near the couch. An easel had been placed next to the coffee table at just the right height so she could sit on the table and paint. Paints of all different colors littered the table, a cup of brushes and a wooden palette among the clutter.

"How did you know that I paint?" she asked as Luci joined her from the bathroom, still naked.

"When I found you, I did a little bit of internet stalking. I saw that painting you did for the county fair three years ago that won an honorable mention."

"Oh." Mina blushed. That piece was not one of her best works. She had completed much better in the years since, but she had not had time to enter them into contests. They sat in her family garage. Waiting.

"You were robbed, by the way. The winning piece was absolute shit."

Mina laughed and shook her head. "You don't have to lie to me."

"I'm not lying," Luci said as he plucked a paintbrush from the cup on the coffee table and handed it to her. "Paint me something?"

She took it from his hand and stared at its pristine bristles.

"Remember how I said I'd need to jump in to save you?" After Mina nodded, Luci continued. "I'm going to do that now."

"You're leaving?"

He shook his head. "I could swap with him, but in this case, it's better that I don't. It would draw too much attention, and then he'd be here with you." He swallowed audibly. "No. I'm just going into his head. I want you close. I need to hold your breathing body while—" he cut himself off.

"While you hold my non-breathing body?"

He nodded. "Paint me something and tell me all about your life. I want to know everything."

"You really want to hear all about hospital supply chains and politics?" Mina tucked the paintbrush behind her ear.

"Yes. And your family. Friends. Pet peeves. There wasn't the internet the last time we met. Hell, there were barely any cars. Do you love or hate the sound of them? Or what about the way asphalt smells?"

"I don't know that I've ever really thought about those things. I guess the sound of traffic can be soothing when it is constant and far enough away." Mina dropped her towel as she started readying her supplies.

She squirted blue, black, green, gold, and amber dollops of paint onto the palette, an idea forming in her mind already.

"The way asphalt smells? Do I really need an opinion on that?"

Luci shrugged, watching her intently.

She sat down at the easel and started on an abstract painting inspired by the personal universe that had graced the ceiling of their cave for a thousand years and the swirling green and gold of his eyes. And while she did, she talked. She told him about the big things, like losing her father and helping to raise Tabitha. She told him about the small things, like the different personalities at work, her favorite quirky professor, and that she preferred tea to coffee.

Just as it had happened that first time, the more she talked, the closer he got, until his thighs bracketed her hips, his chin rested on her shoulder, and his fingers traced gentle circles around her middle. He did his best to stay out of the way of her paintbrush while still being as close to her as possible.

"If you could design your future into anything, what would it look like?" Luci whispered against the shell of her ear.

"Time for family, time to make art. No job draining my energy. I've saved some money for a down payment on a house. It would be nice to have my own space. But someplace still near my family."

Luci hummed contemplatively.

"Luci, why?" She darted her eyes to the side, trying to catch a look at his face.

"No reason."

She peeked at him out of the corner of her eye. "Uh-huh. Totally believable."

"Don't worry about it."

Mina let out a deflated sigh and glanced back at her painting.

"It's done," she said as she set aside her palette and paintbrush.

"Do you mind if I put it in my office?"

"Do I get to see your office?"

"If there's time. After you meet my friends."

"What should I expect from your friends?"

"Well, they're demons, obviously."

"Obviously."

"And as such, they are all definitely going to want to fuck you. I mean, they would want to fuck you if you were just a regular old human. But you're Mina, so they'll probably want to fuck you more than once."

"Oh!" Surprise and elation thrummed through her. "Have you shared me with them before?"

Mina felt Luci nod against her cheek.

She turned to see him more clearly.

"Demons aren't great at expressing their emotions. Well, not the positive ones. If you are willing, the pleasure they'll give you—it's their way of saying they care for you."

Mina couldn't suppress her blush or her excitement. But before she could piece together all that was racing through her mind, Luci changed the subject.

"I owe you for the painting. What do you want?"

"Tell me about your life. What will a typical day be like for you once I've left?"

Luci shrugged. "That's not payment enough."

"It's the payment I want, Luci. Please tell me."

He let out a loud breath and reseated his arms around her waist, tugging her tighter. "I'll make sure that the process here runs smoothly. Check in with each department. Make a report about how backed up the reincarnation pipeline is, ask advice from my department heads about how to lessen it, be told there's nothing we can do. Or they might surprise me and suggest something we've already tried. Then maybe spend a little bit of time with friends, if we can stand to be in the same room together."

"What do you mean?"

"You'd have to ask them." He averted his gaze.

"Okay, maybe I will."

"Mina?" His eyes flashed back to hers.

"Yes?"

"Kiss me?"

Mina turned in his arm, hooking her leg over his thigh, and pressed her lips to his. The kiss was slow, gentle, mournful. Like the beginning of a long goodbye. Bittersweet. Mina had no idea how long they stayed that way, letting their passions simmer as they leisurely explored one another. As if they could stay in that moment for the rest of eternity.

And then he was pulling her down onto the rug. They joined and rocked together, mapping one another with their hands, memorizing each other with their minds, until release left them both breathless.

Eleven

ONCE AGAIN, MINA WORE her simple sundress and sandals, the large butt plug that Luci had inserted at the end of their bath, and a simple pair of panties hidden beneath the pink floral cloth. Comforted by how full she felt, that it was their little secret, Mina reveled privately.

They had spent the rest of their day snuggling, talking, and making love. Luci had been gentle, attentive, and sweet, and it felt a bit as if it were the calm before the storm. Given Luci's suggestion that morning that she meet some of his friends, she had her suspicions about what the storm might look like.

He stood beside her now, his hand clasped in hers as he took her along a dark cavern path.

"Everyone will be so happy to see you," Luci said. "Once again you will be reunited with my legion." He was wearing one of his infectious smiles, and Mina felt the warmth of it in her heart.

The warmth receded quickly, though, as her anxiety gripped her. Who or what would she find among his legion? A pack of demons? Or loyal friends?

Worst of all, everyone would know her, but she didn't remember any of them. What if her current iteration fell short of the Mina they were expecting?

"You are walking so slowly, Mina. You aren't nervous, are you?"

"How could I not be? I'm one tiny human, and you are legion," she stopped walking entirely and worried her bottom lip.

"Oh, yes, how could little old Mina take on all these demons on her own? Surely your soul will be lost." He interrupted her startled laugh with a kiss.

"My soul has been lost to you for a long, long time."

Luci jerked back as if she had stabbed him, clutching at his chest playfully. "How can you say such a thing? I would never be so careless with your soul as to lose it."

Mina grabbed at his arms and pounced on him with a kiss. "You are such a goofball."

He nodded, wrapping his arm around her shoulder and tugging her along with him down the path. "You love it."

They heard the patter of feet long before they saw the young, white woman rushing at them. She had long, red hair and purple eyes that glowed with mischief, an athletic build, and an easy smile. Freckles cluttered her cheekbones and the bridge of her nose.

"Mina!" she shouted as she came upon them, flinging her arms around the surprised human in a tight hug. "You're here! You're here!"

Luci chuckled. "Mina, this is Sindy."

"Let me get a look at you." Sindy held Mina out at arms length and stared at her intently, her eyes darting all over as she took Mina in.

"Do I get a hug?" Luci asked.

"Hell no you don't. I'm mad at you."

"What did I do?"

"You've been hogging Mina here for the last two days." Sindy turned back to Mina. "I can't believe you have been here for two days and I'm just now seeing you. I'm sure Luci told you that you're *his* soulmate and how much *he's* missed you without even thinking to mention me."

Sindy turned, both hands on her hips, and glared at Luci.

"You aren't about to tell me that you're actually my soulmate, are you?" Mina asked, glancing to Luci for help.

"Of course not, silly." Sindy groaned. "You really didn't tell her, did you?" She smacked Luci's arm, and he let out an audible yelp.

"To be fair, we have been busy." Mina shrugged, poorly suppressing a giggle as Luci rubbed his arm. There was no way that Sindy hit him hard enough for it to hurt.

"I'm your best friend," Sindy said, throwing her arms above her head and flashing a toothy grin before spinning around in a circle. "He's been keeping you from your best friend. I have hardly any time with you now. And I have to share you with all the others."

"Oh for fuck's sake, Sindy." Luci shook his head. "Do you think Lilith or Alastor are going to be pleased with you when they find you've made such a claim?"

"Well, sure, they could say the same, but that doesn't make us any less of best friends." Sindy brought her arm through Mina's and laid her head on her shoulder. "I'm so glad you are here."

"I think you will find, Mina, that many of us love you. You'll never want for friendship as long as you are home," Luci said, taking her other arm in his.

Their pace quickened as they made their way to the assembly hall. After stepping through an archway made of human skulls, they entered an enlarged cavern, and Mina took in the stadium seating that surrounded them. There had to be at least enough seats to hold one-hundred thousand. Mina imagined the stadium full of demons shouting for their king. How many angels had he convinced to follow him into hell? If he was that charismatic, maybe she shouldn't be so quick to trust him.

When she glanced over at Luci, she must not have done a great job of hiding her shock or suspicion because he frowned at her.

Sindy ran off to the table set up on the far end of the stadium where three other beings sat, leaving them alone.

"What are you thinking, my love?" Luci asked, placing his body between her and his friends.

"Nothing, really. It's just the power of this place. Thinking of your legions gathered here, following you—it's intimidating."

"That was all over and done with long ago. There aren't as many of us here now. Only a few hundred. The rest scattered to Earth or were destroyed in the many skirmishes between Hell and Heaven."

"Do you miss all the adoration?"

"Oh, they never adored me. Feared me, maybe. But mostly they were just interested in what I had to offer—a safe place to hate humankind. You did ruin that, I suppose." He gave her a small smack on the ass and laughed when she jumped. "I'll keep punishing you for it, but only because you like it," he said with a wink. "Come, meet my family—our family. I promise that you're safe with me." He took her hand in his and led her to the table.

And she believed him. Because of course she did.

"Mina!" a green giant said, knocking his chair backwards in his eagerness to stand. He was larger than any man she had ever seen and all muscle. He bent down to hug her and practically had to kneel, but his embrace was gentle. "It is good to see you!"

"Mina, this is Alastor," Sindy said, bouncing up and down on the balls of her feet.

Alastor was shirtless, and she half expected to find him in torn, purple shorts. But he was wearing black jeans not unlike the pair Luci seemed to be so fond of. He wasn't quite as green as the comic book character, with only a tint to his warm skin, and he had a lovely face with delicate features and glowing, green-yellow eyes. There was something about him that felt woodsy, and Mina wondered whether he enjoyed strolls through the park.

"Move out of the way, you big lug," a woman's voice sounded from behind Alastor. He blushed lightly and stepped to the side. The feminine demon whom Alastor had been hiding was an absolutely drop-dead gorgeous Black woman. But even that description felt like an understatement. She curved and bounced in all the right places. Her pitch-black hair was pulled back from her face in thick braids, heightening the appearance of her slender neck, high cheekbones, and shapely nose.

"I'm Lilith," she said, eyeing Mina up and down, a small curve to her lips and a dangerous sparkle in her eye, before shifting her gaze to Luci. "She always gets the best bodies."

Mina looked down at her body and shrugged. "It's not as good as yours." Lilith's height, her flawless dark-brown skin, and her expressive deep-brown eyes entranced Mina. Her curves were juxtaposed with arms and legs carved with muscle. She looked like she would be ready for battle at a moment's notice.

Luci shook his head, and Lilith chuckled. Mina wondered if she was *the* Lilith. Adam's first wife. It would make sense seeing as Lilith appeared the most human out of all of them.

The last member of the group sat to the right of the head of the table. He had remained seated, one ankle resting on his knee, arms crossed. Although not as large as Alastor, he was definitely not small. His black hair and blue eyes contrasted nicely with his almost alabaster skin. But his cheekbones were inhumanly high and sharp. Two tiny horns protruded from either side of his forehead. Mina admitted to herself that he was very handsome, in a living nightmare sort of way.

"This sourpuss is Beelzebub," Sindy said, hopping over to the seated man and giving him a swift kiss on the cheek. He glared at her in response. "Oh, he's always in a foul mood!" Sindy flicked her wrist at him.

Mina moved over to Beelzebub and held out her hand. He grabbed it and shook, pulling her down to him slightly so he could whisper, "Please call me Bellz."

"It's nice to meet you," Mina said. His lips twitched as he reluctantly released her hand, but he did not smile. "It's nice to meet all of you."

They sat down together. Luci took the seat at the head of the table and guided Mina to the chair on his left. The spread of food before them made for an impressive meal, the first meal that Mina had had since coming to Hell. With the food piled high in front of her, she realized that she should have been starving long before now, but she still didn't have much of an appetite.

"No one eats in Hell for sustenance," Lilith said, noticing Mina's tepid response to the feast. "We eat to have something to do, or because we like the taste and the sensation."

"Isn't there some rule about not eating food in the underworld?" Mina asked as Luci offered her a strawberry. "I'm pretty sure that's how Hades tricked Persephone."

"I would never trick you," Luci said.

"That's a laugh," Alastor said. "You trick her all the time."

"Not about something as important as this," Luci said. "Wherever you decide to stay, I'm behind you." Mina used her lips to take the strawberry from Luci's fingers, flicking her tongue out against him briefly as she did. She saw his eyes spark, and he growled just loud enough for her to hear.

"So, instead of spending lots of time talking about pointless things like what Mina does for a living, I thought we could play a game," Luci said.

"Oh, dear." Sindy rubbed her hands through her hair. The smile that had been plastered to her face since Mina first saw her faded in an instant as Sindy stared blankly at the food on her plate.

"Wait, my occupation is pointless?" Mina asked but was ignored.

"You don't have to play, Sindy. I know how much you hate games, and we need a referee," Luci said, reaching over to pat Sindy's hand. Her smile returned as quickly as it had vanished.

"What's the game, Luci?" Beelzebub asked. He was glaring at everyone at the table except Mina, whom he had seemed to be pointedly ignoring since they shook hands.

"A labyrinth," Luci said.

"That old one we have lying around?" Alastor asked, clearly unimpressed.

"No one has used it in years. Who knows what's hiding in it?" Lilith said, giving Beelzebub a look Mina couldn't quite read, and gave a little shudder. Not of fear, Mina realized as Lilith's arms twitched, but in anticipation of a fight.

Beelzebub rolled his eyes, "I suppose you want me to be the Minotaur and chase you all down."

"No. Definitely not. It's my game. I'll be the Minotaur. But you'll all be my helpers." He glanced around the room, making eye contact with each of his friends. "Mina will be playing our virginal sacrifice."

"Luci, I'm hardly a virgin," Mina said in a dry tone.

"Virginal. Virginal. You are the closest to a virgin among us," Luci said. "Your goal, my love, will be to get to the center of the maze without being caught. If you are caught, whoever has captured you will be able to do whatever they want to you for a full fifteen minutes. Then they have to release you and wait another fifteen minutes to rejoin the festivities."

"Am I allowed to try to get away before the fifteen minutes are up?" Mina asked. Her heart was pounding faster. She knew next to nothing about her opponents. Their strengths and weaknesses were a complete mystery. But, for better or worse, she trusted Luci, and she knew he would not let any harm come to her.

"I suppose if we are stupid enough to not hold on to you, then you are free to escape," Luci said. "But whoever you escape from will not have to sit out the fifteen minutes. They'll be free to come right after you."

"What's off the table, Luci?" Alastor asked.

"Alastor and Bellz are not allowed to penetrate any holes with their dicks aside from Mina's beautiful mouth," Luci said, leaning over the table to kiss her lips. "But you can use whatever else you like for penetration. No permanent marks. No blood or excessive pain. And if Mina is ever in distress, we stop."

"Is this what you meant when you said you didn't mind sharing me?" Mina asked, searching for some reassurance in his gaze.

"This is one of the things I meant, but I don't think we've played this specific game before." Luci peered at her, and when their eyes met, Mina felt like she could read his thoughts, if only for a moment. His desire for her threatened to consume him completely, and he was determined to make their last day together count. He'd make sure she'd never be able to get him out of her system.

"You enjoy having me at a disadvantage, don't you?" Mina asked.

"We all do," Luci said, nodding toward the others. They were all looking at her, even Beelzebub, and he had a hungry glint in his eye that gave Mina the chills.

Sindy, who was sitting to Mina's right, patted her arm comfortingly. "I promise to make sure they don't get too out of line. I've never really been one to participate in these kinds of games."

"Sindy is basically celibate," Lilith said.

Sindy gasped. "That's not true!"

"You haven't had sex for literal ages," Lilith replied.

'Nuh-uh! Just not since Mina was here last." Sindy crossed her arms across her chest.

"Eat up, Mina," Alastor said. "You are going to need your strength to stand a chance against us."

"Do I want to stand a chance against any of you? Might be more fun to lose."

"Wow, you've spoiled her already, Luci," Lilith said.

That set Sindy into a giggle fit.

"Am I wrong?" Mina asked Luci.

"I guess you'll see," Luci replied. "It's no fun if I tell you."

She bit her lip, her eyes meeting Luci's.

He smiled. "You game?"

"Yeah," she nodded. "I'm game."

Twelve

AFTER THEY'D EATEN THEIR fill, Mina and her demons gathered at the entrance to the labyrinth. The walls, made of blue brick, towered over them all, even Alastor.

"Alright, Mina, you get a fifteen minute head start," Sindy said. "And it starts right now."

Before Mina had a chance to take off, Luci grabbed her hand and pulled her back to him. "I love you, Mina." He pressed his lips to hers.

"You're cheating," Mina said, but she kissed him briefly anyway before pushing away.

"Wait, Mina," Lilith grabbed her arm, leaning down to her ear to whisper. "Don't let Beelzebub catch you. It's likely he won't let you go."

Every muscle in Mina's body froze, her mouth gaping as she stared blankly at Lilith, trying to make sense of what she had just said. And how it made her feel, a little dewy beneath her panties. The sharp pain of Lilith's hand connecting with Mina's ass brought her back to the moment.

"Go! You've already wasted three minutes."

Mina took off into the labyrinth, shoving down the tidbit about Bellz, hoping they were messing with her. It was surprising how *not* furious she was about all this. She should be fuming. Shouldn't she? They were treating her like a toy—nothing more than a plaything. But she could already feel herself getting wetter at the thought of being trapped in this game with them. It would all be worth examining more closely later, because right now she had a maze to beat.

She knew there was a trick to solving these things. Something about taking right turns until you couldn't anymore? Or you got back to something you recognized? That was a laugh in this place, though. It all looked exactly the same. She wound her way around to a dead end and threw up her hands.

Retracing her steps, she took a path she really hoped she hadn't taken before. If only she could get on top of the wall. Then she could easily find her way. Keeping an eye out for a place in the bricks that she could grip and haul herself up, Mina was too preoccupied to notice that she was about to walk right into Alastor until it was too late.

He tucked her against him and chuckled as she got close. "Aha, I get you first, it seems." His large hand covered her rib cage and his thumb brushed against the side of her breast.

"Have fifteen minutes really passed already?"

"They sure have," Alastor said, laughing heartily. He picked Mina up and twirled her around. "What to do with you first?" He set her back on her feet and turned her so she was facing him.

"Kissing seems like the normal place to start," Mina suggested.

Alastor nodded, bending down to peer into her eyes. One large palm covered her jaw as he leaned toward her, almost bringing his lips to hers. Right as she was sure he was about to close the final distance between them, he tipped his forehead against hers. His face filled with glee.

"Normal is boring." He snapped his fingers and let go of her. Her mind tried to tell her body to move, but she wasn't fast enough in heeding the warning. Thick, grayish-green vines sprouted from the wall behind her and wrapped themselves around her legs and arms.

She couldn't help it. She screamed, and Alastor sneered at her, his eyes dancing with excitement. The vines pulled her back until she was flush with the wall, brick and mortar biting lightly into her flesh. Alastor snapped his fingers once more and Mina's clothes disappeared. Only her sandals were spared.

As Alastor devoured her with his eyes, Mina wondered if she would have to finish this game nude, even after Alastor was through with her. He took a step forward, brushed her hair off her shoulders, and caressed her breast. Then he flicked her nipple with his green fingers.

"Really shortsighted of Luci to keep you to himself." He knelt in front of her, bringing him to her eye level. Tenderly, he pulled her hair back from her face, gathering it up in his fist into a ponytail. "We have all been craving you for so long."

He tugged on her hair until her head was at an uncomfortable angle then lovingly kissed her neck and beneath her ear. He bit into her earlobe. It hurt, in an exciting way, but she didn't feel any blood when he let go.

"We've missed you," he whispered. "I've missed you." He kissed her then. It was a pleasant kiss. Not the mind bending, earth shattering kisses of Luci, but it still easily made her top ten list. The vines pulled Mina further up the wall until she was above the kneeling Alastor. Her legs were pulled apart, giving the green giant an open view of her core. Alastor lapped at her, chuckling for a moment and then tapping on the base of her butt plug.

He pulled her clit between his lips and slid one of his thick fingers into her. As her desire rose, it became abundantly clear that Mina was in over her head. Alastor increased the pace of his thrusting finger, and she was surprised to discover yet another creature who could easily play her like a fiddle. He twisted his finger as he thrust it, making sure to push against her g-spot at irregular intervals.

"Alastor," she moaned. He pulled his finger from her and stood up. She was held high enough on the wall now that she could easily make eye contact with him, although he still had a couple inches on her.

"I think I'd like to sit back and watch." He leaned casually against the far wall. As he pointed a finger, one of the vines holding her legs started to grow. It inched along her thigh toward her exposed sex, sprouting a few tendrils from the main vine. Mina gasped, unable to tear her eyes away.

The thickest vine plunged into her, while one of the smaller vines crept up to her clit and twirled itself around it. The second tendril moved to the base of her butt plug, wrapped around the flared base, and tugged on it with just enough force that Mina could feel the bulbous head pushing down on her anus. Another tug and the bottom portion of her plug escaped. Reversing course, the vine shoved it back into place before setting a regular rhythm, fucking her with the insertable.

The limb inside her thrust with abandon while the bit around her clit began pulsing. All the while Alastor stood by and watched, a hungry look on his face. Mina's focus narrowed down to his hand as he released the button on his black jeans and tugged down the zipper.

With that same hand, he lazily gestured toward the plant, which pulled Mina horizontal and face down, more greenery sprouting from the wall to help support the weight of her body, and lowered her. Alastor gathered her hair in his hand and pulled her head up. His green cock was large—hentai monster large. Despite herself, Mina began to struggle.

She wanted that cock. Oh, how she wanted it. But she hadn't completely lost her grip on reality. There was no way she could handle it without suffocating or permanently dislocating her jaw.

"Shshsh," Alastor strummed beneath her ear with his thumb. "The flora will be rough, but I want you in control here." He tapped her lips with his large mushroom tip. "I want you to make love to my cock with your gorgeous mouth."

Mina was overcome with relief. And desire. She flicked her tongue out against the head of his cock, tasting him and the small amount of pre-cum that had gathered. Then she planted kisses all over him, anywhere she could reach. He shifted toward her and lifted his cock up so she could kiss the underside of him and the tops of his testicles.

He sighed in pleasure, eyes rolling back. And the vine in her pussy picked up the pace. Shoving as far into her as it could, it nudged at her cervix. At first, she hissed her discomfort, but soon she was anticipating it, reaching for it as fractionally as her bonds would allow.

Struggling with the bindings that held her arms, she took as much of Alastor's cock into her mouth as she could, about a fourth of the tip. If she could get a hand free, then she could stroke him too. But the tendrils didn't budge. Despite her whimpered frustration, she wouldn't be deterred. Instead, she changed tactics, licking him like an ice cream cone. She would leave no part of him untasted.

The plant limb around her other leg grew and climbed up to the entrance of her pussy, pushing in alongside its twin. They twined around one another, creating ribbing and expanding their width, then fucked her in tandem.

The sensations were too much. Pleasure overwhelmed her and undid her. As she came, she redoubled her efforts on Alastor's cock.

"Times up!" Sindy said, clapping her hands together once. Mina found herself clothed, unbound, and feet firmly on the ground once more. She rubbed at her wrists and looked around for Sindy, who was sitting on the wall above her, legs dangling youthfully. Alastor nowhere to be seen.

"Alastor hadn't finished," Mina protested, on his behalf as well as her own. She had been very driven to see him come.

"That's his problem," Sindy said in a sing-song voice, kicking her feet and flinging her arms around.

"Can you at least give me a minute warning next time?"

"Sure!"

Mina pouted but continued on her way, hoping that she was still pointed in the same direction. Her time with Alastor had definitely been disorienting. A bit bummed that she wouldn't be able to purposely let him catch her again so they could finish, what with him being out of the game for the next fifteen minutes, Mina did not realize that her steps had significantly slowed.

The path she was on twisted and turned for a long time. Most of the side paths were very obviously false ends, and she knew that if she found that this was a dead end as well, she'd have to backtrack a long way before she found another viable option. Of course, being in Hell and all, moments after having the thought, she found herself at just such a dreaded spot.

When she turned around to make her long trek back, Lilith stood in her path wearing a red corset, thong, and high heels.

"Lilith!" she gasped. "You scared me."

Lilith's serpentine expression was in no way reassuring, yet it was still a surprise when Lilith pounced on Mina like a cat. She would have banged her head on the ground, but Lilith had anticipated that and cradled Mina's head in her hand.

Sharp claws tore at Mina's sundress, leaving it in tatters. Mina tried to wiggle free, but Lilith kept her weight in just the right places to hold her prey in place without causing pain.

"You better not run from me, little girl," Lilith said as she moved down Mina's exposed body. She dipped her head to Mina's right breast and circled her nipple with her tongue.

"I won't run," Mina gasped as Lilith continued making her way down Mina's body.

"Promise?"

"I promise."

"Oh, I'm going to make you regret that," Lilith said as she slashed through Mina's panties, leaving her completely naked. Lilith fell on Mina's clit, sucking on it violently and biting down.

Mina's scream was loud and long but quickly dissolved into a low moan as the shock of pain morphed into pleasure. Lilith let up and Mina whimpered as the blood rushed back into her nub. After a quick kiss to her thigh, Lilith grinned up at her.

"I see Luci prepared you for today." Lilith pulled on the base of the butt plug. "I think you're ready for another size up, thanks to Alastor. It's really not doing much anymore." Lilith pulled it out and set it aside. "Oh, nice gape going."

Lilith slipped three of her manicured fingers into Mina's ass and spread them, stretching the orifice. Mina arched her back and bent her legs, hoping to give Lilith more access.

"Have you ever been with another woman, Mina?"

"Just once, but it was a pretty brief encounter."

"I suspect that will change if you go back up top." Lilith was now fucking Mina's ass with her fingers, pulling out just to plunge back in. "Anything you'd like to explore with me first?"

"Can I try to make you cum?" Mina asked shyly.

"Aw, are you feeling guilty you didn't finish Alastor? Not to worry." Lilith stood up, pulled off her scrap of underwear, and, turning so she still had access to Mina's body, straddled her face. Lilith lowered herself within Mina's reach and slipped three fingers back into Mina's anal passage. "There's always an aftercare party."

Mina stared in awe at Lilith's pussy. She had large labia minora that peeked out between her labia majora, and her clit stood out like a pearl. In an attempt to not overthink it, Mina dove right in, feasting on Lilith's pussy, lapping her tongue around her lips, prodding at her entrance with the tip of her tongue, and sucking gently on her clit.

Lilith bit down gently on Mina's clit again before tugging it into her mouth and sucking on it furiously at the same time that she added another finger to her ass, giving Mina just enough time to adjust before plowing into her.

The pleasure was intense, and Mina did her best to stay focused on giving Lilith pleasure. She brought her hand up and slipped one of her fingers into Lilith's vagina, taking her time to explore and find that tight bundle of nerves. Mina was slow, gentle, and attentive while Lilith fucked her ass harder. Although Mina liked it rough, she really didn't know how to dish it out herself.

But her gentle loving seemed to be doing it for Lilith. After Mina slowly added a second finger while tonguing her lover's clit with a steady pressure, the demoness shook above Mina. The fingers in Mina's ass stilled as Lilith rode her climax to completion.

"That was fabulous, my pet," Lilith said as she moved positions once more so they were face to face. Lilith's arm squeezed between their bodies, her hand still working away. "I've missed your little kisses." Lilith gently pressed their lips together. Mina pushed her chest against Lilith's, moaning in desire as their breasts met. Lilith was soft and so different from Luci's firm body.

A clear vision of being surrounded by both Lilith and Luci, feeling Lilith's soft breast in one hand and Luci's muscular chest in the other. The thought of having them both together was almost more than Mina could handle.

"I want to fist your holes, but I think Luci will be mad at me if I do that without him." Lilith crawled back down between Mina's legs. "So maybe I'll just do one." Lilith pulled her fingers from Mina's ass. "And I bet he hasn't fucked your ass yet. So we will save that for later."

Mina sucked in air as she realized what Lilith was saying. "You're going to fist me?"

"And you are going to love it," Lilith said, working the three fingers from her other hand into Mina's vagina. She stretched her fingers out like she had in her ass, and fucked her savagely, slapping her clit with the palm of her free hand.

"One minute!" Sindy said cheerily from behind them.

Lilith growled, but Mina was already in action. She pushed Lilith off of her and got to her feet. Lilith's eyes expanded in rage as Mina got to her feet and dashed away. "You promised you wouldn't run, you little bitch!"

"Well, I guess you better come get me," Mina called over her shoulder as she turned the corner. She was beaming, and she hoped that Lilith would catch on to her plan. If she ran now, with a minute left, Lilith was sure to snatch her back up, and they'd get an extra fifteen minutes.

Lilith jumped down in front of Mina. She must have run across the top of the wall. Mina tripped over Lilith and the two tumbled to the ground together.

"I got us more time," Mina whispered to Lilith who was sprawled out beneath her. Mina straddled her and bent to suck on Lilith's nipple, which had slipped out of her corset in the scuffle.

"Naughty girl." Lilith hooked her leg around Mina's and used her hip to dislodge her and flip her on her back. "But I captured you, so I'm going to stay in control." Lilith adjusted her top. "Now where were we?"

Mina obediently spread her legs for Lilith without having to be asked, and Lilith hummed with approval. She placed her fingers back at Mina's entrance and slowly worked them in.

Twisting her wrist, Lilith worked to open Mina's pussy before she slipped in a fourth finger.

The pressure was tight, and Mina felt very full, even though Lilith's hands weren't that large. She wasn't sure how much more would fit, but Lilith managed to tuck her thumb into her hand and again pushed forward. Lilith hadn't made much progress before she frowned, getting stuck on the final set of knuckles.

"I see you came equipped with a tight, little pussy this time around," Lilith said. "But I'm not giving up just yet." With that, she laid down on the ground so that her head was between Mina's legs. She pulled Mina's clit between her lips and nursed until Mina succumbed to another orgasm, the clenching of her full cunt spiraling her release higher. But Lilith didn't let up, continuing to pump her hand into Mina, who came again, issuing forth a torrent of fluids.

And, yet, it wasn't enough. Lilith's fist remained only as far as it had been before.

Lilith grumbled in frustration but slipped two fingers into Mina's back passage. Mina wasn't sure she could handle any more. She felt so intensely full. Her toes curled, and as Lilith started to move her hand again, Mina exploded once more. Another orgasm and she was fairly certain she would pass out.

"Time!" Sindy said.

"The fuck it is," Lilith said.

"Well, I'm issuing a penalty for Mina's blatant manipulation of the rules and misuse of my kindness." Sindy stood over the pair, her arms crossed and a comical pout on her face. There was a fire in those purple eyes that Mina had not seen before, and she was unsure how she should interpret it. "I've given you an extra five minutes. I'm quite sure you don't deserve the full fifteen."

"You are playing this all wrong, Sindy," Lilith said as she kept trying to force more of her hand into Mina. The knuckles were only barely starting to slip inside but got stuck at their highest point. She wiggled her fingers in Mina's ass. "Why don't you come show her how bad a girl she's been? Get in on this?"

Sindy bit her bottom lip, and Mina realized that the emotion she had read was lust. Sindy nodded and took two steps toward the couple on the ground. "Flip her over. I want her on her hands and knees."

"You heard her, virginal sacrifice," Lilith said as she slipped out of Mina.

Mina quickly got into position. "Ass up." Lilith smacked Mina's butt cheek. "Good girl."

"Mmm," Sindy said. "What should I do?"

"Why don't you spank her while I keep trying to work my fist into her naughty, tight cunt." When Mina felt the pressure of Lilith's hand at her entrance this time, it wasn't gentle. Even so, Lilith had no better luck. "Did Luci put a lock on this thing or something?"

Sindy's spanks were a distraction from the pressure of Lilith's hand, and they sent tingles up Mina's spine. They weren't nearly as hard as Luci's spanks, but every once in a while, Sindy would deliberately scratch her with her nails after a slap.

"I wanna fuck her," Sindy said.

"Go right ahead," Lilith said, and, as she kept her hand in place, slid under Mina so she wouldn't be in Sindy's way. Mina glanced back and saw that Sindy was wearing a blue strap-on about five inches long and an inch in diameter.

Sindy crouched behind Mina and gently nudged the tip of the strap-on into her ass. Slowly, she pushed her way in until her hips hit Mina's ass. Then Sindy eagerly fucked.

Mina came once more, her back arching as she jerked with the force of it. And her prediction proved correct. Her body gave out, going limp on the hard brick beneath them.

The demons responded quickly, Lilith's hand slipping free at the same time that Sindy pulled out. Lilith tugged Mina to her chest, wrapping her arms around her. Sindy, not to be left out, collapsed on top of Mina.

Thirteen

As Mina snuggled with Lilith and Sindy in their afterglow, glimpses of memory teased. She remembered a thick vine around her waist, animal slobber, and the color purple.

Once Mina was alone again, and naked, her clothes having failed to return, the memory solidified. Gaps existed between the new recollection and meeting Luci, but when she tried to recall them, she failed.

"I can't leave you alone, Mina, but I also can't take you to Beelzebub this time either. I need him," Luci had said as he guided her through a ravine she hadn't seen before.

Mina couldn't decide whether she was relieved or disappointed. Her time with Beelzebub had been an intense but mostly positive experience. Even so, she wasn't sure if she was ready for more just yet.

"With whom will I be staying this time? Why are you leaving again so soon? I thought the meetings with your lieutenants had gone well."

"They have. One of them found a lead on a power source."
He stopped before a natural archway in the rock and turned to
face her.

Mina's eyes went wide, and she grasped Luci's hands in her
own.

"Don't get too excited. It could be a dead end."

Mina nodded, but the hope that Luci would no longer be a
pawn in God's sick game, that she could see her family again,
that they might find a way out of all this pain for humans and
demons alike, wouldn't be denied.

Normally, she would have prayed in a moment like this.
She wanted to scream at how helpless and lost she felt with no
higher power to turn to. But recent events had made it obvious
that that higher power had been little more than illusion. Any
hardship she had written off as being part of God's grand design
she now saw as neglect. God was just too narcissistic to care.

Luci swooped an arm around her lower back and pulled her
toward him. He lowered his face, resting his forehead against
hers. "Even if this comes to nothing, we will keep looking. We
will find a way out for all of us."

She placed her palm flat against his chest and felt the steady
beating of his heart. At least she had this, had Luci.

He leaned in and kissed her passionately, pulling her through
the archway one step at a time. They were several feet into a
large cavern when he broke the kiss and turned her around so
her back was to his chest.

A young-looking demon with red hair and freckles sat on
the ground, the head of a pink tiger in her lap. She swept a
brush through the tiger's fur, and the animal purred.

"Mina, this is Sindy."

Sindy looked up. Her bright smile lit up her purple eyes as she waved her free hand.

"She's agreed to help keep an eye on you."

"Hi! The others will be here soon. Come say hi to Sunrise."

Mina approached cautiously, crouching and holding out her hand for Sunrise to sniff. The large cat lifted his head, sniffed at Mina's fingers, and then nuzzled against her palm.

"He likes you. No surprise there from what I've heard."

"I'll be back as quickly as I can, Mina," Luci said as he bent over to place a kiss on her forehead. "You're in good hands."

"Please be safe," Mina responded as Luci turned and walked away.

Half an hour later, Lilith arrived. In that time, Mina had learned that Sindy was in charge of all the animals of Hell, most of which she had created. The first time Luci had asked her to create a creature for him, Sindy hadn't realized that he only had need of them occasionally and that she probably should have not made them permanent fixtures. But by the time her mistake became obvious, she'd already grown attached to them anyway. As a result, she spent much of her time taking care of and entertaining them.

"You brought a giant ball of yarn!" Sindy squealed. Sunrise jumped to his paws and pranced toward Lilith.

"Nope," Lilith said, pointing first at Sunrise then the ground. The tiger stopped immediately and sat, tail flicking slightly in irritation at being denied. "Okay. Come here." Sunrise padded over slowly, and Lilith held out the yarn.

Swiping it out of Lilith's hand, the large cat batted it around on his circuitous path back to Sindy.

"Alastor should be here any minute," Sindy announced.

"You invited Alastor?" Lilith sounded less than pleased. She took a seat on the hard ground between Mina and Sindy, creating a triangle between the three of them.

"He wanted to meet Mina, too."

Lilith shook her head. "Speaking of which, it's nice to meet you, Mina." Lilith reached out her hand and Mina took it. She expected Lilith to shake it, but Lilith turned her hand over and stared down at Mina's palm.

"Oh, don't do that, Lilith," Sindy said.

"What are you doing?" Mina asked.

"Looking at your love and life lines," Lilith said, her forehead scrunching as she concentrated. "They are very strange. Long, yet fractured."

Sindy leaned over to look. "Must be because she's Lucifer's soulmate."

"I suppose so." Lilith shrugged, brushing her thumb over Mina's palm once before dropping her hand.

When Alastor arrived, Sindy greeted him by running at him full tilt and jumping into his arms. He caught her and spun her around with a low chuckle that Mina could feel vibrate lightly through the rock floor.

He carried Sindy to the remaining trio and greeted first Sunrise and then Lilith. Shyly, he mumbled her name and nodded in her direction, only briefly making eye contact with the demoness.

"Alastor, meet Mina," Lilith grumbled with crossed arms and an annoyed shake of her head.

"Hello," Mina said.

"So this is Lucifer's lady love. It is a pleasure to meet you." Alastor sat down and crossed his legs in a failed attempt to appear smaller. Mina found it endearing that he at least tried to make himself less intimidating. "I hardly recognize the man since you came into his life."

"Is that a good thing?" Mina asked.

"Yes. Yes, of course." Alastor nodded.

"He's happy, Mina," Lilith said. "I didn't know him when he was one of God's angels, so I can't say for sure, but I don't think he's ever been this happy."

"You would have to ask Beelzebub," Alastor said. "I was once human, many, many years ago. Lilith has been wandering Hell since she was kicked out of Eden. And Sindy, of course, was created shortly after The Fall."

Lilith rolled her eyes and mumbled, "I wasn't kicked out of Eden. There was no Eden."

"You were created?" Mina asked Sindy.

"Oh, yes. There was a giant orgy, and I just kind of popped out at the end."

"Which makes it all the more odd that you're practically celibate."

"I am not, Lilith!" Sindy pouted and crossed her arms. "I just don't like playing your games."

Lilith reached out and tugged a strand of Sindy's hair. "I wish you would play with me."

Sindy and Lilith locked eyes, and Alastor gulped audibly. They stared at one another until Sunrise's loud, feline yawn broke the tension.

"Where's the rest of your menagerie, Sindy?" Alastor asked.

"Berith has them. They are testing a theory about repressed fears and generational trauma."

"That sounds fascinating." Lilith smirked.

"I know!" Sindy giggled. "Berith is such an egghead."

A growl of distress started in Sunrise's throat, taking them all by surprise. He stood up, back arched. The displaced air from his forcefully flicking tail blew Mina's hair from her face.

"What's gotten into him?" Alastor asked. He moved into a crouch facing the direction in which the cat was growling with one hand pressed against the earth.

"I don't know," Sindy said, rising to her feet in alarm.

Lilith rose too, hooking her arm through Mina's and pulling her up as well. Drawing a sword, she positioned herself between Mina and whatever had Sunrise on high alert.

The ground rumbled. Something was coming. Something very, very large. The closer it got, the more the earth shook beneath their feet, fissures in the ground spreading out around them.

Rock split, and Mina fell. Lava bubbled beneath her, coming at her too quickly. There was no time to react and barely enough to conjure Luci's face before the heat became too oppressive to breathe.

A vine wrapped around her waist as another hooked around her right arm. Gravity fought against the tendrils, but the plants won. Not without jerking Mina around a bit, though; her stomach threatening to empty itself. Then Alastor had her in his arms and Lilith dragged them both back from the newly formed gorge.

From across the lava that now separated them, Sindy screamed Alastor's name, her face contorted in fear, Sunrise huddled at her feet.

Alastor's vines unwound themselves from Mina and shot across the gorge. They picked up Sindy and her tiger and brought them swiftly over right as a towering dog the size of a small mountain came into view.

It dipped its head to peer at them but did not try to cross the ravine. The canine sniffed Lilith, Alastor, Sindy, and finally Mina. With three short whiffs and one long, the dog smelled Mina again. A second head descended, and Mina thought at first it was a second dog. But its neck connected to the body of the first dog. The second head seemed mostly interested in Mina as well.

When a third head dipped down, Mina couldn't help but let out a small, startled scream. A rhythmic tap, tap, tap started, as if something heavy was hitting rock.

"Call it off, Sindy," Lilith demanded. "Call it off."

"I can't." Sindy said, shaking her head wildly. "It isn't mine."

The third head brushed against Mina's torso, nearly knocking her off balance. If Alastor hadn't been there to hold her up, she surely would have fallen.

It nipped at her, almost playfully.

"Sindy, for fuck's sake, please try!" Lilith shouted.

Sindy reached out her hand to the beast's first head, but it ignored her. Lilith brought her sword up to strike.

"Wait," Mina said. The dog's eyes were kind. That rhythmic sound—he was wagging his tail. She patted the third head's nose. It licked her, leaving a line of slobber from her chest to her hairline. All three heads snapped up. Then the beast turned and bounded away.

"What was that?" Lilith asked, sending an accusing look Sindy's way.

"It wasn't one of mine," Sindy said.

At the same time, Alastor said, "I don't know, but we had better find Lucifer."

Now nude and lonely, Mina recognized the dog from her memory to be Cerberus. Pet and guard dog to Hades. Obviously there was a lot that Luci hadn't told her. She hoped they'd have time for all her unanswered questions, but she wasn't sure how. Unless she could enact her plans to summon him.

Mina wandered the maze for what had to be at least fifteen minutes, trying to make sense of what she had remembered. Trying to remember more.

She took heart in knowing that Lilith and Alastor had to have rejoined the game by now. Perhaps she could ask them about it if one of them captured her again.

Mina glanced up, her eyes running along the tops of the brick walls. Sindy was nowhere in sight.

Two hands, white as snow, grasped her shoulders, pulling her back against a stone-hard chest. One arm snaked around her waist, tugging her closer as the other applied pressure to the back of her neck.

"I need your safe word, Mina," Beelzebub breathed against her ear.

"My safe word?"

"You say it, and the game stops. I deliver you to Luci. He might not need one, having a bit of your soul like he does, but I won't risk it. Safe word, now."

"Milton."

As soon as the word slipped past her lips, Bellz moved through a hidden doorway in the wall that closed behind them.

Fourteen

A s the flogger whooshed before landing a stinging kiss to her inner thigh, Mina slipped further into subspace. Bellz had worked her over for some time, leaving her warm, tingly, just shy of bruised, and so aroused.

She was strapped to a St. Andrew's cross made of simple wood. Looking down, she could see that her skin was a dark pink, and as Beelzebub lifted the flogger again, landing another blow, she'd realized she'd lost track of how long he'd been at it. Still, each new thud heightened her pleasure.

After flicking it across her breasts, then her stomach, and then up between her legs, Bellz tossed the flogger aside, stepped toward her, and tilted the furniture along with her up to meet him. His cool hands soothed her aching skin, tracing each faint mark he'd left, and he pressed his lips to her.

Taking her gently, he lingered as if trying to commit her taste to memory. He slid his tongue across her bottom lip before dipping it into her mouth. His hand in her hair cupped the base of her skull. He nibbled at her playfully before breaking the kiss.

"Don't leave us, Mina," Beelzebub said, his blue eyes piercing.

She blinked at him as the reality of giving up everything she'd just gained set in. And the cost to keep it. So, instead of addressing any of it, she changed the subject.

"Where did you take me?" On the way, Mina had been so shocked by how safe she had felt nestled against Bellz that she hadn't paid much attention to where they were going. And once he'd hung her from the cross, she'd been too preoccupied to care.

"Lilith turned you into such easy prey." Bellz traced his finger beneath Mina's chin. "I had been tracking you the entire time, so it wasn't hard for me to take you when I had the chance." His fingers tickled down her neck and over her collarbone. "We're under the Labyrinth, and we have until they find us. But I think that might be a while." His finger danced lazily around her nipple. "I'm not sure why Luci picked this location. He knows I come here to get away."

"How long have we been here?" As Mina came back to herself, panic set in. They were running out of time before she had to get back. If the window closed before Luci found her, she'd be stuck in Hell.

"Twenty minutes, tops," he whispered. "Worried that you won't make it home to your family?" His tongue darted out, hitting that sensitive spot beneath her ear. "That's just silly, Mina. You're with your family. You are finally home." He dipped his head to her breast and sucked on one nipple before switching to the other.

"That might be true, Bellz," Mina said on a gasp as he bit down. "I suspect that it is, given how I feel with you. But is it fair to expect me to upend my entire life when we've all only just met?"

"We haven't only just met, Mina. We've known each other for lifetimes. You just don't remember." His brow creased with frustration. "You don't know how much it hurts every time you go. Luci is a wreck, regardless of what he says about supporting you. You bring joy, hope, and life to this place." Bellz caressed her cheek, running the pad of his thumb over her bottom lip.

"Could we maybe have this conversation without me chained down?" She rattled the manacles on her wrists for emphasis.

"I don't want you running away," Bellz said. "And I'm not convinced that you won't."

"Then handcuff me to you."

Bellz breathed out heavily through his nose and then nodded. Immediately, Mina found herself huddled against Bellz' chest. She wasn't handcuffed, but he had a death grip on her. They were sitting on a very deep couch, Mina tucked into his side. Although she was still naked, it was a vast improvement.

"I don't want to leave any of you. I really don't want to leave Luci," Mina felt Bellz stiffen beside her. "What?"

"Nothing," Bellz mumbled.

"No, that wasn't nothing." Mina moved so her legs were under her and turned so she could more easily look at him. She grabbed one of his large hands in both of hers.

"It's hard to talk about." He tightened the arm wrapped around her back.

"Okay, but you're with a friend. A friend without a stitch of clothing, I might add." She bit her lip as she tipped her chin, attempting to get him to look at her. "I hope this is a safe space."

Bellz only nodded while he defied her every attempt to make eye contact.

"Then talk to me, Bellz." Mina rose up to her knees and took his face in her hands, gently turning him to face her. He sucked in air sharply.

"Luci isn't the only one who fell in love with you back then." Bellz looked sheepish, and Mina immediately let go of him and sank back down.

"Oh."

"We all love you, and we all think you are sexy as fuck," Bellz said. "But I've always loved you a little more than the rest. Except for Luci."

"I feel like Sindy would have feelings about that claim," Mina said.

"Sindy hates being competitive. She designated herself as your best friend because she knew the rest of us were gunning for something more," Bellz said. He rolled his eyes, but there was a fondness in his expression. A fondness for Sindy? "Maybe I'm just being an ass."

"It's confusing," Mina said.

"You love him the most, Mina. You always have. I learned a long time ago not to try to get in between you two."

"Then what are you doing now?"

Bellz sighed. "Trying to keep you around. For everyone. Not just for myself this time."

"Do you think you could help me, Bellz, figure out how to summon Luci to Earth? He's reluctant to give me any details on how to do it, but having a plan on how I could see you all again will make leaving a bit more bearable." Mina unconsciously traced her finger along Bellz' black t-shirt. "I know you don't want me to leave at all, but I don't have a choice. You don't understand. My family, my sister, my mother, my niece, they need me."

"I don't know. That sort of thing is dangerous, a lot more dangerous now than it was before. Luci has lost a lot of support. He doesn't control his legion like he used to." With unsteady fingers, Bellz tucked her hair behind her ear.

"The thought of being without him, it's too much, Bellz," Mina said as a few tears escaped down her cheeks.

"Don't cry, Mina," Bellz said, placing a kiss on the top of her head. "I'll help, even though Luci is going to kill me for it. There are places you can go, nightclubs mostly, that cater to our kind and our followers on Earth. As far as summoning goes, I don't know all the ins and outs of the ceremonies, but it is possible. I think there are numerous methods. If you start looking, you'll find it."

"How can I recognize the nightclubs?"

Bellz shrugged. "It's not like they are marked. You'll have to just go to a bunch until you get lucky. But I do know that at least one exists in San Jose. That's where you're living now, right? I think there's also a coffee shop or a bookstore in Petaluma."

"They aren't even all nightclubs?"

Bellz squeezed her side. "We are all drawn to you, Mina. Not just the five of us. I mean all of us are drawn to you."

"Why? Because of the sliver of Luci's soul I possess?"

Bellz shook his head, his hand tracing intricate designs on her hip. "That won't matter to as many of us as it once would have. You stood up to God; even if we don't all like the outcome, we still recognize your power. We crave it, and we'll do anything for a taste." The tip of his finger caressed the crease between her hip and leg. "This desire we all have, it should protect you from being killed. At least at first. But it won't protect your loved ones, and it won't protect your virtue. To summon a demon, even one of us, is asking for sex whether you want it or not."

"Whether I want it or not?" Mina looked Bellz up and down. "If they all look like you—"

"They don't."

Mina shuffled around uncomfortably. Her fluids, thick and viscous, pooled between her legs. "Holy crap, I'm wet."

Bellz laughed and finally dared to meet her eyes. "I see my warm-up is finally catching up to you. You have always been a bit of a pain slut."

"Have not." Mina punched his arm ineffectually.

Bellz growled, pinning Mina beneath him in seconds. "Don't provoke me." He dipped his head and bit down on the flesh connecting her neck and shoulder.

"Eek! Bellz, that hurts," Mina stilled despite the pain. For one thing, she could feel herself getting, inexplicably, even wetter. For another, she didn't want to rile him up any more than she already had.

"Get off of her, Bellz," Luci said. "You've had way longer than your allotted time."

Fifteen

Luci had found her. She let out a sigh of relief as she spotted him across the room. As he checked her over, he gave her a small, reassuring smile.

Bellz looked up at Luci then back down at Mina. He flashed a predatory grin and kissed her. This kiss was nothing like the last one. It was fierce, almost angry, and definitely possessive.

Bellz was trying to piss off Luci.

"Bellz," Luci snarled. He flung his wrist and Bellz was pulled into the air, but he was faster than Luci anticipated, clutching Mina to him so that she was pulled along.

"You're the one who is always preaching to me about sharing," Bellz said, lowering them both to their feet. "So let me have a little longer." He moved his hands down Mina's body, cupping her vulva in one hand and squeezing her ass in the other while he sucked noisily on her neck.

"If you insist on sharing, then we are going to share, Brother." Luci's voice came from right behind her, and she could feel his warmth on her back. He placed one hand on her hip and the other on her left breast, took another step forward, and buried his face in the other side of her neck.

I am going to be covered in hickeys, Mina thought, but she couldn't resist them. Not separately and definitely not together.

She brought both hands up and held Luci's and Bellz' heads to her, sliding her fingers through their hair. Relishing in the surround sound of their groans.

"What would you like us to do to you, Mina?" Luci whispered into her ear before pulling her earlobe into his mouth.

"I think you know my answer already, my love. Whatever you want." Mina thrust her breasts out toward Bellz as he was once again playing with them, sucking on a nipple while he flicked the other with his powerful fingers.

"Very well," Luci said as Mina's hands were tugged upwards, wrapped in rough rope, and tied to an eye bolt anchored in the ceiling. Both Bellz and Luci stepped away from her.

"Should I continue with the flogger?" Bellz asked, shuffling over to where it now hung on the wall. It was either a different flogger or he had used his magic to put it back in its proper place. "Or maybe a paddle?"

Silently, Luci circled Mina. The ropes tugged upwards so that she had to stand on her toes, the balls of her feet just barely elevated above the floor. "We have this human girl completely at our mercy. And she just gave us permission to do whatever we like."

"That's true," Bellz said, leaving the flogger and the paddle on their hooks. He turned back toward her. "Her flesh is very soft, inviting."

"It's already got a warm glow to it," Luci said, voice husky. "I think I'd like to feel that warmth beneath my hands."

Mina whimpered, waiting for the impact. She focused on their breathing as anticipation built. Three sets of ragged breathing. They craved her as badly as she did them.

Luci swatted her ass with his open palm. As she waited for his hand to land again, Bellz smacked her breasts with the back of his. They took turns beating her ass, the back of her thighs, her breasts, her labia, her clit. Sometimes they hit her hard enough to almost knock the breath from her lungs, sometimes only hard enough to warm her. They never delivered a blow she couldn't handle, didn't gladly invite, and as they continued, what she could take, what she needed, increased.

Bellz brought his hand to her pussy in a sharp spank, and her wetness splattered against him. "I think she's ready," he said. When her bonds disappeared, her legs gave out. Luci scooped her up, carried her back to the very large couch, and tossed her onto it, face down.

She squeaked, and Luci climbed behind her, pulling her ass up into the air and bringing his face between her legs. He tasted her with his tongue and then shoved three fingers into her vagina. She whined, her orgasm just out of reach.

"Not yet, little cum slut," Luci said as he removed his fingers from her pussy and plunged them into her ass. "I'm going to fuck you here, and Bellz is going to fuck your pussy, and we want you to save your cum for that." Luci slid another finger into her ass and ravished her.

Mina could make out Bellz in the corner of her eye. She saw him watching what Luci was doing in rapt attention while he stroked his cock. It had to be larger than Luci's, and she quivered at the thought of him stretching her. Only Alastor's mammoth was larger.

Luci wrapped his other hand around Mina's waist and tugged her up so her back was pressed to his front. Manhandling her breast, he tweaked her nipple and tugged on it. With an incline of his head, he cued Bellz to climb onto the couch.

Bellz laid down in front of them so when Luci dropped Mina, Bellz was there to catch her. He helped her to straddle him, the tip of his cock right below her entrance.

"Ride me, Mina," Bellz said, then smacked her ass. "Now."

Mina slowly lowered herself onto Bellz. Oh, yes, he definitely stretched her. With him only about half way into her warm tunnel, she whimpered and stopped moving while she adjusted to the size. Bellz growled as Luci pushed down on her from behind, fully impaling her on Bellz. He was almost too much, the sound escaping her throat unfamiliar. She rocked as much as she was able against him, trying to bring friction to her apex.

"Don't you fucking come yet," Luci spat at her, pulling his fingers from her ass. She felt him against her, lovingly rubbing her breasts, her hips, her clit, his touch in stark contrast with his tone. "I want to feel it when you do." She felt the tip of his penis against her rosebud and froze.

Bellz thrust into her and pushed her back onto Luci's cock. His tip slid into her ass, and once started, he didn't stop. In moments she was fully impaled on both cocks. Forget the attempted fisting from earlier; this was as full as she had ever felt.

There was no way she would last long.

Then her demons started moving, taking turns thrusting. She felt like a puddle of sensation, held together by the will of her two lovers alone. Soon they were slamming into her, Bellz into her cervix, and Luci as far into her as he could get. The pressure against her cervix hurt, but it tethered her, heightened her pleasure. Bellz sucked on a breast, and Luci rubbed her clit.

Mina's sudden climax hit hard, her cunt clamping down on Bellz' cock.

Bellz and Luci stilled. Mina could hear Luci's calming breaths behind her as Bellz' tickled the hair behind her ear. She felt them both twitch. They were close.

Bellz reached his hand around her ass where he slipped a finger into her alongside Luci's cock at the same time that Luci slipped a finger inside of Mina's pussy, filling her even more. They began to move again, in tandem. Their thrusts were slow, deliberate. She came again, and this time both demons came with her.

She collapsed on top of Bellz, and Luci crushed her between them until she wiggled and grunted, and he shifted his weight off of them. His arm and a leg remained draped over Mina's body. Luci's head rested on Bellz' shoulder.

Bellz' chest rose and fell underneath her in heavy pants. "Stay," he whispered.

Mina whimpered at the request. Every fiber of her being begged her to obey, to give in.

Bellz rolled to his side, and Mina found herself wedged between her lovers. Luci's front was pressed to her back and Bellz' nose rested against her cheek.

"Stay," Luci whispered into her ear.

Mina closed her eyes, willing the building tears not to spill, not to give her away.

Luci said, "No one on Earth will ever love you the way that I do." A pause. "Or, hell, even the way this guy does."

Mina laughed, but it was a shaky sound, vulnerable in a way she wasn't quite yet ready to face.

So instead she kissed Bellz, a swift but hard kiss, hoping to distract him from the disobedient tear that rolled down her cheek.

She didn't want to say it, but she had to. She owed them honesty. She didn't have a choice. There was only one option.

But she would bottle this all up so that once she was back on Earth she could savor it during the countless lonely nights in her future. At least her demons would still have each other. If only she could help them see that, appreciate it for the gift it was.

"I'll be gone by morning, but there is no use dwelling on it. Lilith promised me an after party."

"You still haven't solved the Labyrinth." Luci softly kissed her shoulder, his arm draped over her and resting on Bellz' side.

"Everyone has had a turn with me. I think it's safe to say that I lost." Mina grabbed Luci's hand and brought it to her mouth. She sucked on his finger while making sure to maintain eye contact with Bellz.

When Bellz gulped and Luci stiffened behind her, Mina lowered her lashes. Sensuously, Mina pulled Luci's finger from her mouth and said, "Ravage me at the after party."

"I don't want to share her with the rest of them, Luci," Bellz said. "Sharing her with you is bad enough."

"Try, Bellz," Mina kissed his neck. "For me."

"You might see my beastly side before you leave, Mina," Bellz said. His smile didn't quite reach his eyes. Was she asking too much of him? She shook the thought aside. She didn't want to celebrate without him.

"I'll keep you in check, Brother," Luci vowed.

Sixteen

LUCI LED MINA, DRESSED in nothing more than a silk robe, by the hand through the maze of the Labyrinth until they reached its center. They entered a large area with a hot tub, a humongous bed, and a table piled with food. Bellz trailed behind them, his arms crossed over his chest. Even though he wasn't actually pouting, he was giving off a lot of upset-toddler energy.

The rest of the gang wasn't here yet, Mina needed to cheer up Bellz, and inspiration had just struck. She turned to Luci and kissed him. "Why don't you go gather the others?"

Luci glanced from Bellz to Mina then nodded his head and disappeared.

She padded over to where Bellz lingered by the doorway. She reached out, grabbed his hand, and tugged on it. Reluctantly, he stepped toward her.

"Are you mad that I want to share you, or are you mad that I'm leaving?"

"I'm not mad, Mina. I'm heartbroken."

"You don't know how I can summon you, do you?" She brought her hands up to his head and buried her fingers in his hair, nudging him gently to look at her.

"You want to summon me?"

"You think it's only going to be hard for me to say good-bye to Luci?" She raised up on her toes and kissed him. His large hands closed around her waist and pulled her into him.

"I was once summoned through a spirit board by this young, blond teenager home from college," he whispered as he picked her up and carried her to the bed.

"What did you do to them?" Mina asked.

"I couldn't do anything to her myself since the connection was only through the board. But I gave her very specific instructions on what she should do to herself."

"You sexted via spirit board?"

Bellz nodded as he placed Mina on the bed.

"What did you tell her to do?"

"I had her fuck herself with whatever she had handy. A TV remote, a candlestick, a vegetable or two from the kitchen." Bellz tugged Mina's robe down over her shoulder and exposed her left breast. He bent down and lapped at her. "I'd love to do that to you now. Fill you up with whatever I can find."

But they could hear the others talking and laughing loudly as they made their way to the center of the maze. Bellz pulled Mina's robe over her shoulder, covering her up once more, and left the bed. She quickly sat up and brought her legs around so that they hung over the edge.

Bellz smiled at her once before the rest of the group invaded their quiet time, and she feared it was the last time she would see it in this lifetime. She vowed then and there that she would do whatever was in her power to reach out to them from Earth. There was no way she was going to spend her life without any of them.

As Sindy, Alastor, and Lilith, with Luci behind them, came into the doorway, Mina jumped down from the bed, skipped over to Bellz, and kissed him on the cheek before running to greet the others.

"Mina!" Alastor's bass baritone rattled the room as he picked her up in his arms and swung her around.

"Alastor, I think I owe you something." Mina blushed as he placed her back on her feet.

"You owe me nothing, little one. Giving you pleasure is always enough for me."

Mina pouted. "But what if it wasn't enough for me?"

Alastor chuckled then bent over and picked Mina up by her hips and swung her over his shoulder. "Anyone else hear that we haven't satisfied our queen?"

"I definitely heard that," Lilith said, and Mina felt the brush of Lilith's hand along her thigh, clawed fingernails lightly tickling skin.

"It sure sounded like it," Luci said. "Although I can't imagine that it's true. How many times have you come in the last few days, my love?"

"But surely Mina wouldn't lie to us," Sindy said.

"Take her to the bed," Bellz commanded.

After Alastor deposited her onto the mattress, her limbs were pulled into four different directions and clipped into padded cuffs attached to metal link chains that clinked against each other every time Mina moved. Someone untied her robe and pulled it open.

"Um, guys, this isn't exactly what I had in mind," Mina said.

"But you said that you weren't satisfied," Sindy said as she sat next to Mina's head and brushed her fingers through Mina's hair.

"No. I'm unsatisfied that some of you have gone unsatisfied."

"Yeah," Lilith quipped, climbing on top of the bed and straddling Mina's hips, "that makes no sense to us."

"Well, I got you to come, Lilith," Mina said. "But Alastor and Sindy haven't yet."

"Sure we did!" Sindy said. "Bellz had you, though, so you missed it."

"Hmm, well, one more for all of us seems fair," Mina, more than a bit bummed she missed out, suggested.

"I think for each of ours, it's only fair that you get one, my love," Luci said.

Lilith slid down Mina's body, slipping between her spread legs. She lowered her lips to Mina's clit and gave it a gentle kiss. Luci climbed on top of Mina's chest before guiding his penis between her breasts. Grabbing hold of one mound of flesh in each hand, he pushed them together and guided his hard tool between them.

Alastor stood above her head and lowered his large cock to Mina's mouth where she kissed and licked him, blissfully continuing her penis worship from before. Sindy, who still sat next to Mina on the bed, lowered her lips and began lapping at Alastor's cock from above.

Slowly, Sindy worked her way down so that her tongue flicked against Mina's. Alastor groaned and pulled back out of their reach, and Sindy fell on Mina with a passionate kiss.

When Alastor brought his dick back between them, Sindy and Mina tried to continue their make-out session around

Alastor, which resulted in them covering his cock with slobber, kisses, and licks. Their lips could only meet when Alastor pulled back so that just his tip was between them. They created a seal around him as their tongues flicked against his beautifully monstrous dick on their way to each other.

Alastor worked his hips, timing his thrusts with Luci so that they wouldn't get in each other's way. Meanwhile, Lilith covered Mina's clit and labia with gentle kisses. She slid a single finger into her and swirled it around, gently prodding at her g-spot and inner walls.

Mina whimpered her need, and Luci stopped his movements to turn and look back at Lilith. "What are you doing back there?"

"Giving Mina a taste of her own sweet medicine," Lilith said between kisses.

"While I love your instincts, we don't have time for it. Come help me with her tits. Bellz, what are you doing just standing there? Take Lilith's spot." Luci's commanding tone had Mina's cunt clenching down right as Lilith retreated, and she gasped at the emptiness.

Lilith climbed up to Mina's side, opposite Sindy.

"Oh, good call, Luci," Lilith said before planting a gentle kiss on his mouth. "This is where the show is happening." Lilith clamped down on Mina's nipples, sending a shock of enticing pain to the human's core, and used her grip to pull Mina's breasts up and together. Luci picked up his pace.

With everyone crowded around her head, Mina couldn't see Bellz as he replaced Lilith between her legs, but she could feel the mattress dip. At first, he picked up where Lilith had left off, covering her in soft kisses, but then sucked violently on her clit, forced three of his digits into her, and fucked her. She came instantly.

"Good job, Bellz," Luci said.

"That's one for me," Mina said breathlessly. "Now I want one for one of you." Mina rattled her chains. Even though she was frustrated that she couldn't touch them in return, she resumed her adoration for Alastor's cock and Sindy's mouth.

"Luci, I think your lady is greedy for our cum," Alastor said as Sindy began to work her mouth over the head of his cock. It put her at a bit of an awkward angle above Mina but also between Luci and Alastor. "Pardon me, Mina," Alastor shifted to the side so that Sindy could more easily get her mouth on him.

Mina watched wide-eyed as Sindy took the giant's green length into her mouth and then her throat. Sindy appeared part serpent the way her jaw distended to fit him.

With the snap of Luci's fingers, Mina's chains disappeared. The weight of him perched above her held her in place, but she gripped the back of Lilith's head with one hand and pulled her down. Lilith let go of Mina's nipples as she tried to catch herself. When their lips met, Lilith happily returned Mina's kiss.

Luci groaned at the sight, and Mina felt his cock harden, if that were possible, against her chest. He brought her tits together once more and resumed using them as his personal cock sleeve. But he only managed for a moment before getting frustrated and grabbing Lilith by her hair, yanking her out of the way.

"And I thought Bellz was bad at sharing," Lilith grumbled, anger in her eyes at having been interrupted again. In response, Luci slammed his mouth against Lilith's. They growled as their teeth mashed, fighting to get closer to one another or to defeat the other in their passionate battle.

"I want to see you fist her," Luci said, his lips brushing against Lilith's as he spoke. Mina's stomach tightened with desire at the sight of them.

"I'm going to need some help," Lilith said. "She was too tight earlier."

"What about what I want?" Mina asked.

Luci shot her an incredulous look. "I already know what you want."

"And what is that?" Mina asked. She was frustrated at her lack of control. More often than not, her helplessness in the hands of her lover was intoxicating. But right now, when she would be leaving soon and might not get the opportunity again, she wanted to show them all how much they meant to her. They needed to know that she would miss them just as much as they would her.

"Everything I'm willing to give you," Luci said, stooping down to kiss her with enough heat that she almost forgot her objections.

It took all her strength, but Mina pushed Luci off of her. He careened into Sindy and Alastor and the couple broke apart. Sindy burst into giggles, which started Alastor chuckling. Lilith calmly sat in place, a smug look on her face as if she were happy to see someone finally push Luci around a little.

"What was that?" Luci asked, clearly shocked.

Mina sat up quickly and tucked her legs under her so that she was squatting, ready to pounce. "What about what I want to give to you?" With a growl, Mina flung herself at Luci. He landed on his back as she straddled him. He couldn't disguise his smile.

"I will take whatever you want to give me," Luci said as he reached around to grab her ass. This time, Mina kissed him.

He opened his mouth to her, and her tongue danced with his. She was lost in it and never wanted to be found, willing time to stop for a while longer.

After grinding her hips against Luci's hard tool, she positioned her entrance at his tip and pressed down. Her toes curled as she sank down onto him.

She sat up and arched her back as she rode him. The others in the room were entranced, and it seemed like none of them remembered how to breathe, Luci least of all. He didn't move beneath her as she rode him. Even as she grew more frantic, her moans getting louder, he lay as still as stone.

Mina had almost begun to worry that he had actually turned to rock when he came inside her, spurting his seed into her womb. All at once his breath returned to him, and he gulped down air and moaned her name.

He pulled her down against him and then flipped her over so that he was on top of her. "Is that what you wanted?" He kissed her neck. "To make love to me in front of everyone?"

"I want you to know that I love you." Mina kissed the top of his head, his forehead, his temple. "I want you all to know that I care." She turned to look at Sindy, Alastor, and Lilith. Finally, her eyes met Bellz, and she was surprised by the longing she saw there. Before thinking about it, she reached out a hand to him and he took it. She kissed his palm.

Luci moved out of the way so that Bellz could claim his spot on top of her. She cupped the back of Bellz' head and pulled him toward her. As he slipped into her she whispered, "You are worthy of love, Bellz. I care for you deeply." He buried his face into the crook of her neck and let her thrust up against him.

Mina turned her head to the side and glanced at Sindy sitting snuggled up against Lilith. Sindy's gaze was clouded with longing, and her eyes were glued to Bellz. Mina wondered why Lilith had claimed that Sindy was celibate, yet it hadn't taken much to get her to join them. Perhaps Sindy was protecting her heart. But from whom?

"Roll over, Bellz?" Mina asked, and Bellz complied. She rode him for a moment or two, mostly to watch Sindy's reaction, before climbing off of him. "Stay there, please."

Mina held her hand out to Sindy, and Sindy squeaked, shaking her head.

"Trust me," Mina said, crawling over to the two female demons. Pressing the palm of her hand to Sindy's cheek, she kissed her sweetly. Bellz growled behind her, and she reached back to place her hand on his arm. Mina broke the kiss and held her hand out to Sindy again. This time Sindy took it.

Mina helped Sindy climb on top of Bellz. The two of them seemed to be in a daze and would do no more than she directed. With patience, Mina lined Bellz's erect member with Sindy's wet entrance. Very slowly, she pushed down on Sindy's shoulders until Sindy was completely impaled.

Sindy and Bellz moaned their pleasure in unison, and Mina couldn't help the upward curve to her lips. It made sense, this union. Bellz didn't like to share, and Sindy wasn't overly fond of playing games. Besides the fact that Mina was pretty sure

Sindy had wanted this for a very long time. And, if the look in Bellz' eyes was any indication, he had too.

Still, the couple didn't move. They only stared into each other's eyes, as if the raw emotion was more than they could comprehend. Mina straddled Bellz' legs and pressed her body against Sindy's. She wrapped her arms around her and placed one hand on Sindy's hip and the other below her breast.

"Follow me," Mina said as she pulled Sindy up and then plunged her back down. "Roll your hips a little. Feel him inside of you, and let your desire build with his, slowly."

As she continued to move with Sindy, her hand wandering down to rub Sindy's clit in gentle circles, Mina made eye contact with Luci. He was gazing at her in awe and adoration, and she couldn't bring herself to break their connection. If only she could live in his gaze forever.

Bellz began with small thrusts. His hands came up to grip Sindy's hips, and he rolled into her. Sindy gasped his name. And then they both came apart together. Mina let Sindy go, and the demoness fell forward against Bellz' chest. His hands roamed her back, pressing Sindy to him so tightly that his fingertips made indentations in her skin.

Luci plucked Mina from the bed and held her cradled in his arms.

"What?" she asked. He nodded toward where Lilith and Alastor clung together on the bed. Lilith lay on her back and Alastor between her legs. He slowly inserted himself into her, and they lay motionless, clutched around each other for a long moment before moving together tenderly.

"You keep teaching us new things." Luci kissed her shoulder.

"You already know how to love me like that," Mina said.

"Yes, but I don't do it enough." He carried her to a large armchair. It seemed to appear out of nowhere—or perhaps Mina hadn't noticed it before, but she doubted that. It existed now because Luci needed it to. She wondered if he'd keep these powers if she managed to summon him to Earth.

He sat down on the chair. "Straddle me, Mina. I want to feel you around me once more."

"What about my fisting?" Mina asked.

"It will have to wait for another lifetime, I suppose," Luci said, and she could see the tears standing in his eyes. "It's good to have things to look forward to."

In that moment, Mina didn't just understand the strength of Luci's devotion to her. She felt it. It came hurtling down on top of her like a ton of lovely bricks, and it was her turn to forgot how to breathe.

Mina slipped down onto his rigidness and clenched him with her muscles, letting her walls ripple against him while otherwise staying motionless. She bent her head to kiss his neck. She infused her love into each press of her lips. She had to make sure that he would have enough of her love to last him.

"I will love you until then and beyond," she whispered into his ear.

He thrust up into her lightly, rubbing his body against her core. They came together, their orgasms rolling on as Mina continued to trace Luci's upper body with her lips. As they came back down, panting, caressing each other, Mina stilled and found Luci's face streaked with tears, beads of water reflecting off the greenness of his eyes.

She kissed his tears, "Please don't cry, master of all that is evil, villainous, and diabolical. You have all of my love. If you asked for what of my soul you don't already own, I would willingly give it to you."

"Then stay." Luci held onto her fiercely. She could feel him getting hard inside of her again, as if his hard member could keep her in place.

"I can't, Luci, but you can take it out on me—the disappointment, the urge to chain me down and keep me forever. You can fuck me now," Mina said.

Luci shook his head. "I promised to support you, and I won't allow that to have been a lie."

"It won't be, so long as you let me go."

"No, Mina. I want you to remember my love. Not my darker self."

"I love every bit of you, especially your darker side." Mina pressed her lips to his as he stood up, slipping out of her, and carried her back to the bed where Lilith and Alastor had just finished, still entwined with one another, Alastor with the silliest grin plastered across his face.

"I've never experienced anything like that, Mina," Sindy said from where she was spooning with Bellz. His head rested on hers, dozing happily.

"Incoming," Luci yelled as he tossed Mina into the air at the snoozing group. Alastor caught her and held her to his chest. He laid back on the bed, and she collapsed next to him, her knee resting on his thigh. Luci climbed up onto the bed behind her and spooned her. Lilith laid on her back and placed her head on Alastor's chest. Mina traced Lilith's shoulder and arm in adoring caresses. Sindy climbed over Luci and Mina to slip in between her and Alastor, resting her head on Mina's hip. Bellz scooted over, draping himself against Luci's back. With his left arm, he reached across Luci and Mina to clasp hands with Sindy.

Mina felt content, safe, and warm, and she knew she'd never feel quite this way again. She clutched the arm Luci had draped over her.

"I love you, Luci. I love you all," she mumbled as sleepiness took her. The steady rise and fall of Alastor's chest and Luci's breath on her shoulder lolled her into deep sleep.

Seventeen

P AIN. SO. MUCH. PAIN.

Mina's lungs burned. The left side of her body ached. A throbbing in her head left her dizzy and confused. And underneath it all, her heart had been fractured into shards. She'd left them behind. She had left Luci, and it hurt to breathe.

Hesitantly, she opened her eyes and found herself in a hospital bed. Although fancy, the room was fairly nondescript. It wasn't a medical institution in the network she worked for but likely a private facility associated with the matchmaker or one of her clients. The curtains were drawn, yet Mina could see sunshine peeking around the edges. Her mother sat at her bedside, a well-loved romance novel lying open in her lap.

Luci had only been a dream? Of course he had been a delusion her mind had created to make sense of trauma. Mina closed her eyes against a sharp, new pain splintering her heart further. He wasn't real.

Opening her eyes again, Mina focused on her very real mother. "Mom, you've ruined that book." Her voice came out raw, and she coughed before she could continue. "That spine is so broken."

"You're awake!" Sandra smiled at her daughter before placing the back of her hand against Mina's forehead. "And I think your fever has gone down."

"What happened?"

"You fell over the railing. But, luckily, that very nice man didn't waste a moment before jumping in after you. It was a harrowing rescue, from what I've been told. More importantly," Sandra said, lifting one eyebrow, "he didn't make any love matches on the cruise." Wiggling her shoulders, Sandra waited a beat, but when Mina didn't respond, she drooped and leveled her daughter with a stare. "He's still single."

"I almost die, and you are still trying to set me up," Mina said, attempting to prop herself up in bed and failing. Sandra stood, setting her book in her chair, and stacked pillows behind Mina's back.

"Can you blame a mother for wanting grandchildren?"

"You have a granddaughter."

"And I would like more," Sandra said, arms crossed. "I thought that maybe your near-death experience would shift your priorities. There wasn't a white light and a long-dead family member there to tell you the meaning of life?"

Mina laughed. "What would the meaning of life be, Mom?"

"To settle down and have kids, of course."

"The meaning of life is to beget more life? Yeah, that actually tracks, I guess." Mina sighed but winced at the ache that followed. "Unfortunately, there was no white light. I did dream I was in Hell, though." Mina shrugged.

"Hell? What have you been doing that got you sent to Hell?"

"Relax, Mom. It was just a dream. And I only remember some of it." Mina winced at the lie. She remembered it vividly.

The memory of Luci's lips and his weight on top of her rushed back all at once, and she flushed.

It had definitely been a dream, right? There was no way that any of that could be real. Mina gasped as anguish washed over her. She didn't want it to be just a dream, but it had been. Of course it had.

She couldn't have met her soulmate in Hell, and she certainly didn't have an orgy with him and all his best friends. Her toes curled as she remembered all the sex her mind had conjured. But it had to have been a dream. Being desired by so many would never be her reality.

A man with dark brown hair and green eyes poked his head around the corner of the door frame. He smiled when he saw Mina sitting up in bed. "Pardon me, but I wanted to check in on Mina. Can I pop in?"

Sandra nodded. "Please do. Mina, this is Victor. He was the young man who rescued you." Victor made his way to the bedside, and Sandra vacated her chair. "I'll just give you two some privacy." Mina's mother slipped from the room with nothing more than a wink in her daughter's direction.

The man was tall and lanky, with enough muscular definition and wavy locks of hair to be considered handsome. He was currently wearing slacks and a sweater vest, though, and it wasn't doing much to flatter him. Maybe he had dressed to impress her mother.

Mina rubbed between her eyes. Her headache had returned.

"You must be dehydrated," Victor said as he poured a glass of water for her from the pitcher sitting on a side table. When he handed her the cup, his fingers lightly brushed hers.

"What possessed you to jump in after me?"

"I didn't really think about it. When I was a kid, we had a tradition to jump into our neighborhood lake every spring after the ice melted. I've been in colder waters." He flashed her a lopsided grin.

"Well, thank you." Mina took a sip of the water. She hadn't realized how parched she was, and the cool water soothed her throat.

"I was hoping that you might contemplate thanking me with more than words." Victor's cheeks reddened.

"Excuse me?" The effects of her dream had not exactly worn off yet, and she couldn't shake the notion that he was propositioning her.

"Oh, no," Victor's blush deepened until it looked like a sunburn, "I just meant that you would hopefully consider letting me take you out on a date once you are feeling better."

Mina laughed and nodded.

His blush faded and was replaced with a warm smile that only barely filled his eyes.

Having accomplished his goal, Victor didn't linger. He mumbled an awkward goodbye after they'd exchanged numbers and exited the room.

Mina settled against her pillows and sighed. Whereas the prospect of a date with another man didn't provide much of a balm to soothe her heartache at being without Luci, it did give a direction in which to go. That seemed like reason enough to say yes. Maybe it would turn into something, but, at a minimum, it would provide a distraction. Her mother, at least, would be thrilled.

A South Asian woman with thick, black hair highlighted with gray knocked on the open door, flashing a badge. Mina waved her in, and the woman stepped inside.

"Hi, Mina. I'm Detective Jacobs," the woman said, stopping at the foot of the bed. "Your mother sent me up. It's nice to see that you are awake. How are you feeling?"

"Like I plunged two stories into the Pacific Ocean, I suppose," Mina said, shrugging. "Honestly, I'm happy to be alive." Mina debated whether that statement was true. Maybe she would have preferred to stay in her Hellish fantasy.

"Do you remember at all what happened?"

"I was talking to my sister. A large group of people moved past me, and I felt someone grab me." Mina shook her head.

"That corroborates what your sister told us. She heard you say, 'Get off me,' and a scream before the call went out. Our current theory is that someone helped you over that railing. Given your height, the railing was too tall for you to have fallen over."

"I flattened myself against the railing to make more room. I definitely didn't climb it. But why would someone want to push me overboard?"

"Our leading theory? A misguided prank," Officer Jacobs said, nodding to the chair. "Mind if I sit?"

"Oh, please do."

Officer Jacobs moved to the chair and sat down. "Did you make any connections on the boat?"

"Not really," Mina said. "Although Victor just asked me out on a date. Should I be concerned?"

"Oh, no," Officer Jacobs shook her head, working her bottom lip between her teeth. "I don't think so. Victor's the one who saved you."

"Oh, okay," Mina said. Even to herself she sounded unconvinced.

"But here's my card." Officer Jacobs held out her business card, and Mina took it. "Feel free to call me if you remember anything of significance, or if Victor makes you uncomfortable."

"So, you're saying there's a possibility he could be the culprit?"

"Of course there's a possibility, but after having interviewed him, I believe it to be a remote one."

"Okay," Mina said, staring at the card in her hand without really seeing it. She couldn't help feeling like a sacrificial lamb being led to the slaughter. Although Mina had to suppress a chuckle at the thought of timid, vest-wearing Victor being a predator.

"My cell phone number is written on the back. You can reach me there any time."

Sandra chose that moment to return to the room, a bag of fast food in her hand, and Officer Jacobs took it as her cue to leave.

"Mom, have you cleared that food with the doctor?"

"Of course," Sandra said.

"Oh, thank God. I'm starving."

Eighteen

THE FIRST TWO DATES with Victor had gone well. Really well, surprisingly. She hadn't had high expectations, but when Victor showed up in a smart business suit to take her to the opera on the first night, she had swooned. She'd learned that he was an investment banker who dabbled in real estate. Although he came from money, he prided himself on the fact that he earned most of his wealth.

He had kissed her on her doorstep at the end of the night, and she had had to stop herself from inviting him in.

The second date, a picnic in the park, had gone just as well. They had spread a blanket under a tree with leaves just starting to turn to a deep red, drank wine, and cuddled as they'd gotten to know each other better. His timidness had completely disappeared. Mina found his confidence and his occasionally demanding demeanor very sexy.

So she wasn't terribly shocked when Victor had called her out of the blue two nights later and asked her to meet up at a nightclub. Any fears she had had that he had been the one to toss her into the ocean had been forgotten. Which led her to this moment, breathless from hours of dancing and sitting on a low loveseat off the side of the popping dance floor while Victor made his way back to her with two drinks in hand.

He placed the drinks on the table in front of them and slinked down onto the couch next to her, wrapping an arm around her shoulders.

"You didn't spike it, did you?" Mina asked, not waiting for an answer before she took a swig of her double rum and coke.

Victor chuckled. "What if I told you that I had?" He slipped his hand down her back and let it rest on her waist, his pinky tickling over her bare hip.

"Hmm," Mina smiled seductively at him before taking another generous gulp. "Maybe I want to be at your mercy."

He pulled her drink from her hand and placed it on the table before tugging on her hip, rotating her, and pulling her over him so she was straddling his lap. He gave her a tiny smack on the ass. "You're feisty today."

She nodded and nuzzled against his neck. "Wanna dance?"

"Let's go back to my place, and then we can dance for as long as you want," he whispered before nibbling on her earlobe.

Mina stood and offered him her hand. He took it and rose, snagging their drinks. He downed his whiskey in one gulp while he thrust her glass out to her. "Finish it."

Victor's eyes remained plastered on her bobbing throat while she chugged the sweet fluid. She placed the empty cup next to his. Victor pulled out his phone and called them a cab.

"The car's ten minutes away." Victor pulled Mina to the dance floor where he flipped her around and pulled her ass into his groin. They rubbed against each other, his hand tickling the sides of her breasts. She reached above her, getting lost in the locks of his shoulder-length hair.

As they danced, the recently imbibed rum set in, intensifying her buzz to full inebriation. There was only Victor's hard body pressed against her, and she groaned as he grasped her right breast in his hand, unconcerned that the revelers around her might notice.

"Our car is here, gorgeous," Victor said as he untangled their bodies. Their hands loosely clasped, he led her through the doors of the nightclub and into the crisp night air to the waiting car.

The back seat was spacious, and, after a little chitchat with the male driver, Victor pulled Mina closer to him and kissed her. His hand made its way under her tight shirt, but there wasn't enough space to move. He quickly gave up, choosing instead to slowly lift her shirt up until her breasts were free of it. She wasn't wearing a bra.

Mina glanced at the driver, who was staring intently at the road.

"Don't worry about him," Victor said. "He knows that if he wants a good tip, he can't look. You are a lady."

Mina tried to hold in her snort but it came out anyway. A lady? Really? She was practically throwing herself at Victor. Third date rule or not, she felt nothing like a lady.

"Are you not? Should I ask him to turn back and look at your breasts?" Victor asked, raising a brow at her, as he leaned down and kissed a nipple. "Regardless, you're mine tonight, and I do not share."

Mina blinked at him, taken back to her dream. To Bellz and his intoxicating possessiveness, and how it crumbled—for her. She swallowed, remembering Sindy's warmth as Mina fucked Bellz with the demoness. When she pulled herself from her memory, Victor was staring at her intently.

"You like it when I call you mine." Victor's smile was frightening, and she didn't dare correct him. It had been the memory—was it a memory?—of her demons that had dilated her eyes and heightened her arousal. But it seemed that Victor liked the reaction, so she would let him believe what he wanted.

Victor tugged Mina's shirt back down and opened the car door. They had stopped in front of a large, two-story home. Victor helped Mina from the vehicle and waved to the driver as he pulled away. Leading Mina inside, Victor closed and locked the door behind her.

As he turned right into the dinning room to pour drinks, Mina wandered the first floor. There was an office on her left and stairs leading to the second floor in front of her. Past the staircase was a short hallway that led to a family room and the kitchen to the right of that.

In the kitchen, Mina found a door that was padlocked. She assumed it went to the basement. The house looped around so that the kitchen dumped back into the dinning room at the front of the house.

"What's behind the locked door? A sex dungeon?" Mina asked as she approached Victor at the bar.

"Sounds like you would like it to be a sex dungeon." Victor slid a glass across the bar to her. She took a sip without asking what it was and was pleasantly surprised by the warm honey flavor that filled her senses. The drink burned ever so slightly on the way down.

"My kink showing already?" Mina asked, wincing. "I usually try to save that for the fifth date."

"I don't believe a lady like you has a kinky bone in her body."

"Is that your kink? Would you enjoy corrupting me?" Even though she sat on the tall stool with her back to the bar, her mind was transported back through lifetimes to Luci warning her that his game would be a challenge for a virgin who'd never so much as orgasmed.

Victor came around in front of her. He pushed her legs apart and then knelt, bringing his head between them. Only a skimpy thong stood between him and his prize, her short skirt preserving no modesty.

Victor pulled the straps of her thong down her legs and over her black high heels. With a solid grip on her calves, he tugged so that she was just barely perched on the bar stool before descending on her apex. Mina kicked off her shoes and hooked her legs over Victor's shoulders to help her keep her balance.

He sloppily slurped her clit into his mouth before lapping his tongue along her slit. She gasped when he nudged the tip of his tongue inside of her. "You taste delicious." He dove in for more, devouring her clit while he slipped a finger into her.

Just as Mina's toes were starting to curl, Victor stood up and yanked her onto unstable feet before leading her upstairs to his bedroom.

They descended onto the bed together, removing the rest of their clothing in a frenzy. Victor forced her onto her back so he could look at her with not a stitch on. "You really are gorgeous."

Mina traced her fingers down Victor's chest then tickled his abs with her fingernails. "You aren't so bad yourself." His cock was long and thin. With it rigid as it was, Mina was impressed how far out it stood from his body.

Victor kissed her again, his hands pinning hers to the bed. Mina moaned when he began to tie her down. He bound her wrists together with white strips of fabric that had maybe once been a t-shirt before fixing the opposite end to a central rod of his headboard but left her legs unbound. She wished they were Alastor's vines, and when she closed her eyes, she could almost imagine they were. In response, her thighs clenched, and she writhed, thrilling at the tug of the restraints.

"My safe word is 'Milton'," she whispered, some part of her mind reminding her that this was reality. Precautions needed to be taken.

Victor quirked a brow and gave a half nod. His near indifference left her longing for Lilith.

On his knees, he nudged her legs apart with one leg and fingered her clumsily. It was the ghost of Lilith's touch that fed her desire.

When he slapped her tit, hard, she gasped, but the accumulating moisture slipped between her cheeks. He felt it too, and his eyes went dark.

"You liked that?" he asked before smacking her other breast. Once again, fluid gushed from her. "What a little whore. I'm surprised."

"Is it a good surprise?" Mina asked, fear pushing at the edges of her mind. She probably would have felt it more keenly had she not been drunk on booze and lust. The dream invading her mind at even the slightest persuasion.

Victor slapped her vulva. Her clit. She gushed. "I have to say, Mina, that you aren't what I expected. I have never *saved* a life before. It was thrilling, but now I think you belong to me in a way the others couldn't. Your life is mine." He kissed her neck before sucking on it and then bit her. She screamed at the pain, and he stopped short of breaking her skin, barely. Then he shoved a gag into her mouth, securing it with another strip of cloth tied around her head. He pulled out a condom from the bedside table and slipped it on, but he didn't enter her. Instead, he speared her with three digits.

"Look at you, only getting wetter." He rammed his long fingers into her cervix. Determined that she'd take all of them, Victor thrust into her with abandon, unconcerned with whether she derived any pleasure. Surely that was a red flag. But the danger felt too similar to the maze, where she'd been hunted and captured. She wanted more. She wanted to be back there, and this was the next best thing.

Mina whimpered when he removed his hand. Was he done already? She wasn't sure what she wanted. That fear was getting louder, and she was starting to suspect that, at the very least, she would be left unsatisfied tonight. Victor grabbed her roughly by the hips and flipped her over so she was flat on her stomach. And she was face first on the table in Hell again, Luci shoving her skirts over her head. She wiggled in anticipation.

"I think that last position was too easy for you," Victor said as he held her in place with his body weight, clumsily splitting her folds and impaling her with his fingers. She had no way to retreat as he began to hammer away. Although she could feel his insistent need against her hip, he made no move to fuck her.

He wrapped his hand around her throat and squeezed.

Usually that was all Mina needed to surrender completely, but Victor didn't hold her throat, easing her into the subservient role she craved. His fingernails bit into her sensitive skin. He cut off the circulation of her blood flow, and although she could still breathe, she was quickly growing lightheaded. Then he tightened his hold, restricting airflow. His other hand never ceased as she fought for consciousness, her vision narrowing to a pinprick.

She called out around the gag, her safe word a mumbled mess.

"Oh, are you trying to tap out? Cute of you to think your safe word means a damn with me."

She started to struggle in earnest, hoping to dislodge him enough that he would have to release her to regain his balance. But he only moaned, called her a bitch, and told her to struggle all she liked.

Right as Mina was about to black out, she felt Victor's hand tighten once more. He was going to crush her windpipe. Terror consumed her. She couldn't fight him much longer, and nothing she had done so far had worked. Damn it. She had chosen not to leave her family even in her fantasy. She would not leave them now. With the last of her energy, she screamed into the gag, into her mind.

The pressure was gone. She coughed. She was empty, and she didn't feel Victor's weight either.

Strong hands helped to turn her over. When she opened her eyes, green greeted her—green speckled with amber and gold. A gentle hand came up to cup her face as Mina regarded the blond man gazing down at her, his face stricken with worry.

Nineteen

TEARS BLURRED HER VISION. "Luci?" She struggled against the material holding her to the headboard. She needed to touch him. *He's real. He's real. He's real.*

"I'm here, Mina," Luci said as he tugged her wrists free and pulled her into his lap. "I'm so sorry."

"You're sorry? For what?" Even the hoarse sound of her voice did not deter her from reaching for him. She was shocked to find his cheek damp with tears.

"I should never have used him to get to you. I should have waited for another option."

"Who? What?" Mina croaked, voice raw. Fuck, it hurt to talk.

"Victor," Luci spit out his name like it left a vile taste in his mouth. "He was going to kill you, Mina. If I hadn't been able to stop him in time, he would have succeeded."

Mina cautiously prodded at her throat with her fingertips, assessing the damage, before locking eyes with Luci. She would definitely be sporting bruises. "I don't care. You're here." She turned so she could straddle her naked demon. He was real, and he was underneath her. Touching her. Wrapping her mind around the rest of it was, at the moment, both impossible and unimportant.

She kissed him deeply, flicking her tongue insistently against his bottom lip until he parted his lips for her. Their tongues frolicked together before she asked, "How are you here?"

Luci gripped her hip in one hand while he tenderly cupped the back of her head with the other. "Victor sold his soul to me—well, technically, an underling. One of the conditions is that I can swap places with him whenever I want. Right now he's in Hell, and I'm here. When we switch back, he won't remember anything. He'll just think he blacked out."

"That's right. You told me that's how you were able to send me over the railing of that yacht, and how you were able to rescue me. Which, by the way, he totally took credit for. It's the only reason why I let him take me out," Mina said. "That and I think I was looking for a distraction for this unexplainable grief. I thought you were a dream, Luci."

"Fuck, Mina." He clutched her close, stroking her hair.

"Is it always this dangerous?" Mina's vulva brushed against Luci's placid cock as she shifted her weight. It twitched in response.

"No, but I don't usually decide to put you in the path of a serial killer."

"Um. What?" Mina stilled. "Did he sell his soul for that?"

"He sold his soul in exchange for being untouchable." Luci kissed her throat soothingly.

"Well, it doesn't matter. He can just stay in Hell, and you can stay with me."

Luci chuckled and tucked a piece of hair behind her ear. "I wish it worked that way."

Mina grumbled and shrugged. Reaching beneath her, she located Luci's semi-hard erection. "Can I?" When he nodded, she tugged on him until he was fully aroused. "I need you inside me."

"Are you sure? You don't need a minute?" He brought his face level with hers, concern etched on his face.

"No. Claim me. Please. Fill me."

He grasped her hips in a punishing grip and pulled her onto his erection so gently it left her panting at the juxtaposition.

"Luci, you feel so good. So perfect."

This is what she needed. Every inch of Luci set Mina's blood on fire. Every molecule came alive with delight. She didn't wait for him to set the pace. She couldn't hold herself back from riding him without rhythm.

Luci stopped trying to keep up. He went still, staring at her in awe. "You are being very forward," he said with amusement as Mina continued to writhe. Luci grabbed her hips and held her in place so he could set the pace.

"It's the alcohol," Mina gasped between moans. She had forgotten how good he felt. Her nerve endings danced under his touch. The sensations chased away the fog the alcohol had brought and the heaviness of almost being choked to death. The pain ebbed away.

"I've never had you drunk before." Luci's eyes sparkled, any sign of his earlier distress gone. He was rock hard inside of Mina as she rocked against him.

"Of course you have." Mina covered his neck with kisses, grinding her clit into him. "A billion lifetimes and we never got drunk together?" Mina moaned. "Not once?" She whimpered as her peak beckoned. "I find that hard to believe."

"There isn't alcohol in Hell, and we very rarely spend time on Earth together." Luci's breathing was even, but Mina could hear the slight hitch in his voice as she pleasured herself on him.

"Oh!" Mina popped off of Luci's cock and jumped out of bed. "Let's go raid Victor's bar then." Denying her own pleasure only brought tingles to the base of her spine. She had been so close, but she didn't want to come too quickly. She needed this to last.

Luci frowned at her then down at his cock. "Can't it wait?"

"No, I want to know what drunk Luci is like. We can fuck while you drink." She tilted over to the side, precariously standing on one leg, yanked a blanket off of the bed, and wrapped it around herself.

"Now you are covering yourself up? I just saved your life, Mina. The least you can do is show some skin."

Mina stuck her tongue out at him but dipped one shoulder so the blanket fell to expose her down to the collarbone on one side. "If you tell me that you own me now because you saved my life, then you need to get in line." She made her way out the door and to the top of the stairs, completely confident that Luci would follow her.

He grabbed her hips from behind and twirled her around to look at him, stepping into her space until her back pressed against the banister. Mina felt Luci's possessiveness in her toes. She liked it. "Did Victor tell you that?"

"He has a serious ego problem, Luci. He also really wanted to tell me how kinky I was allowed to be."

"That fool."

"I guess that's why he decided to kill me—I was kinkier in reality than he wanted me to be. He became incensed that I got wetter after a little bit of spanking." Mina shrugged.

"Mmm." Luci gazed down at her, beaming with desire and adoration. "Damned fool."

"Well, of course you would say that. You're my soulmate." She tugged on his arm lightly to remind him that they had been heading downstairs. As she took the first step, her foot slipped on the blanket and she started to tumble.

Luci catapulted himself over her and landed on the stair beneath her with unnatural grace, catching her before she could fall. He scooped her up and carried her to the safety of the first floor.

"Thank you," Mina whispered.

"Drunk Mina is stubborn, willful, and clumsy," Luci said.

"Uh-huh. And madly in love with you." Mina kissed Luci's cheek and then laughed aloud at his blush. "The dining room is on the left."

Once more, Mina found herself perched on top of a bar stool. This time it was Luci rummaging through the bar looking for something to drink, the pile of unacceptable options growing on the bar top.

"He had mead. Find the mead."

Luci gave a grunt of approval and finally produced the bottle from the bar. "He had it tucked into a corner. I'm guessing he doesn't break this out for just anyone. Do you want some?" he asked.

"Nope. I have had enough for the night, I think." Mina hopped off of the bar stool and moved to close the blinds and curtains. Once she was satisfied that they had adequate privacy, she dropped her blanket and sat down on the edge of the dining room table.

Luci shrugged and took a sip from the bottle. He sloshed the liquid around in his mouth before swallowing it then put the bottle down and stared at it for a moment. "Eh, I've had better."

"There's a whole bar full of booze, and you don't want any of it?"

"God used to throw the most insane parties with the best drugs. Everything since? Just eh."

Mina shook her head and hopped off the table. "Find me shot glasses," she said as she rummaged through the bottles he had passed over. "Aha!" She grabbed the bottle of rum, her favorite brand even. Luci placed two shot glasses on the counter, and Mina filled them. "There you go. Down these, and maybe two more?"

"One of these isn't for you?"

"No. I'm sloshed already," Mina said as she grabbed a shot and downed it. "Oh, fuck."

Luci took the bottle of rum and moved both shot glasses out of her reach.

"I have no impulse control. Add that to the list," Mina said.

Luci poorly suppressed a laugh as he refilled the second shot glass and took both shots. He filled them again and did two more. "That rum is too sweet. It's unnatural."

"No. It's perfect."

"Huh, I didn't realize you had such bad taste in alcohol when I declared you my soulmate. Is it too late to trade you in for a different model?"

"Oh, that's funny." Mina glared and punched Luci's shoulder. "We get lucky enough for a little more time together, and this is how you want to spend it? Insulting me?"

"We didn't get lucky, Mina. You almost died." He threw the rum bottle against the wall, and it exploded. The sugary alcoholic scent filled the room. "I put you in the path of that maniac, and he could have killed you." Luci stomped over, clasping her arms and pulling her into his embrace. "Don't you dare think I would be okay if you died after I just found you."

"Luci, what does it matter? I'm glad I didn't die. But you and I are eternal. If I had bit the big one, you'd find me again."

"You don't understand, Mina, what it's like for me in those years before I find you. The last few years in Hell I've been more myself. More grounded. I make better decisions, am more level headed, and am happier when I know where you are."

"Oh," Mina smiled. "That's pretty sweet."

"That's your takeaway?"

"Uh-huh." Mina kissed from Luci's chin down to his collarbone.

"Mina, losing you—"

"Misplacing me," Mina interrupted.

"It's utter torture. I have half a mind to storm back into Hell and rip that man apart."

"I definitely won't be sleeping with humans from here on out, that's for fucking sure." Mina kissed her way to his bellybutton, bending over her hip to reach him. She then abruptly stood up as a thought hit her. "Wait. How long has passed for you in Hell since I've been back?"

"About forty-seven years, I think."

"Oh. Wow." Mina stabilized herself with a hand on his bicep.

"That's nothing when you've been around for three Earth millennia, give or take a millennium."

Mina bit her lip, a frown creasing her forehead. "There's nothing in your contract with Victor that allows you to punish him?"

Luci pursed his lips in contemplation. "I suppose I could null and void his contract. He is technically in violation of the clause that protects my private interests."

"Am I your private interest?"

"Damn right you are." Luci's eyes clouded over in a haze as he stared at her. Was the alcohol starting to hit his system? It became clear that his outburst with the rum bottle had just been a precursor as he pushed her back until her butt was against the dining room table. He picked her up by her hips and practically threw her back onto the table.

She landed on her ass, and the table rattled underneath her, obviously not the sturdiest of furniture. Victor probably bought it from one of those discount furniture places where everything looked really nice from afar but like crap up close.

As Luci climbed onto the table on all fours, Mina spread herself for him. His eyes wandered. They bore into her like, given half a chance, they'd devour her soul. He was predator. She prey. Would he hurry up and catch her already? *Fuck it*, she thought and twined her fingers though the hair on the back of his head and pulled him into a kiss.

He growled. "You are mine."

"I am my own." Mina watched for Luci's reaction. He offered her none, only staring at her as he had been. There was no flicker of anger, confusion, or surprise. It was a breath of fresh air after the way Victor had treated her. "But I am also yours, freely given."

Luci mashed his lips into hers. Mina massaged her lips against Luci's in response before opening her mouth in offering. Luci wasted no time diving in.

Mina's fingertips danced along Luci's spine as she made her way to his ass, where she clutched him firmly. She thrust up at him, trying to remind him that there was more to her than just her mouth, which he had thoroughly explored.

Luci broke the kiss. "Did you want something?"

"Yes. Your cock. Inside me."

"What would you do to have my cock inside you?" Luci kissed from Mina's neck down to her nipples, lapping at them, then continued down to her clit. He circled it with his tongue, applying slightly more pressure with each rotation. Mina squealed and, even though she knew it would make Luci want to tie her down, couldn't stop herself from squirming beneath him.

"Anything. Except remain still." Mina said, and Luci smirked. "What? It's physically impossible when you're eating me so well."

"I don't have my powers this time, so I can't bind you." Luci bent back to her, licking every part of her, from her clit to her labia. He slipped two fingers into her, pressing his fingertips into her sweet bundle of nerves.

"Oh, Luci, of course you can. You just have to do it the old fashioned way."

"That takes too long." He began to fuck her with his fingers in slow thrusts that only left Mina craving more. He brought his thumb to her clit. "Besides, we don't have any rope."

"Oh! Sex dungeon!" Mina pushed Luci off of her and rolled on top of him, giving him a brief kiss before leaping off the table.

"Oh my god, woman. You cannot stay put." Luci's angry growl quickly dissolved into laughter as he followed her into the kitchen.

"Crap, I forgot." Mina jangled the padlock. "He put a chastity belt on the sex dungeon. Who does that?"

"Um, Mina, I don't think that's locked because it's a *sex dungeon*."

Mina, gasping, dropped the padlock and took a jump back. Luci had said that Victor was a serial killer. Mina had heard him say it, but she had only registered that fact superficially. The real world consequences had been too terrible to contemplate.

She turned to stare at Luci in complete shock, a chill running down her spine. "What if someone is down there?"

Luci sighed heavily. "It's highly likely."

"We have to help them."

"Mina, we will. But what do you want to do about Victor?"

"He should go to jail, Luci. This all needs to come to light. Who knows how many victims he's had? Their families deserve closure."

Luci sighed again.

"And if it had been me? Would you let my mom wonder what happened to me? It's exactly like not knowing where I am, Luci. Except that at least you get to know that I'm alive."

Luci grunted his acceptance. "We'll do this the whole way, but that means I'll need to leave soon. Victor will need to be here when the cops arrive."

"I'll need to call them. Is my neck bruising yet?"

"Yes." The anger in Luci's voice sent chills down her spine.

"Good. Now, what will Victor remember when he comes back? I think I need to tell the cops a story that is as close to the truth as possible and also plausible to Victor." Mina paced the faux-wood vinyl floor.

"He'll most likely be pretty confused. He'll remember the urge to kill you." Luci stepped into her path, halting her, and traced the bruising on her throat with a fingertip. "The way your flesh felt against his fingers, the way you struggled under him." Luci's eyes were deep and glossy as Mina met them.

"And then what?" Mina reached up and wiped a tear that fell down Luci's cheek.

"And then he'll remember nothing." He turned his head and placed a kiss to the palm of her hand.

"Will he be unconscious when you switch back?" Mina frowned at the thought of losing Luci again. At least this time she would know that he was more than just a creation of her subconscious.

Luci nodded. "It's a lot for a human mind to take, so unconsciousness is the only way we can prevent mental breakdowns."

"Okay, I think I know what to tell the cops." Mina headed back to the dining room, where she recovered the blanket and wrapped it around herself, careful this time to hold up the bottom so she wouldn't trip when she made her way up the stairs and back into the bedroom.

She didn't realize that Luci had been on her heels until after she had pulled her cellphone from the pocket of her skirt, threw the skirt on the bed, and turned around. She jumped in surprise.

"Sorry." Luci sheepishly bit one side of his lip. "I'm not letting you out of my sight." He shoved her onto the bed and climbed over her before her heart had settled. He pulled her legs apart, caressing her labia, circling her entrance, and slipping three fingers inside. "Try not to move." Although he made love to her, pressing against her walls like he was memorizing her every texture, he wasn't gentle as he gave her the friction she needed, and Mina's eyes rolled back into her head.

Mina abandoned her phone where it had fallen on the pillow next to her and brought her hands up to clutch the rails of the headboard as Luci devoured her clit, lightly pulling it between his teeth. Her synapses exploded in an unexpected orgasm. She hadn't felt it building, so it must have been just around the corner for a long time. Luci carried her through it, one clit nibble at a time.

Luci joined her at the head of the bed, wrapping his arms around her and tucking her against him. "Make that phone call."

As Mina picked up her phone to call 9-1-1, she hesitated, remembering the phone number she had for Detective Jacobs. Something about her interaction with the woman had prompted her to add her as a contact. And now she was glad she had.

It rang three times before Detective Jacobs picked up with a curt greeting. Once Mina had announced herself, the detective's tone changed immediately.

After sharing her location, Mina explained that she had accompanied Victor home, that he had tied her down during what had started as a consensual interlude. That it had slowly turned darker until he ignored her safe word and tried to strangle her to death.

"It was very lucky he passed out when he did," Mina concluded.

A sob escaped, and a surprise jolt zapped through her. She was terrified, and she had started shaking. Victor would have killed her. Had killed others.

She was thankful for Luci's strong arms holding her together. He tucked his chin over her shoulder, and the weight kept her tethered.

"Did you manage to untie yourself?" Detective Jacobs asked.

"Yes. It took some doing, and my wrists are bruised all to hell, but I'm free."

"That's good. You did good, Mina," Detective Jacobs said.

"I think there's someone in the basement. It's padlocked, but I think I heard someone crying."

"I'm on my way to you right now, Mina."

"Please, hurry. I'm not sure how much longer he'll be out."

"Can you leave?" Detective Jacobs asked.

"I need to let you in, and I won't leave someone in the basement. If I'm here and he wakes up, I can at least create a distraction."

Luci squeezed Mina's hand in support, kissing away the tears that landed on her cheeks.

"Hold on, Mina," Detective Jacobs said, and Mina could hear Jacobs on her car radio.

"I've called it in. An ambulance and uniformed police officers are on their way. Hang tight. Try to stay near the front door in case you need to make a hasty exit. I'm about fifteen minutes out, and I'm the closest. I'm going to stay on the line until I'm there."

"What if he hears us and wakes up?"

"I will put my phone on mute. That way I'll be able to hear your end, but he won't hear me."

"Okay," Mina said, and then after a moment added, "Thank you."

Mina muted the call and carefully placed her phone on the bedside table. "Fifteen minutes." She started to cry in earnest then. It wasn't enough time, not nearly enough.

"I'll stay with you for as long as I can before making the switch." Luci rubbed his thumb across the back of her hand in soothing circles.

Their eyes met, and the rest of the world slowed. They crashed into one another, lips meeting in a maelstrom of passion. He was hard when she grasped him and lowered herself onto him. They were in a similar position as they had been before going downstairs. Mina cursed herself for ever having left this room. How much time had they lost?

Luci shifted his hips so he could toss Mina onto her back without relinquishing his place inside her. The strips of shirt were still tied to the headboard. Luci wrapped them around each of Mina's wrists in a loose knot. She wrapped her fingers around the cloth so she wouldn't squirm out of them.

"Fuck me, Luci," Mina begged. "Please, make me feel it for days."

Luci smirked at her, an evil glint in his eyes that thrilled her. When he began to move, his thrusts were urgent and demanding. He grunted with the effort, trying to get deeper. She hooked her ankles together as high as she could around his

Twenty

I T HAD BEEN THREE months since Luci and Mina had brought down the serial killer the news coined The Bachelor. Apparently Victor, independently wealthy, owned homes all across the West Coast. He wasn't at all the self-made man he had claimed to be. Authorities had uncovered the bodies of twenty-three women so far, and properties were still being excavated.

The idea that a person, not that much older than her, had already had the time to wreak such mayhem and cruelty left Mina reeling.

She had trouble sleeping thanks to the memories of what she had seen that night. Detective Jacobs had shown up first, beating the ambulance and uniformed officers by several minutes. When Mina had opened the door, the detective gasped at the bruising on her neck.

"Where is he?" she had asked.

"Upstairs," Mina replied. "The bedroom at the top of the landing." Mina anxiously stood at the bottom of the stairs as she watched Jacobs climb to the second story and disappear into the bedroom.

"Do you need any help?" Mina croaked. An unexpected tightness in the throat doubled her over as she coughed uncontrollably. She spent several minutes trying to get the spasms under control before Jacobs placed a reassuring hand on her back.

"We need to get you checked out."

"Thanks," Mina said, straightening. "I'm just a little raw."

"Not surprising."

"Is he secured?" Mina asked, glancing upstairs.

"He's handcuffed to the bed frame, still asleep. I hope he stays that way for now."

"I think we need to check out the basement. There's a padlock on the door."

"I have bolt cutters in the car," Jacobs said as she pulled out a dining room chair for Mina. "Sit."

Mina did, waiting anxiously. When the detective returned, Mina grasped Jacobs' hand and led her into the kitchen.

They stopped before the basement door.

"We really should wait," Jacobs said. "Uniforms are en route. There's no reason to do this before they get here."

"I think someone's down—" Mina stopped abruptly. "What was that?" It sounded like muffled sobbing.

"Fuck. I heard it." Jacobs wasted no time cutting through the lock with the bolt cutters and pulling open the basement door. "Stay here."

"No way. You might need me," Mina rasped.

Jacobs gave Mina an annoyed look. "Fine. But don't touch anything. This is a crime scene."

Mina tiptoed down the stairs after Jacobs. She brought her hands to her mouth to cover a gasp at the sight of a young blond woman chained to a wall with nothing but a threadbare mattress between her and the cement floor.

She was dirty, her clothes almost non-existent. She only wore a torn, white tank top. Her bare legs and feet did nothing to protect her from the chill in the room.

Mina rushed to the woman's side, crouching down beside her. Her lips were chapped, tear stains highlighting the dirtiness of her face.

"It's going to be okay," Mina whispered as Jacobs used the bolt cutters to break the chains from the wall.

When the woman slumped forward, Mina caught her.

"What's your name?" Jacobs asked as she slipped an arm around the woman's waist and helped Mina ease her to her feet.

"Kathryn."

"Kathryn," Mina said, forcing a smile. "I'm Mina, and this is Detective Jacobs. We are going to get you out of here, get you some water, and maybe a nice cheeseburger. How does that sound?"

"We have to hurry. He'll be back soon," Kathryn said, trembling in their arms.

"He's handcuffed upstairs. He's not going anywhere near you," Jacobs said. They made their way back to the stairs one agonizing step at a time. Kathryn had no strength, which was unsurprising, Mina found out later, as Kathryn had been held captive for two weeks with little food or water. Two weeks in which her wealthy and well-connected parents had pulled every string they could to try to locate their daughter and still could do nothing for her. Two weeks at the mercy of a monster way worse than any demon Mina had ever met.

Finally back in the dining room, Mina, Kathryn, and Jacobs had all collapsed into chairs as they waited for the ambulance. They didn't have to wait long. The cute EMTs took Kathryn out on a stretcher while they escorted Mina to check her injuries.

By the time Mina had given her statement, the place was crawling with police. Even the feds had come out, and Mina overheard them talking about multiple bodies and cadaver dogs.

If she ever got the opportunity to talk to Luci again, she would definitely be bringing up the practice of demons enabling this amount of human devastation. Victor had been allowed to execute his evil proclivities with no fear of retribution. How many lives had he destroyed? All with Hell's stamp of approval.

Luci had seemed so neutral about the whole situation. That thought left her cold. She remembered her regret at having had to call the cops and a jolt of guilt speared her. The whole time she'd been with Luci, Kathryn had been suffering. How could she have, for even a second, thought that her time with Luci was more important than getting Kathryn help?

Mina had been sitting in the backseat of Jacobs' unmarked squad car, her legs hanging out the door, when an officer brought Victor out of the house. As he got close to her, he yanked out of the officer's grasp. "This will never stick," he said. "And when I'm out, you'll get what's coming to you."

"What makes you think that?" Mina asked. She stood, placing her hand on the roof of the vehicle for support. Her adrenaline-exhausted legs weren't going to cut it.

"I've got friends in low places, baby," Victor said, hate in his eyes. His voice dripped with vitriol. He stood up straighter, no doubt thinking about his pact.

The officer caught up and clasped Victor's arm. Mina held up a hand so he wouldn't pull him away just yet. She leaned into Victor and whispered into his ear. "When you make a pact with the devil, it's important to read the fine print. Satan is my soulmate, asshole, and he's pissed as fuck at you."

Victor had looked at her with shock as the officer pulled him away. Then he had called her a witch, screaming that she would burn in Hell for all eternity.

Mina shook her head. Three months had passed since that night, and she was still second guessing herself. It had been stupid to tell him anything. She had just been so angry. Angry that he thought he was above the law, that women's lives only had value in the pleasure they could provide him, that he thought he had anything on her. She needed, in that moment, to bring him down to size.

After Victor had been driven away, Mina had begged Jacobs to take her to the hospital where Kathryn had been admitted. Later, she would acknowledge to herself that she had done it in part to assuage her guilt. But in the moment, it just felt like the right thing to do.

Either fate had worked very hard to make sure that her path crossed with Kathryn's right when Kathryn needed it most, or it had been a complete coincidence. But one that size should not be ignored. Like life evolving from a single-celled organism, this random-chance occurrence could potentially have profound consequences.

And so Mina had been allowed into Kathryn's emergency room, and she'd stayed with her through all the IVs, the blood tests, and the constant barrage of questions from nurses and police officers.

"My dad owns a chain of fast food restaurants," Kathryn said when she was starting to feel more like herself. She had demanded that Mina make good on her promise for a burger, but a veggie burger, please, as Kathryn had been a vegetarian for ten years. The two women sat together on the sleeper couch the hospital provided for overnight guests, a roller table between them and two brown-paper bags full of greasy food before them. "He also owns a small chain of high-end hotels, a car dealership, and an insurance company."

"That's a lot," Mina said, frowning. "Are you saying that my food contribution is a bit underwhelming?"

Kathryn laughed and shook her head. "Just the opposite. It's nice to just be with someone who doesn't put on airs. Although you probably didn't know who I was, and I just ruined it."

"No," Mina said, placing her hand over Kathryn's. "I don't care who your dad is, or what he owns. I'm here because I'm worried about you. You just went through something traumatic, and your dad is out of town. You shouldn't be alone."

Kathryn sighed. "I know I should call a friend or something. Let you get out of here, but—"

"But you don't want to have to explain to them what happened?"

Kathryn nodded. "I need time to process."

"And you don't have to explain anything to me. I'm not going anywhere. Unless you want me to."

"Thank you, Mina."

They ate and surfed bad cable TV, then fell asleep propped against each other on the couch until a nurse came in and scolded Kathryn for not being in the hospital bed.

In the morning, Kathryn's father arrived. He was in a state, his expensive suit rumpled and his unbrushed, white hair pointing in every direction. He embraced Kathryn and refused to let her go for a solid ten minutes, all the while thanking Mina profusely for finding his little girl.

Mina slipped away but not before making sure Kathryn had her number and they had scheduled a day to hang out and check in on one another's mental state.

Three months had passed, and Mina still had trouble sleeping at night. Her mind refused to stop running through all the scenarios for the victims she hadn't saved. What had been the last thought of each of those women? Were they working toward acceptance and peace in Hell right now? Would they be reunited with their loved ones in the next lifetime?

As Mina snuggled into her pillows, pulling her blanket up to her chin, she felt Luci's love surround her. This moment, although it often took a little longer to come than it had before Victor, soothed her just as it did every night. He would always be there for her, even if only briefly. Surrounded in his love, all her fears of human monsters disappeared. At least for long enough for her to drift to sleep.

Twenty-One

L IFE HAD FINALLY STARTED settling out. The reward money that Kathryn's father had insisted Mina take, despite her numerous attempts to turn it down, had provided her with options. She had quit her job so she could focus on her art and purchased a townhouse only a few miles from her family home.

Although she hadn't been able to keep her name out of the papers completely, the public's focus had quickly shifted to Kathryn, who basked in the limelight. Mina was thankful to maintain her anonymity. Unfortunately, The Bachelor was everywhere. That man didn't deserve all the attention, but it was human nature to stare at horrors.

Mina hadn't told her mother any of what had happened, but she hadn't been able to keep it from her sister. Which, of course, meant that it made it back to her mother anyway. That was reason enough to stay silent about her time with Luci in Hell. Besides, her sister would either freak out or refuse to believe her—probably both—and Mina didn't want to cause a rift in their relationship.

"You know, Mom keeps saying how lucky you are that you stopped going out with that Victor creep," Dahlia said. She stood in front of a glass display case filled with antique toys.

They were at their neighborhood indoor flea market. A normal Saturday morning outing while Sandra spent some one-on-one time with her granddaughter.

"Crap. She is pretty heavily in denial."

"Eh." Dahlia shrugged. "Maybe it's better this way? She probably can't handle the guilt of having thrown you at him."

"She didn't, though. Not any more than she would throw me at anyone."

The two wandered the aisles until they came to a bookcase overburdened with old board games. On a small table to the right of it sat an old spirit board and planchette. Engraved with a delicate font, the set was simple, with the usual sun and moon. But there was a raven engraved on one side and a butterfly on the other. A spattering of stars tied the antique board together. The price tag, tied around a foot of the planchette, read fifty dollars in a handwritten scrawl.

"I think I'm buying this," Mina said, scooping up the board and balancing the planchette on it.

"You can't be serious," Dahlia said, shaking her head. "Remember that time at Tina's house when we were in middle school? You couldn't sleep for a week."

"Yeah, well, Tina was moving it," Mina said. "I just like the look of it. It's perfect for my coffee table."

"Uh-huh, it will totally fit in with that whole goth thing you've got going," Dahlia said, voice dripping with sarcasm.

Mina looked down at her pink cardigan and floral print skirt and laughed. "You don't know me." With a flick of her hair, she turned on her heel and went straight to the checkout counter. The business owner put it in a plain paper bag large enough to hide it from view. Handy. She wouldn't have to explain her purchase to her superstitious mother when they met up for lunch.

After a lovely lunch with her family, Mina sat on the floor in the living room of her new suburban townhome, her spirit board on the carpet before her. With the couch at her back, the coffee table in front of her, and the chaise flanking her left, Mina had almost everything she needed. She turned the planchette over in her hands absentmindedly while she summoned the courage to try it. It wasn't fear of success stopping her. Quite the opposite. The worst-case scenario wouldn't just leave her feeling like a fool. There was a real possibility that her heart would break all over again.

With a deep breath, she braced herself for what was most likely to be crushing disappointment and placed the planchette on the board. She moved the window of the planchette over the letters "H" and "I" with a barely perceivable nudge then moved it back to the empty space in the center of the board and waited.

From experience, Mina knew that with additional people she would more easily get results, but she also knew that those results would be nothing less than suspect. It was so easy to move the planchette without even realizing you were doing it. All her energy was focused on not doing so now and giving herself false hope.

Five minutes went by and nothing moved. Mina sighed and admonished herself. What had she been thinking? Of course these things were nothing more than wood. Had she really thought she could reach Hell so easily?

Mina stared down at the palm of her hand. Everything had a cost. Hadn't Luci said that?

When Bellz had told her she could summon demons, he had talked about being on the receiving end of a spirit board communication.

She knew that demons liked sex, at least the ones she had met. But there were other things they craved, things that they happily made deals for. Thinking about all the bloodshed The Bachelor had caused, an idea started to form.

With shaky legs, Mina made her way into the kitchen and pulled a small paring knife from the block on the counter. Rummaging through her junk drawer, Mina found a pack of band-aids covered in tiny dinosaurs, a housewarming gift from Tabitha. Cautiously, she padded back to the living room.

Once more sitting on the floor, Mina extended a trembling hand over the spirit board. She pricked her finger with the paring knife and hissed at the pain. The blood came faster than she had expected and fell in the center of the board. Cursing under her breath, Mina placed her thumb over the cut so she could position it. Then she let a single drop fall on the sun, the moon, "Yes," "No," "Goodbye," the butterfly, and the raven. Finally, she let her blood land on the planchette just below the window.

"Please, Luci," she whispered before pressing a band-aid over her wound. The bleeding had slowed, but she didn't want to risk dripping blood on her floor. "Come back to me."

Slowly, the wood absorbed the blood until not a blemish remained.

Creepy, but a good sign.

Mina flexed her hands before placing her fingertips back on the planchette. It jerked violently, spelling out her name.

"Luci?" she asked aloud.

The planchette responded with a "No."

"Who is it?"

B-E-L-L-Z

"Well, hey there, sexy."

"We miss you," Bellz said through the spirit board.

"I miss you too."

"Games suck without you."

Mina laughed. "Can I talk to him? To the others?"

"Maybe."

"Did Luci tell you about Victor?"

"Yes."

"You are so monosyllabic. I guess that's good for a spirit board conversation, but it really makes me wish I could see your face, that I could feel you."

"Close your eyes."

Without hesitation, Mina complied, keeping her fingers on the planchette. One by one, Bellz lifted her fingers, planting gentle kisses on the pad of each, even over the bandage.

Bellz' voice materialized in her ear, "Keep 'em closed." He kissed her ear. "Sindy is seeing who she can scrounge up. They should be able to use my connection to you to establish their own."

"What happens if I open my eyes?"

"Then you won't feel or hear me until you close them again."

"I will keep them closed, then, unless you need me to get something."

"You pricked your finger to reach us, didn't you?" Bellz moved his hand over her shoulders, down her arms, and grasped her hands in his.

"It only worked after I used my blood."

"Listen, Mina, your blood woke this board. It's connected to you now, and you may not like everything that finds its way through. Find an iron box to store it in when you aren't using it."

Mina nodded.

"If the iron box isn't enough, line the box with salt."

"Okay." She slipped her fingers through Bellz', thrilled that she could touch him as well. "How's it going with Sindy? It sounds like she was with you when I called."

"You think that because you set us up you're entitled to status updates?" Bellz dropped one of her hands and gave her a light pat on the hip.

"Uh-huh. I'm pretty sure it was in the contract. Always read the fine print, Bellz. That's Demoning 101."

"We are having a lot of fun," Bellz said. "Until one of us remembers that we can't share all we've learned with you. Luci is constantly sulking." Bellz slipped behind Mina and pulled her hair to the side before planting a gentle kiss on her neck.

"You guys have to remind him that he's loved when I'm not around."

"He doesn't love us like he loves you."

"Okay, but there are more of you. Surely the love of the four of you makes up for my absence."

"No, nothing could."

"Please don't say that." Mina leaned into Bellz, who in turn wrapped his arms around her shoulders.

"Sindy is back. Can she join us?"

"Yes, please."

Sindy gripped Mina's hips and slid small arms around her waist, pressing her head against Mina's chest while Mina stroked Sindy's hair.

"Luci is on his way," Sindy said. "He asked that we keep you company."

Mina sighed at the sound of Sindy's voice. It felt wonderful to be surrounded by her friends once more. Trying to figure out how to bring Luci to earth had monopolized so much of her time that she hadn't given herself a chance to mourn the loss of everyone else she had left behind.

"Did he sound angry?"

"Definitely not," Sindy said, nuzzling into her cleavage.

"How did he sound?" Mina placed a gentle kiss on Sindy's head and then on Bellz' arm.

"Frustrated that he was stuck in a meeting."

"A meeting? What meeting?"

"Luci has been calling his crossroads and Faustian demons together to review their practices. I think he's curious how many more Bachelors are out there running amok with deals that make them basically invincible," Bellz supplied.

"He's been obsessing about putting an end to it," Sindy elaborated.

"No way," Mina said. Luci never stopped surprising her. "You guys wanna join me on the couch?"

"Sure," Sindy said. Both Bellz and Sindy stepped away from her so she'd have the space to move.

"Uh, I might need to open my eyes to find it, though," Mina said as she stumbled through her living room. Soon, she'd have this place memorized well enough not to turn on a light when she needed water in the middle of the night.

"Oh! We can see," Sindy said cheerily. "I mean, mostly. We can see you perfectly. There's a couch shaped blob just behind you."

"Oh, no, that's my dining room table shaped like a couch. It's all the rage."

"Wow, humans are so weird."

"I'm kidding, Sindy. That's my couch. I don't even own a dining room table yet."

Bellz chuckled then tossed Mina over his shoulder, taking three long steps to the couch and setting her back down on it. Sindy pounced on Mina as soon as her butt hit the cushion.

"Sindy!" Mina giggled as Sindy tickled her neck with gentle kisses.

"You know I don't like sharing, but you guys are pretty hot," Bellz said.

Mina blindly groped for him. "Help me out here, Bellz, I can't see you. And you need to join us. You have to participate to share."

Bellz picked up both girls like they weighed nothing and slid under them. "Proceed," he said.

"Sindy," Mina stage whispered, "What is he expecting us to do?"

"Sexy things," Sindy squealed, tugging Mina's t-shirt over her head.

"I'm not sure I agreed to that. I was kind of hoping for some Netflix and chill," Mina said.

"Netflix and chill? I don't know that human colloquialism," Bellz said, tracing his fingertips along the waistband of Mina's pajama bottoms.

Mina attempted to answer but was distracted by the trail of kisses Sindy was leaving down her body. Between kisses Sindy said, "That's code for sex. She was making a joke."

"Eesh," Mina said. "Not funny if you have to explain it. Although even Netflix and chill starts with a movie. But you can't see well enough to watch a movie, and I can't open my eyes. So I'm happy moving right to the sex part."

Bellz grumbled underneath her.

"What?"

"I've never seen a movie," Bellz said. "It would have been nice."

Both Sindy and Mina turned their attention to him. Sindy slid off Mina so Mina could turn around and settle into Bellz' arms, straddling his stomach. She wasn't sure where Sindy had gone because she couldn't feel her anymore.

"I can still put a movie on, Bellz. You could listen to one."

"Eh, next time you briefly die, just make sure to bring one with you," Bellz said as Mina kissed his cheek.

"Or maybe I find a different way to summon all of you. The spirit board thing definitely has its drawbacks. Where is Sindy?"

"On my cock." Bellz grunted.

"I wanna see." Mina pouted.

"Shh." Bellz rubbed her back in circles. "You can hear her."

And Mina could. It was easy to picture Sindy bobbing up and down on Bellz when she stopped to listen. As Sindy lapped at him, Bellz' breath came faster.

"Wow, you guys are so into each other that my beautiful Mina is being ignored."

Mina's heart stopped at the sound of Luci's voice, and she squeaked with happiness when he wrapped his arms around her and pulled her into a tight embrace, lifting her from Bellz' stomach and placing her on the back of the large chaise lounge where he could stand between her legs.

"Luci," she gasped, wrapping her arms and legs around him and tugging him closer. Keeping her eyes closed, she nuzzled into his chest and breathed him in.

"You got pretty lucky today, I see," Luci said.

"Nuh-uh, no one's fucked me," she purred, 'yet."

"You're lucky Bellz intercepted your call and not one of my many enemies," Luci clarified.

Bellz' chuckle came from Mina's left. "It wasn't that long ago that you and I were enemies, Luci."

"And now you call me Luci and help hold down my woman while I drive her to madness."

"He does?" Mina yelped as Luci pushed her off of the back of the chaise and into Bellz' waiting arms. He laid back with her, twisting them in the chaise so he could rest against the back cushion.

Luci yanked down Mina's pajama bottoms and nudged her legs apart. He growled, a sentiment that Bellz echoed. Bellz kneaded her breasts in his hands, working inwards toward her nipples, pinching and tugging on them.

Luci kissed the inside of Mina's knee, then her thigh, before placing a gentle kiss on her clit. He drank at her, letting his tongue slowly part her labia. Earning her wetness one lick at a time.

Again, she had lost track of Sindy until lips fastened onto a nipple that Bellz had helped harden.

"Sindy, you are so quiet and sneaky," Mina moaned.

Sindy giggled but kept sucking on Mina's nipple as Bellz flicked the other with his forefinger and thumb.

Luci worked his tongue far enough into Mina's channel to nuzzle his nose against her clit. After lubricating a finger with her juices, he pressed against her anus.

The tip of Luci's finger dipped into her. But Mina's moan was replaced by a whimper when all sensations stopped and she fell back in the chaise. Bellz was no longer behind her, and both Sindy and Luci were gone.

"Guys?" she called out and waited for an answer. When she didn't receive one, she opened her eyes. She was alone. Naked, horny, but alone. With a grunt, Mina flung herself back across the living room to the spirit board on the floor.

Placing her fingertips back on the planchette, she took a deep breath and concentrated on the board, desperately willing it to move. Nothing happened. Without really thinking of the risks, Mina picked up the knife once more and pricked her right middle finger, then proceeded to drop her blood on the board and planchette as she had done previously.

The planchette moved almost immediately, before Mina fully touched it. With an agonizingly languid pace it spelled out two words. "Big" and "Mistake."

Twenty-Two

THE SHARP EDGE OF a blade pressed into Mina's neck almost enough to draw blood. Arms tugged her into a standing position before a strong shove between her shoulders forced her onto the coffee table. She caught herself and lessened the impact, but the continued pressure of the blade motivated her to lower herself to the table completely.

Closing her eyes, Mina hoped that she might be able to hear her new assailant. The fact that this demon could touch her when her eyes were open set off alarm bells.

"You're all naked 'n' ready to go," a man with a thick Texas accent said.

"Who are you?" Mina asked. With her eyes closed, she couldn't see him. If she opened her eyes, she still wouldn't see him, but she probably would be unable to hear him either.

"Doesn't matter who I am," he said. "What matters is that I'm gonna destroy you."

"You wouldn't dare," Mina said. Bellz had warned her about this. She had known encountering an unknown demon wasn't just a possibility but a likely outcome.

"Hey, you're the one who invited me in with that sweet tasting blood o' yours. Time to deal with the consequences." His palm landed on her bare ass with a sharp sting, the first of many spanks. He spread them out across her backside, and soon she was writhing on the table.

This demon may have been a surprise, but he wasn't uninvited. Mina had meant it when she'd said she was willing to handle any fallout. And this? Her core throbbed each time his palm connected with her flesh. The anticipation of what he'd do next, she felt down to the soles of her feet.

He flipped her over and captured her hand in his, sucking on the finger she had pricked and moaning deeply at the taste. Her heartbeat pounded through the small wound and reverberated in her clit.

"Do you know who I am?" Mina asked. Bellz had told her that her status as Luci's soulmate would keep her safe from at least the worst of demon depravities. But that wouldn't matter if her tormentor had no idea of her bond with Satan.

"You're clearly a human slut," the demon said. "Naked and wet before I even arrived. Were you preparing yourself for me? Don't think I'll go any easier on you."

How should she play this? She could fight with everything she had against this unknown entity, or she could play along. Bellz had told her that all demons were drawn to her. Maybe she could use that to her advantage. Maybe she didn't need to fear the Texan any more than she feared Luci. His hand on her ass had felt good. Really good. She could have fun. With the decision made, her whole body relaxed.

"Would I have invited you here if I wanted you to go easy on me?" Mina bit her lip.

"You seemed to like the warm up plenty. But I don't think you truly know what you're in for." The demon leaned forward, spreading Mina's legs in a way so similar to how Luci had just done it that she ached to be touched. His hot breath hit her core first, the only warning that he was about to strike. He bit her engorged clit between his front teeth and pulled.

She almost screamed with the sweet torment of it, but she knew her neighbors would hear it. They certainly didn't need the cops banging down the door looking for a domestic disturbance. Swallowing her response had a funny side effect. The pain quickly turned to pleasure, and she could feel herself hurtling toward an intense orgasm.

The Texan sensed it in time and disengaged. "Oh, I don't think so." Then he was silent for a long time. Mina only knew he was still there because of the presence of his hand on her thigh. He absentmindedly stroked light circles into her flesh. Surely he didn't mean to soothe her, yet it had the effect regardless.

"Interesting, very interesting. You aren't just a human slut like I had assumed." The Texan brought his hand down onto her clit in a loud slap, and then he did it again and again until his hand was coming down hard on her core every few seconds.

Her orgasm was back, just around the corner, and this time the demon didn't stop as it approached. He bent back down and once more clamped his teeth onto that sensitive nerve bundle.

Mina exploded.

Her toes curled, her eyes fluttered in her head, and she thought she was going to lose consciousness. But somehow she managed to hold on.

Although her eyes were still tightly closed, Mina could see the room brighten like a bomb had gone off. When she opened them, she saw her demon tormentor before her. He was glowing with power, and the smile on his face was nowhere near malicious.

Tall, handsome, and clad in a cowboy hat and boots, a button up shirt, and jeans, he oozed strength and swagger. The top few buttons of his shirt were left undone, revealing dark chest hair.

"That was beautiful," he said. "The best gift anyone has given me in," he tilted his head to the side while he thought, "a little over a decade."

"I can see you." Mina sat up on the table and reached out to touch his arm.

He looked down at her as if he was only now really seeing her. Then he joined her on the table. "That was a powerful orgasm. You've recharged me. Although recharged might be the wrong word. I'm not sure I've ever been this juiced."

"Glad to be of service, sexy demon guy."

The Texan narrowed his eyes at her. "You weren't trying to reach me at all, were you, little slut?"

"The name's Mina."

"I'm Oz."

"The great and powerful?"

"Ha. Currently that appears to be the case. And sated. It's been years since I've been sated." He shook his head in disbelief. "Are you Lucifer's Mina?"

Nodding, she brushed the back of her knuckles against Oz's cheek in a gentle caress.

"I have long considered Lucifer my enemy. Ever since you came on the scene and started mucking everything up, demons like me haven't had much of a home." Oz shrugged. "But I can now understand why he and so many others find you so enthralling. You take everything we throw at ya in malice and hate but somehow reflect it back at us in love."

Mina moved her thumb against his cheekbone. "And you assumed until now that you were unworthy of it?"

"Once before, I thought I was worthy of something similar, but it turned out I wasn't. No surprise there. I wreak havoc on those who try to contact the other side. It's always been easy for me. It isn't easy on them. And I have many ways of inflicting my torments."

"Torments? Really? That wasn't so bad," Mina said as she wrapped her arms around his and placed her chin on his shoulder.

"Most people don't respond like you did."

"I'm a freak that way." Mina gave his shoulder a small kiss, and Oz, for only a moment, glowed just a bit brighter.

"What can I give you in return? Fair's fair. Let me use some of this newfound power to give you something you desire." He flexed his arm, folding his fingers into a fist.

"Other than that mind-numbing orgasm? I can barely feel my toes."

"Mmhmm," Oz said, eyelids drooping as he gazed at her.

She'd happily go again, if he was willing. But there was something she wanted more.

"I want Lucifer, Sindy, and Beelzebub here with me. In person. Not the half way they were here before," Mina said. She almost asked for Lilith and Alastor too, but they had been too busy to join in earlier, and she refused to inconvenience them.

"They were here before, eh?"

"Yes," Mina said, blushing. "Beelzebub answered me initially, but our call got dropped."

"That asshole is always getting on my last nerve, intercepting calls that by rights belong to me. I'd hate to do him a favor." Oz spit in disgust. "Or Lucifer, that fuckin' goody two shoes." He exhaled heavily. "But I owe you one."

"Thanks, Oz. You need more juice, call on me anytime," Mina said before kissing him gently.

Oz blushed and nodded.

In a flash of bright light, Oz was gone, her spirit board and planchette gone with him. Mina had only a moment to wonder about that before her heart leapt into her throat and all thoughts evaporated.

Luci, Sindy, and Bellz all appeared on the chaise almost exactly where they had been before they left. Mina beamed at them from her spot on the coffee table. They were fully clothed, and although Mina felt suddenly very underdressed, she didn't really care.

"What did you do?" Luci asked as he stood up from the foot of the chaise.

Twenty-Three

LUCI CROSSED THE ROOM and scooped her up. "What did you do?" he repeated.

"I met one of your enemies, and he did me a favor." Mina shrugged. She couldn't tear her eyes from him. He'd been here a moment and already the tension she'd unknowingly been carrying drained away and breath filled her lungs more easily.

"What did you do to warrant a favor?" Luci's voice was gravely with worry. His stern gaze had Mina almost in giggles.

"I orgasmed."

"He touched you?" Bellz asked, immediately at her side.

"Well, yeah," Mina said. "Not that I had much of a choice in that."

Then Sindy was next to her, too, peering at her with stormy, violet eyes. "He raped you?"

"No. I wouldn't call it rape," Mina said as Luci sat down on the couch with her across his lap so that Bellz and Sindy could more easily surround her. Sindy sat under Mina's legs and clutched them to her chest. Bellz draped a leg over Luci's so he could brace Mina's back with his chest.

"Then what would you call it?" Luci asked.

"More like consensual non-consent? There's a line he can't cross, right? He can't cause me excessive bodily harm, like maim me, and he can't kill me. Giving up control in those circumstances, it's thrilling, intoxicating, addictive.

"I knew the risks when I tried to reach you all. And, maybe I'm crazy, but I'm not scared of any demon. I feel like—I don't know." Mina looked at each of them in turn. "I feel like I was built to love you all. Should I really only limit that to the five of you?"

"Yes," Bellz said. "I already don't like sharing you with my family."

"Not all demons are as open to love as we are, Mina," Sindy said.

"Maybe because they haven't met me yet." Blushing, she hid her face between the junction of Luci and Bellz' arms.

"You are a very foolish woman," Bellz said, his tone equal parts censure and delight. Mina uncovered her face and was met with his unreadable expression. He had supported her wishes in this before, even given the dangers. Maybe the reality had changed his mind. What was Luci thinking? How angry would he be?

But when her eyes met Luci's, she found them sparkling with admiration.

"Even after all these lifetimes, you still keep finding ways to surprise me," Luci said as he gently pressed his lips to hers. "I love you, Mina," he whispered against her mouth.

"I love you too, Luci," Mina said. "I'll do anything for more of this." When she returned his kiss, she pressed herself into him, wishing it could go on forever, enjoying the way Luci yielded to her desires. But she still had a bit of a bone to pick with Bellz, so she pushed off of Luci's chest and twisted so she could challenge the grumpy devil head on.

"What?" Bellz asked, his eyes softening when he looked at her. The kindness she saw there shocked her enough that she almost forgot what she was going to say.

"I'm not foolish," she spat out before she lost her focus or nerve. "Or, if I am, then you should be glad for it. Otherwise you wouldn't be here about to watch your very first movie."

"A movie?" Bellz' eyes sparkled, and Mina couldn't help herself. She set her lips to Bellz' in a quick, sweet smooch.

"No fair!" Sindy said. "I want a kiss."

"I'll give you plenty when we are back in Hell," Bellz said.

"Not from you," Sindy said, rolling her eyes. She climbed over Luci to hover in front of Mina. Mina responded by meeting Sindy's sweet mouth with her own. "Yay!"

"I missed you, Sindy."

"Which movie?" Luci asked.

"I know just the one," Mina said. She clumsily rolled off of their laps, barely catching herself before smacking into the floor. Then she popped up to her feet and moved to a cardboard box that had yet to be unpacked.

"*Star Wars*? *Jurassic Park*? Maybe a rom-com?" Luci asked.

Mina shook her head. "It has adventure, comedy, and true love. If only I could find it." She had already removed a sizable stack of films, and the pile was only continuing to grow as she rummaged through the box.

"I've heard much about the *Star Wars*," Bellz said.

"You might only have time for a single movie. It would be cruel to only show you one," Mina said, finally pulling out the movie she was looking for. She popped it in, switched on the TV and the sound bar, and then snuggled in with her demon trio.

As a sick kid sitting in bed and playing an 80's sports video game popped up on the screen, Luci quickly distracted Mina by moving her hair from her neck and placing ticklish kisses along the side. Sindy and Bellz sat cuddled together, their eyes plastered to the screen.

"Luci, you're going to miss the movie," Mina said.

"I've seen it," he whispered into her ear.

"You're holding out on Bellz?"

"He never wants to come to my movie nights."

Mina laughed, and Luci resumed peppering her neck with affection. His soft lips tickled behind her ear, sending sparks of pleasure into the base of her skull. When he captured her earlobe between his lips, the sensation swooped lower, hit harder. His arms, already snugly wrapped around Mina's frame, tightened.

"I want to taste every bit of you," Luci said. Mina stood up and grabbed Luci's hand, leading him into her bedroom just down the hall. Her bed was pretty simple. Just a queen sized mattress on a box spring with no frame. She hadn't gotten around to picking out much furniture since finding her new place.

"This setup is going to make bondage hard," Luci said.

Mina pouted. "But not impossible, right?"

Luci flung Mina over his shoulder before taking two steps to the bed and tossing her down on it. Before she could get her bearings, he had a wrist in each hand and was holding her down, his eyes dark, pupils so large that their green was reduced to a sliver.

"Luci?" Mina asked, taken aback by his fierce intensity.

"You summoned a demon, and you have to accept the consequences of those actions."

"If I get it tattooed to my forehead, will you all stop telling me that?"

Luci growled at her.

"Stop demon-splaining and kiss me."

This time Luci's growl rumbled against her lips. She giggled in response. Her giddiness at feeling his weight and his need for her bubbled up uncontrollably. Mina locked her ankles behind Luci's lower back and thrust up at him, her core brushing against his tight abs.

"God, I missed you, Luci." Mina longed to run her fingers through his blond hair.

"What does God have to do with any of this?" He was still in the process of devouring her soul with his eyes, and she wanted nothing more than to give him every last bit of it.

"Technically the asshole did introduce us."

"Well, he lost any brownie points for that when he treated you the way he did."

"Agreed," Mina said. "Maybe I said it so you'd torment me a bit?"

Luci chuckled. "Trying to manipulate me, human?" Luci pressed a gentle kiss to where Mina's shoulder met her neck. "I suppose I will allow it this time." He released her wrists and slipped his hand between their bodies so he could trace gentle circles around her clit.

Mina tugged Luci's shirt up, awkwardly slipping it past her legs without unclasping them. Luci helped yank it free, tossing it across the room where it landed on her large, stuffed Cerberus.

"Pants, Luci. Pants," Mina pleaded. "Please."

"Not yet." He placed his hands on her thighs and forced them open. Holding her in place, Luci wiggled down the bed, leaving gentle kisses along her skin as he went. When he reached her core, he breathed her in, basking in her scent.

Mina propped herself up on her elbows. "Luci, I get that you want to really take your time here, but I'm not sure how much of that we are going to get. Oz and I didn't really discuss when his favor would end."

"You are not relaxed at all. Didn't you just have a huge orgasm?"

"Uh, yeah. It was intense," Mina said, collapsing back on the bed. "I'm just all in my head about losing you again."

"You'll never lose me," Luci said. "Let's enjoy the time we have and stop worrying about what we can't control. Besides, Oz will totally fuck you again in exchange for a favor."

Mina crossed her arms, her bottom lip jutting out the tiniest bit. "He took my spirit board."

"He what?"

"When he disappeared, so did my spirit board and planchette."

The edge of Luci's mouth twitched up in a smirk. "That bastard."

"What?"

"He was trying to protect you. You truly have an effect on every single one of us, don't you?"

Mina shrugged, tilting her head to the side. "Do I?"

"It doesn't matter when our time is up. You'll find another way to summon me."

"And you're okay with that?"

"Yes, Mina. Now can I get back to devouring you?" He didn't wait for her reply before lapping at her sex and sliding two fingers into her. He angled his fingertips up, hitting her in that earth-shattering spot while licking circles around her clit.

His touch was gentle, so reserved compared to the way he touched her in Hell. It was nice, restorative almost. As if his love was in each touch, in each flick of his tongue.

Mina moaned Luci's name and thrust her hips into him. Her fingers found their way into his hair, and she lightly scraped her nails against his scalp, causing him to hum against her clit. Her clit hummed back.

"More, Luci, please," Mina begged.

Luci nuzzled her thigh then plunged a third finger into her. The muscle in his forearm strained as he fucked her. His lips fastened around her clit.

Her crest neared. Her toes curled, and she let out a loud moan that was bound to draw the attention of Sindy and Bellz in the other room. She careened into it, tumbling into nirvana with only Luci to catch her.

But he didn't let up, pulling every last drop from her orgasm. Mina tugged on his hair and squeaked as the pressure on her sensitive clit became too much.

Luci chuckled evilly as he climbed up her body and collapsed on top of her. He nuzzled into her hair as she wrapped her arms around him.

"I love you, Luci," Mina said. "Wanna fuck me now?"

"I really, really do," Luci said as he unbuttoned his pants and tugged them off. In moments he was inside her, thrusting languidly against her as she writhed under him. He tucked his arms under her, pulling her into his chest. His movements were gentle, full of potent longing.

"Are you feeling okay?" Mina asked, her concern enough of a distraction from his delightful weight and the perfect way his cock worked her.

"Never better." He glanced down at her with a puzzled expression.

"You aren't acting like yourself. I think you're making love to me, Luci."

"You deserve to be made love to." Luci kissed both of her cheeks, her nose, her chin, her forehead, her lips. "I should do it more often."

"Are you trying to kill me?" Mina asked. "My heart is going to explode."

"Not this time."

Luci and Mina's lips met in a quick conflagration of passion as Mina grabbed Luci's ass, meeting his thrusts with her own.

"What do you want more than anything else in the world, little human?"

"Is this what you ask people before they happily hand over their souls?"

"No. This is what I ask the woman I love."

"I want to marry you and have all of your babies." After Mina kissed the corner of his mouth, he turned his head and returned her affection.

"I'm not sure that's worth giving up your immortal soul," Luci teased.

Mina rolled Luci over onto his back and straddled him, managing to keep her fallen angel firmly in place during the maneuver. "My soul already belongs to you."

"Not officially."

"But in all the ways that actually matter." Mina traced her fingers over Luci's strong chest as she moved on top of him, mapping him with her hands.

Luci made a face. "I want to give you my child, Mina. But I won't make you a single parent." He reached up to cup her cheek in his hand.

"We can figure that out after we figure us out," Mina said. "But I do want it. Wait—do we need to worry about birth control?"

Luci laughed and shook his head. "I'm not some mortal who can't control his own body. My seed is only potent when I want it to be."

"Seriously? That's super handy," Mina said, kissing the palm of his hand and then each fingertip. "Now are you going to tie me up and fuck me, or am I going to have to ask Bellz to do it?"

Luci growled and snapped his fingers. She found herself hogtied in the middle of the bed with a ball gag in her mouth. Mina's laugh came out muffled, which only caused her to laugh harder.

"Not what you had in mind?" Luci freed Mina with a quick snap. She hurried to sit up. Luci stood next to the side of the bed with his arms crossed.

"Sorry. That was giddy laughter that you have powers this time," Mina said, rising to her knees. "I liked your bondage choice." She blushed.

"Hmm, I do have my powers." Luci flashed his teeth at her in a knee-weakening grin. "How about a proper bed?" With another snap of his fingers, Mina found herself on a perfect replica of Luci's bed in Hell.

"Luci! I love it!" Mina said, tracing her fingers over the smooth wood of a post. "Can I keep it?"

"It's all yours." Rope had materialized in Luci's hands as he approached her. Once on the bed, he herded Mina onto her back then gently took her wrist in his hands and wrapped it with rope before looping the rope around a post and tying it off.

After repeating the process with her other wrist, Luci stopped to place a chaste kiss on her lip, then each nipple, and lastly her sensitive clit. Kissing his way down one leg, he took her ankle in his hand, looping another rope around it. Then he wrapped the other ankle in more rope and brought both feet up, fastening them to the posts to either side of the headboard where her wrists were already secured, bending her at the waist and leaving her open to him completely.

Luci crawled over her on his way to her bedside table where he found her glass dildo. Small and easy to clean, it was Mina's go-to when she wasn't interested in vibration. Agonizingly slowly, he slid it into her vagina, pumping it in and out of her, letting the upturned end of it drag across her g-spot.

Leaving the toy firmly inserted in her, Luci got off the bed and moved to the door. "I'm going to watch the end of the movie. If I come back and that toy has been dislodged, you'll be in for it." He winked on his way out the door.

Mina lay as still as she could, fearing that the small, glass dildo would easily slip from her wetness if she moved a fraction of an inch. She wasn't alone for long, though, before she heard the soft tiptoeing of feet in the hallway.

Sindy murmured her approval as she joined Mina on the bed, immediately removing the glass dildo. "Luci left you all tied up for me. How nice of him." Sindy slipped two fingers inside of Mina and began to fuck her with them furiously.

She had been close to orgasm when Luci left, and Sindy brought her right back to a sense of heightened pleasure. Although Mina knew her release was a ways off, now at least it was a possibility. Not lessening her pace, Sindy added a third finger.

"I know Lilith wanted to be the first to fist this tight pussy of yours, but she's not here and I'm not sure I can resist," Sindy said as she expanded her fingers, trying to make space for her pinky.

"Sindy," Mina gasped, "I've never—not in this body."

"Don't worry." Sindy flashed Mina a happy-go-lucky smile. Her expression was quickly replaced, however, with a scowl as she focused on spreading her fingers. Finally, Sindy succeeded in adding her pinky.

Gleefully, she fucked Mina for several minutes before tucking her thumb in and poking the tip of it into Mina. She had already felt stretched beyond her limits. The pain only heightening her longing for more, but this burned. The pain overwhelming all else.

"It's too much!"

"If I can't fist this gorgeous pussy then I'm just going to have to fist that sexy ass instead."

"Not without an enema," Mina said. "We are on earth now, where my body has more functions than just sexual ones."

"I don't care about that!" Sindy cocked her head to the side and studied Mina's face. "Although an enema could be fun."

Sindy called into the next room. "Luci, we need an enema kit please!"

It didn't take long for Luci to join them. "This is where you ran off to?" He approached the bed and smirked in approval as he saw the majority of Sindy's fingers inside Mina.

"I can't fist her pussy, so I thought I would try her ass, but my best friend is insisting on an enema."

"She wants to be clean for you." He rubbed kind circles on Sindy's lower back. "But I think we can save that for another time."

"Movie's over!" Bellz called from down the hall. "Can we put on another one?" he asked as he came in through the door. "Oh. Never mind. This looks way more fun."

Somehow Sindy brightened at his presence, and Mina couldn't help but let out a heartfelt chuckle. "You've got it bad." Sindy whipped her head around and blushed.

"Shh," Sindy said, putting a finger still dripping with Mina's juices to her mouth.

Luci leaned in and kissed Sindy, capturing her finger between their mouths. He lapped at her finger, savoring Mina's taste, before dipping into Sindy's mouth.

Tearing her eyes away from the erotic display before her, Mina found Bellz entranced, the pulse in his forehead throbbing.

"Bellz, come here."

His eyes snapped to her, and she could clearly see the barely contained rage within them. He gave her a small nod and walked to her.

"Come here," she said again, softer, and Bellz joined her on the bed.

"Closer," she said, and Bellz rested his head against hers. "You are loved, Bellz. I love you. Sindy loves you. Luci loves you."

Bellz inhaled deeply then exhaled through his mouth. Mina breathed him in.

"You aren't losing out if we all belong to each other," Mina said. "Kiss me, Bellz."

Bellz' lips were firm and demanding against hers, and she moaned as she opened herself to him. All she could do was respond with her mouth, as she was otherwise incapacitated, but she did her damnedest to infuse their kiss with as much love and feeling as she could manage.

Bellz wrapped Mina's hair in his hands, lightly tugging to tilt her head back so he could descend on her neck. It sent chills down Mina's spine, and her skin broke out in goosebumps.

At some point, Sindy and Luci had disengaged and were cuddling on the edge of the bed watching Bellz and Mina. Bellz glared when he noticed them.

"Bellz, you'll never guess what Mina told me she wants more than anything else in the world," Luci said, lazily tracing patterns across Sindy's exposed neck and collarbone.

It was Mina's turn to glare. She hoped that her eyes pierced Luci to the core. "That was private."

Luci smirked at her, his eyes sparkling as if to tell her to trust him. "She wants to have my babies."

Bellz' eyes widened to the size of dinner plates, and then he gulped, turning his gaze on Mina. "That's hot."

"I told her I'm not willing to make her a single mother, but you could give it a shot if you want to."

"Whoa, what?" Mina asked.

Luci winked at her. What was he playing at? There was mischief dancing in his eyes, and Mina was definitely curious to see how it played out. Besides, worst case scenario she'd end up with Bellz' child. Her heart swelled at the thought, and she didn't even try to hide the smile that crept onto her lips.

But a very loud part of her screamed at the wrongness of having Bellz' child before Luci's. "Luci, untie me right now." It was just another game, but she still struggled.

"I don't think I will."

Mina pulled at her bonds in a futile attempt to free herself.

"Calm down, Mina, or you'll hurt yourself," Sindy said soothingly, climbing up the bed and stroking Mina's hair in a motherly fashion.

Bellz devoured Mina with his eyes, lingering on her hips and breasts. He kissed her again, and Mina quickly forgot her protests. He found his way between her legs, and she could feel the tip of his large endowment nudging at her entrance.

Mina was wet from Sindy's fingers and Bellz' kisses and ready for him. He dipped his head to one of her breasts and took a nipple into his mouth while Sindy licked around the other.

Luci sat casually with his back against a post at the foot of the bed. He seemed content to just watch it all unfold. Mina made eye contact with him as Bellz sank into her. She gasped and licked her lips as she tried to process the exquisite feeling of being filled by Bellz' large cock.

When he began to thrust inside of her, she couldn't contain her moan, but she maintained eye contact with Luci. Sindy snuck a hand between their bodies and manipulated Mina's clit, at the same time reaching behind Bellz and massaging his balls.

Bellz picked up the intensity as Mina's orgasm approached. With one more flick of Sindy's talented fingers, it overwhelmed her. Bellz didn't last much longer, shooting his seed into her.

"That was way fast, Bellz," Mina said.

"Mmm," Bellz nuzzled his head into her shoulder as he continued to spurt inside her. "You happened to tap into one of my fetishes."

"Did I?" Mina asked, kissing the top of his head. "You want to impregnate the human race with your demon spawn?"

She felt Bellz twitch inside her.

"Are you starting to get hard again?"

Bellz laughed.

"Impregnate me next!" Sindy said. "Please, Bellz!"

"I told you she loves you," Mina whispered in Bellz' ear. To Luci she requested, "Can you please untie me now. I think my hands are going numb."

Immediately, Luci used his powers to free her limbs. She stretched, bringing her legs down to the mattress. Bellz slipped out of her and reached for Sindy, tossing her onto the bed next to Mina.

Mina crawled to the foot of the bed and wrapped her arms around Luci's middle, snuggling up to him but turning so she could watch Sindy and Bellz.

"Don't worry about getting pregnant," Luci said in not quite a whisper. "You aren't fertile right now."

"You are an ass, you know that?"

"Yes."

Bellz and Sindy were coupling, Sindy on top at first before Bellz flipped her on her back. Sindy wasn't having it, though, and managed to tackle Bellz again.

"Do they always fuck like this?" Mina asked.

"Yeah. Whoa!" Luci rolled Mina away, thrusting her between his body and the post as Bellz and Sindy tumbled into them. "I should have made this bed bigger."

"Yeah, it's not as big as the bed Bellz has," Mina said.

"That's because I fashioned this one after the likeness of our bed, not the group sex bed," Luci said. He leapt over her onto the floor and then helped her down. "Let's go watch a movie and give these guys some room."

"I don't suppose you conjured any extra sheets for this king sized bed. I think they'll need to be changed before I go to sleep tonight."

Luci blinked and new sheets appeared on the chest at the foot of the bed. The chest that was also new.

"You are like my own personal home goods store," Mina said.

Twenty-Four

I F SOMEONE HAD TOLD her a year ago that she could feel so much joy, Mina would have probably told them they were full of shit. Luci had wrapped himself around her, one arm and leg draped heavily over her. His lips trailed along her neck and shoulder. Her skin glowed after another round of lovemaking on the couch, the movie barely a buzz in the background.

"Luci, this is perfect," Mina said. "I hope you stay the rest of the day and through the night." Half the day had gone by, but they still had plenty of daylight left. Mina felt only slightly guilty at the thought of sleeping it away.

"Me too," Luci said. "But since we don't know how much time Oz has given us, I can't promise anything."

"I really should be more specific next time."

Luci's chest rumbled, the sound of his chuckle following. "You know, humans often say that after their first demon deal."

Mina intertwined their fingers and brought the back of his hand to her mouth. She admired the veins, tried to memorize the shape of each knuckle as they sat for a moment in comfortable silence. "Not only have I never felt this way about anyone before, but I didn't even think it was possible."

"Wow, that's a lot to put on a person, Mina."

Mina laughed. She'd said something very similar to him that first day in Hell "I can't believe you are throwing that back in my face, asshole."

"And you love me, so what does that say about you?"

"I think we both know I'm pretty fucked up."

"The Hell you are. You're perfect."

Mina's phone buzzed its way across the armrest, and Luci caught it before it fell.

Mina mouthed a *thank you* as she answered the phone. "Hey, Dahlia. What's up?" Mina turned to face Luci on the couch, idly twirly a blond lock of his hair. "Okay, calm down. Tabitha can come stay with me for the afternoon. Oh, uh, but I do have friends from, uh, out of town over. I can't just kick them out."

Luci gripped Mina's bare ass and tickled the underside of her cheek with a light touch of his fingertips. She squirmed and clamped her hand over her mouth to keep from squealing out loud, shooting Luci a warning look.

"Sure, I'll see you in fifteen minutes. Drive safely. It's going to be okay." Mina glanced down at the phone and shook her head. "She hung up on me."

"What was that?"

"My sister needs me to babysit my niece for the afternoon. Tabitha's school has a scheduled half day today, which my sister planned for, but a work emergency popped up."

"Fun," Luci said, his eyes twinkling with delight. "I haven't met your niece in lifetimes."

"I wonder why we always come back in the same roles," Mina said.

"Most families don't, but I think God has a pretty sick sense of humor when it comes to this endless loop of ours."

"We should get dressed and make sure Bellz and Sindy are decent." Mina sniffed under her arm and then sniffed Luci too. "And maybe squeeze in a speed shower. We smell like sex."

"You say that like it's a bad thing."

Bellz and Sindy were more than happy to join Luci and Mina for a shower. It was a tight fit. The shower stall wasn't small by any means, but Lucifer and his second in command took up a substantial amount of space. Add in their two, albeit much smaller, lovers and it was full to bursting.

They lathered each other up in a mass of limbs. A pair of hands gripped her hips, tugging her back against a hard length.

"That feels amazing, but we have to focus. My twelve-year-old niece is going to be here in five minutes," Mina said, wiggling out of reach.

They were toweling each other off when Mina said, "That might have actually been faster had we gone one at a time."

"But there would have been less touching that way," Sindy said, her bottom lip jutting out the tiniest bit. Mina gave Sindy's pout a quick peck before dashing into the bedroom to put on clean clothes.

By the time the doorbell rang, she was dressed in jeans and an oversized sweatshirt. Yanking a random pair of socks from the top dresser drawer and closing her bedroom door behind her so her devils could get dressed without scaring her niece, Mina ran to the door.

Tabitha greeted her with a tackling hug. "Aunt Mina!"

"Hey, kiddo." Mina wrapped her arms around her niece and lifted her off the ground.

"Thank you, Mina. I'll be back for her around seven," Dahlia said, stress still lacing her voice, and with nothing more than a quick kiss on the cheek for both Mina and Tabitha, she was back in her car and down the road.

"So what do you want to do?"

"Order pizza and watch horror movies," Tabitha said.

Mina chuckled, following Tabitha back into the townhouse. "Your mom might kill me if I send you home with nightmares again."

"That hasn't happened since I was nine."

"It was a PG movie, Tabitha."

"She said you had friends over. I wanna meet them," Tabitha said, glancing around the living room before disappearing into the kitchen, no doubt hoping to track them down.

Luci chose that moment to come out of the bedroom. He closed the door behind him, but not before Mina glanced Bellz and Sindy still half naked and making out.

"Tabitha, I'd like you to meet Luci," Mina said, whipping her head around to make sure her niece hadn't seen what was going on in her bedroom.

Tabitha came tearing out of the kitchen and stopped just short of tumbling into Luci and Mina. "Hi. Isn't Lucy a girl's name?" She then whispered to her aunt, "What are his pronouns?"

"He/him," Mina whispered back. "And a 'girl's name' is just a social construct."

Luci shrugged. "It's a nickname. Also spelled with an 'I.' It's nice to meet you, Tabitha." He held out a hand for her to shake, but Tabitha gave him a hug instead.

"Are you Aunt Mina's boyfriend?"

Luci's eyes grew large with panic. They hadn't had time to discuss how they were going to explain their relationship to Tabitha.

"You are!" Tabitha practically screeched. "You totally are! Does Mom know? Does Grandma?"

"No, no, no, no," Mina said. "I mean, he's my boyfriend." She glanced at Luci, an embarrassed smile tugging at her lips. "But no one knows, and your Mom is going to kill me when she finds out that you knew before she did."

Luci put an arm around Mina's waist.

"I think she'll be more happy than angry, Aunt Mina."

"I guess we'll find out when she picks you up in a few hours." Mina placed her head on Luci's shoulder.

"Did I hear something about horror movies?" He gave Mina a squeeze before letting go and heading over to the TV. He looked a little lost when he got there, and Mina realized he probably didn't know how to get the TV to function without using his demonic skills. She swallowed her mirth.

"Yeah. And pizza," Tabitha said, plopping down on the chaise and bouncing in place.

"Which horror movie should we watch?' Luci asked as he sat down on the floor in front of her partially unpacked box of movies. "*Rosemary's Baby*?" He wiggled his eyebrows at Mina.

"Um, no," Mina said.

"*Alien*?"

"Wow, no."

"*Omen*?"

"Which one? The original or the 2006 release?"

"Either." Luci shrugged, holding up both.

"No and no." Mina stuck her tongue out at him.

"What are you guys talking about?" Sindy asked. She and Bellz had emerged from her bedroom fully clothed, thankfully.

"We are trying to decide which horror movie to watch," Tabitha provided as she jumped off the chaise and ran over to them. "I'm Tabitha. Who are you guys?"

"I'm Sindy, your aunt's best friend." Sindy waved shyly.

"I thought Kathryn was your best friend," Tabitha said, then slapped a hand over her mouth.

"I'm allowed more than one," Mina said.

"I'm Bellz." He crossed his arm over his chest, his familiar glower firmly in place.

"Cool," Tabitha said, rubbing her big toe into the carpet. Her eyes widened at the sight of Bellz' prominent cheekbones. He wore a beanie that covered his small horns. "Bellz is a funny name."

Mina came over to stand next to Bellz and put a hand on his arm. "Bellz and Sindy are lifelong friends of Luci's. And now they are my friends, too."

"Cool," Tabitha said again before retreating to the other side of the room and helping Luci pick through the box of movies.

"Stop glaring at my niece," Mina whispered to Bellz. "She is a little girl, and you are as intimidating as fuck."

Bellz smirked and arched an eyebrow.

"That wasn't a compliment. Be friendly," Mina said, poking his chest with her pointer finger. "Sindy, help me out here."

Sindy took Bellz' arm. "I'll keep an eye on him." The look on her face betrayed her happiness to have an excuse to stay by his side.

When Mina went to check on Luci and Tabitha's progress, she found Luci holding a copy of *Carnival of Souls*. He looked up at her, a twinkle in his eye.

"That the one?" Mina asked.

"Yes," Luci said. "Definitely."

"Why are you looking at me like that?"

"No reason," Luci said.

Tabitha's attention ping-ponged between them, her mouth open like a fish. "He's not just your boyfriend."

Mina, Luci, Bellz, and Sindy could only gape back at her. What exactly had she picked up on?

"You're in love," Tabitha said. "How long have you been dating?"

"Why do you ask?" Sindy asked, narrowing her eyes at Tabby.

"I can't figure it out. It's like it's brand new, but, uh, ancient all at the same time," Tabitha said.

"Are you having a witchy moment?" Mina asked, kneeling on the floor next to her. She tucked a piece of Tabitha's hair behind her ear.

"It *is* ancient," Tabitha said, a tear rolling down her cheek. Mina brushed it away with the pad of her thumb. Tabitha had always had a way of intuiting things she couldn't possibly have known. And sometimes when a truth hit her, especially one with earth-shattering consequences for those she loved, it was a bit much for her to handle.

Mina could see no way around telling her niece as much of the truth as she dared.

"Remember when I had my accident on the yacht?"

"Yeah," Tabitha said.

Mina took a deep breath. "I died, Tabby. Not for very long, but long enough for me to find Luci."

"It's a nickname," Tabitha said, gasping as the pieces fell into place. "Lucifer." Tabitha scooted away from him until her back hit the chaise. "Get away from us. Leave my aunt alone."

"Oh, Tabitha, he's not evil," Mina said.

"But Grandma—" Tabitha said.

"Yes," Mina said. "Grandma has a lot of ideas about Hell, and she wasn't wrong about those realities centuries ago. But Hell has changed. Lucifer has changed."

"Thanks to Mina," Luci said. "She showed me what love was and made everything better, including me."

Mina's heart soared. "Or I happened to be at the right place and time when you decided you were ready to change."

Tabitha still eyed Luci with caution, but her shoulders had relaxed and her jaw no longer twitched.

"You just hugged him. What did you sense?"

"I don't know. I might need to hug him again," Tabitha said.

Luci stood up and walked over to Tabitha, holding out a hand to help her up, which she took. He then wrapped her up in a brotherly hug. Hesitantly, Tabitha hugged him back and took a deep breath.

She laughed, pulling away so she could stare up at him. "You love her every lifetime?"

"Every single one," Luci said.

"I don't think I can tell Mom about this," Tabitha said. "She'd freak."

"It's a lot to process," Mina said, tucking Tabitha against her. "Let's get the movie started, and I'll order pizza."

"Then ice cream at the place around the corner?" Tabitha asked as she and Mina sat down on the couch together.

"Absolutely," Luci said. "I love ice cream."

"Can't get that in Hell? Always melts too fast?" Tabitha giggled.

Sindy did too, and Tabitha jumped a bit as if she had forgotten there were two other people in the room.

"Are they also from Hell?"

"They are, but they are two of the best friends a girl could ask for. Bellz can be a little grumpy, but he has a good heart. And you are going to love Sindy."

"Can I braid your hair?" Sindy asked Tabitha, coming around to join them on the couch. "Oh, and we can paint our nails too."

"Not while I'm here. That smell." Bellz grimaced as he sat down on the chaise. Or maybe his face was just stuck that way.

Luci fumbled with the DVD player but finally managed to get it to work. Mina ordered pizza using an app on her phone, and they all settled in for the movie. Bellz and Luci shared the chaise, cuddling even.

Mina's heart warmed at the sight. They were both so handsome, both unafraid to show their affection. The thought that she might be responsible for their open display shot warmth down to her toes.

Twenty-Five

THE FOOD COMA HAD set in long ago. Mina may have over-ordered pizza, but still they had managed to finish almost all of it. The triple scoops at the ice cream parlor definitely didn't help. An hour before Dahlia came by to pick up Tabitha, the girl had passed out on the couch, her head in Sindy's lap.

Bellz stood over her, arms crossed. He was still glaring, but the extra wrinkle in his forehead suggested that he was mulling something over.

"What's up?" Mina asked, twining her arm through his.

"I don't like how tuned in she is to our wavelengths. It leaves her vulnerable."

Luci came up behind Mina, wrapping his arms around her waist and placing his chin on the top of her head. "We should provide her with protection."

Bellz gave a curt nod then turned on his heel and headed for the kitchen. He came back moments later with a bowl and a small, sharp knife. Kneeling on the carpet, he set the bowl before him. Calmly, he pressed the tip of the blade against the pad of his thumb and let his blood, a deep red so dark it almost looked black, drain into the bowl.

Luci did the same. Bellz held the bowl out for Sindy, who followed suit, gracefully avoiding jostling Tabitha or dripping any blood on the upholstery.

"Can we borrow a little bit of your blood as well, Mina?" Bellz asked. "You're special, and I think it might add some oomph to the protection."

Mina nodded, holding out her hand. Bellz reached for it, but Luci smacked him away.

"I've got this. Just hold the bowl out," Luci said as he grabbed Mina's hand and turned it palm up. He rubbed his thumb over her palm in reassuring circles then pressed the knife into the tip of her thumb until a bead of blood bloomed. Only three drops fell into the bowl before Luci brought his lips to Mina's thumb and sucked lightly, staunching the flow and healing the small wound with his demonic powers.

Her fingertips would definitely need a few days to recover after all she had put them through today. It would make painting a little difficult, but she would manage. At least it would remind her of this. Of them. Of him. Her gaze drifted upward and caught on Luci's.

The mixture, which began to smoke a bit and coagulate into a black paste, held Luci's attention. Bellz scooped it out of the bowl and used the substance to trace runes on Tabitha's forehead.

"Well, that's going to be a little hard to explain to Dahlia," Mina said.

Bellz, Luci, and then Sindy all pressed a kiss to Tabitha's forehead before instructing Mina to do the same. Tabitha's skin absorbed the runes until they disappeared completely, all trace of them gone.

Tabitha's eyes opened and she rubbed her temples, "Ugh, brain freeze." She looked at each one of them in turn. "What did you all just do?"

"Placed a protection on you. Nothing from the hell realm can harm you," Bellz said.

"Put your tongue on the roof of your mouth, Tabby," Mina said.

Tabitha's face relaxed as her brain freeze began to dissipate.

"Did she get any of her homework done?" Dahlia asked an hour later.

"Of course not," Mina said. "It's a Friday, and she was spending time with her cool aunt."

Sindy and Bellz had once more retreated to the privacy of Mina's bedroom, but Luci sat on the chaise reading one of the romance novels that Mina's mother had lent her. He seemed pretty engrossed in it, but that didn't stop Tabitha from pulling on his arm and demanding he come meet her mom.

"Mom, you have to meet Mina's new boyfriend," Tabitha said as she approached the entryway with Luci in tow, willingly or not. His body language gave nothing away.

"No way," Dahlia said. "He's hot," she mouthed to her sister as if Luci couldn't easily read her lips.

"Dahlia, this is Luci. We've been dating for a month or so. Luci, this is my sister, Dahlia."

"It's so nice to meet you," Luci said, holding out a hand. Dahlia ignored it and hugged him instead, clearly a Cadere family trait. Luci hesitated only a second before hugging her back.

"Eesh, when did our family get so huggy?" Mina asked.

"So, how did you meet?" Dahlia asked. "Put your backpack down, Tabitha. We can hang out for a bit."

"Actually," Mina said, shooting Luci a panicked look. "Luci needs to leave in a few, and we were hoping for some alone time."

Luci's time on Earth could run out at any moment. If he disappeared with Dahlia still hanging around, she'd have more questions than Mina was ready to answer. No thank you to that sitcom drama.

"Oh, yeah, sure," Dahlia said. "Another time. It was nice to meet you, Luci."

"You too," Luci said.

After they had said their goodbyes, Mina and Luci settled on the couch, and she let herself breathe again.

"You okay?" Luci asked. He pulled Mina against him so her back was pressed to his chest then eased them down into a partial reclining position.

"I introduced you to two family members. I'm kind of freaking out a little. Tabitha knows way more than she should. I'm fine pulling myself into the path of stupid, oncoming danger, but I don't want them involved."

"It might be hard to keep them out of it entirely."

"Maybe I should have stayed with you—"

"Your family needs you."

"Not if I'm going to be bringing demons into their lives."

"We aren't so bad, are we?"

"You definitely aren't." Mina arched into Luci, twisting until her mouth made contact with his cheek, and she caressed the underside of his chin with her lips. "But what happens when I meet a demon who—" Mina stopped herself from saying more. It was ridiculous, delusional, to think that she had some magical pull with all demon-kind. Somehow she had managed to get Luci to buy into it.

"Who doesn't immediately find you irresistible? Impossible." Luci teased her ear with his teeth, his tongue. "Have you remembered anything else about our first life together?"

Mina shook her head.

"Being with Bellz didn't shake any memories loose, huh?" Luci tugged the neck of Mina's sweatshirt to the side and kissed her shoulder, sending tingles down her spine. His hand slid down her stomach. With a flick, her jeans were unbuttoned, and Luci tugged down the zipper.

"Nope."

He slid his hand into the front of her pants.

"Well, my point is that if you could tame him, you can tame anyone. And you certainly managed it." His lips brushed behind her ear.

"Tell me," Mina said.

"I love you, Mina," Luci said.

"I love you, too," Mina said, patiently waiting for Luci to regale her with the story he had hinted at.

Mina's patience was rewarded with silence. It was a comfortable silence, at least.

"Are you going to tell me?"

"I just did," Luci said, pausing to kiss her again, "but I will gladly tell you every moment that you exist."

Mina laughed. "I should have been more specific. Tell me about Bellz."

"Oh. Ha!" He pulled her earlobe between his teeth and nibbled gently. "Not long after we met and fell irrevocably in love, I asked Bellz to watch you while I was in some meeting. Who remembers what it was about, but it was a bunch of my lieutenants. And I wasn't ready for anyone to find out about you yet."

"So you asked Bellz to babysit me," Mina said.

"Oof. I guess I did," Luci said. "He's always been my best friend, even when he was my worst enemy. If I could trust anyone with such a delicate secret, it was him. I definitely didn't foresee him getting so attached to you, though."

As Luci delved into his story, Mina began to remember. Each word brought back a fresh recollection that left her breathless with its vividness.

Twenty-Six

"**Y**OU'RE LEAVING? AFTER THAT?**" Mina had asked, a bit in disbelief. Feeling had only just started to return to her toes after the serious tupping in which she and her demon lover had just engaged. The declarations of love they had shared were still ringing in Mina's ears and singing in her heart. And he was telling her he was leaving?

"I've got a meeting. It's been on the books for decades. I can't skip it. Not without raising some serious eyebrows. Serious, bushy, demonic eyebrows. In some cases, eye ridges."

"Oh." Despite the goofy grin on Lucifer's face, Mina couldn't keep the frown from creeping onto hers. She pulled the sheet up to her chin and snuggled back into the pillows piled behind her. Stars twinkled on the ceiling of the cave. Luci had filled their home with couches, pillows, and blankets and topped it off with a giant bed covered in even more pillows and blankets.

"Don't you do that," Luci said, joining Mina on the bed. "Don't look so sad. I can't handle it."

Mina's reply was cut short by Luci's lips on hers as he pressed her back into the bed.

"Crap."

"Language."

"My language offends you? After everything I just did to you? You're adorable."

"I suppose you need to spend more time corrupting me. Which you can't do if you leave."

"I've thought of this. That's why my dear friend Beelzebub will be stepping in to keep you company and corrupt you further while I'm gone."

"Excuse me. What?"

"Beelzebub," Luci said as if he'd completely addressed her reservations.

"I don't want anyone else to corrupt me, Luci."

"Well, at least meet him first before you make up your mind completely. He should really be here by now." Luci glanced at the gap in the cavern wall that served as the main entryway and shook his head. "You'll like him. He's just like me."

"Did you just claim that we are anything alike?" A tall demon, broad of shoulder and dark of hair, stepped into Mina and Luci's love den.

Luci hopped off the bed and grabbed Beelzebub's shoulder in greeting. He stood between Mina and his demon friend so that Mina could only see those broad shoulders and the top of Beelzebub's head. He had a few inches on Luci.

"The fuck," Beelzebub said. "Did you just touch me?"

"I need you to watch Mina while I go to that head of staff meeting."

"Who?"

"Mina," Luci said, stepping to the side. Mina yelped and clutched the sheet tighter. Why hadn't Luci given her time to get dressed?

"A human? Really, Luci?" At least Mina could see him now. He had two small horns on either side of his forehead. His cheekbones stood out prominently against the rest of his perfectly sculpted face. Piercing blue eyes seemed to see straight through the thin sheet. Mina swallowed hard.

"Hi," she said before turning to Luci. "I think my clothes are on the other side of the room."

"I'll get them," Luci said. "Sorry, I should have thought of that sooner." When he returned with her clothes, he asked Beelzebub to turn around and then helped Mina don her dress and fasten it.

At some point Beelzebub had turned back around, because when Mina looked up he was watching her.

"Who is she?" Beelzebub asked Luci.

"She's my love," Luci said.

"You are in love with a human?" The bile in Beelzebub's voice stung like acid.

"God brought her here, and she stood up to him."

"I think I heard something about that, actually," Beelzebub said, shaking his head.

"He trapped her here, Beelzebub. He condemned her for disagreeing just like he condemned us."

"And that made you decide to fall in love with her?"

"I didn't decide anything. I fell in love with her. Oh, that's right. You've never been in love before, so how the fuck would you know?"

"You're deluding yourself, Lucifer. You want to believe that you love her because you are seeing yourself in her. You are in love with the story of her because it parallels yours. You aren't in love with a human. You, brother, could only ever be in love with yourself."

"This really feels like a conversation I shouldn't be around for," Mina said, mostly under her breath. Luci heard, though, his head snapping back to her, eyes full of concern.

"I'm sorry, love." Luci wrapped one arm around Mina's waist, tugging her to him until their chests met, and caressed her check. "I know you don't want to hear this."

"You want to leave me here with him?" Mina asked, her voice hushed in the hopes that they wouldn't be overheard.

"He'll spend a little time with you, and you'll win him over."

Mina peered around Luci's shoulder. Beelzebub had wandered over to the farthest couch and was examining a pillow whose fabric twinkled in the light of the artificial stars above them.

"I've really got to go, Mina. I'm already late." Luci paired his parting words with a dangerous kiss that left Mina in a deep pit of desire. By the time she opened her eyes, her dark prince had gone.

It seemed rude to leave Beelzebub alone on the other side of the room, so she made her way toward him. He really was quite tall, and Mina stopped farther from him partly out of fear and uncertainty, but mostly so she could meet his gaze without giving herself a crick in the neck.

"You love my boy?"

"Your boy?" she asked, puzzled for a moment before it clicked. "Oh. Luci? Yes." Mina's heart warmed thinking of how quickly her love had come about. Had this happened a year ago with a human man, she would have doubted that the emotion was more than infatuation. But something about this place and all that had happened since she left her quiet hovel of a home cemented the attraction. "Very much. I know it's a little hard to believe. But I've never felt this way about anyone. He just left, and I already can feel the fissures beginning in my heart."

"Luci? You've given him a nickname?" Beelzebub snarled at her, and before she could process that he had moved, his hands were wrapped around her arms in a death grip.

Mina's bottom lip trembled. Despite her trepidation, she met his gaze.

"His name is Lucifer. He's a demon, the worst of us all. He could destroy your soul with the blink of an eye or damn you to eternal suffering with the flick of his wrist. Don't be mistaken. He's not some human man you've fallen for." Beelzebub's face reddened and his eyes dilated as he leaned down and sniffed her hair.

"What are you doing?" Mina asked.

"Maybe I should remind you of what we are," Beelzebub said as he swept his leg behind her and pushed her back, knocking her off balance and lowering her to the couch. He settled on top of her, pinning her arms to her sides and parting her legs with a thigh.

"Beelzebub, please stop," Mina said. "I don't think this is what Luci intended."

"He knew what would happen the moment he left you alone with me. He knows what I am. He knows what we are. You are the one mistaken." Beelzebub clasped his mouth to the side of Mina's neck, sucking and nipping at her delicate flesh. She tried to shrug him off, but he eluded her, succeeding in branding her with pleasure.

"He trusts you," Mina said, whimpering as his tongue lapped at the spot just below her earlobe.

Beelzebub pulled back to look at her. His smirk disarmed her, and all thoughts of protest briefly left Mina's mind. "He knows me, little human. He knew what I'd do. He must have wanted it to happen."

"But what about what I want?" Mina asked.

"I don't need your consent, human."

"It will be better with it," she said, dangling the notion in front of him like forbidden fruit.

Beelzebub pushed off of the couch and took a step back, tilting his head to the side, his face almost unreadable. It looked like he was working hard to make sense of what she had said. "I'm sorry," he said as if he were posing a question.

Mina sat up and readjusted her dress to cover her legs. She patted the spot on the couch to her right, inviting him to sit. When he did, he was careful not to touch her.

"I liked what you were doing. But it's nice to be asked. Especially since I'm not really sure we should be doing it." Mina risked a glance in Beelzebub's direction.

He had a gentle grin on his face, and he stretched his arm out behind her as he scooted closer to her. They still weren't touching, but he was only a fraction of an inch away. "Lucifer wouldn't mind. He's never been possessive. And we've loved each other for a long time."

"Yeah?" Mina turned, bringing one leg onto the cushion so her shin brushed Beelzebub's muscular thigh. "Did you love him before the fall?"

"I did." Beelzebub's fingertips brushed along her shoulder blade.

"Is that why you chose to follow him?"

"I didn't so much follow him as arrive after him. I would have stood up to God if he hadn't."

"I'm sorry you had to go through it at all."

"I'm pretty sure we played right into God's plan anyway. Pretty infuriating, but at least I get to take that frustration out on human souls."

"And is that satisfying? Torturing us?" Mina swallowed as she remembered all the things that Luci had done to her under the guise of torture.

"Honestly? No." Beelzebub closed his eyes and inhaled her scent. "Torturing you, however, is going to be another story."

"Luci did say that you would be furthering my corruption," Mina said, biting her bottom lip. "Maybe that's what he meant."

"Wait a minute. Lucifer told you that before he left, and you didn't think that he was giving us his blessing?"

Mina laughed "Blessing? That's a funny choice of word."

"You don't think demons can bless things? Of course we can."

"I don't think so. I'm pretty sure that blessings are a heavenly thing."

"I bless you with long and many orgasms." Beelzebub pulled Mina into his lap and brought his mouth down on hers. His tongue brushed against her bottom lip, and when she gasped, he plunged into her mouth.

Mina slipped her fingers through his hair and massaged his scalp as he cupped her bottom in a firm grasp, pulling her against him. His hardness pushed against her core, causing her to call out. He swallowed her moan with his kiss before responding with a pained groan.

"Tell me, little human, what has Luci done to you so far?"

"That's private," Mina said, blushing as she thought about how Lucifer had inserted the tip of his finger into her anus during their lovemaking earlier.

"Lucifer won't mind," Beelzebub said.

"But I do," Mina said. "He's special to me, Beelzebub. My time with him." She shook her head. "Besides, you were going to show me that you're a real demon."

"Are you really sure you want to play that game?"

"Are you telling me that you can be anything other than a big, bad demon?"

"You are playing with fire."

"When in Hell." She shrugged.

His grip on her ass tightened. He tilted her onto her back and hovered over her. Beelzebub's intent blue gaze pulled her in, intoxicating her with a lusty haze. There was a hunger in his eyes that threatened to devour her. And she wanted it to.

"Are you sure about this?" Beelzebub asked, brushing a strand of Mina's hair from her forehead. "Once we start, I won't be able to stop."

"Are you going to cause me permanent harm?"

"Not permanent."

"Then I'm sure."

"Alright. We aren't doing it here, though." Beelzebub stood up and offered Mina his arm.

Twenty-Seven

TOGETHER, BEELZEBUB AND MINA walked through Hell. Mina hadn't been out of the cave much, and the change of scenery should have been nice. Except the souls seemed so aimless. Luci had ended the use of torture the week after her arrival, but no system had yet been agreed upon to replace it.

"Where are we going?"

"To my corner of Hell." Disgust painted his ever-present grimace even more sour. "This place is a mess. Your doing, by the way. I'd heard rumblings that Lucifer was no longer tormenting souls, but I had no idea it was because a little human got him all mixed up."

Mina stopped in her tracks, digging her heels in. "You are still torturing people in your corner of Hell, I take it."

"Of course."

"Nope. I'm not going there."

"I gave you the chance to back out." Beelzebub whirled on her.

Mina held up her hands in surrender. "That's true, but consent doesn't really work that way. It can be revoked at any time. Besides, you did promise no permanent harm." She tapped the tip of her toe against the rock ground, trying to work out a solution so she could still go with him. Because, shockingly, she still wanted to. "Just don't take me near anything I can't unsee."

Beelzebub wrapped his arm around Mina's shoulder and tucked her against him so her breasts brushed his chest. Those striking blue eyes pulled her in until she was unaware of anything else around her.

She didn't notice that their surroundings were slowly dissolving and rearranging themselves, not until they'd been replaced completely.

"We're here." Beelzebub stepped away to reveal a room full of the oddest contraptions Mina had ever seen.

Two large planks of wood crossed to form a towering "X" with manacles attached at each point. Stocks stood open as if in anticipation of their next victim. A piece of furniture that almost resembled an ottoman except for its long legs and hard surface hovered in the corner. Whips, canes, crops, and floggers of all different colors, materials, and sizes hung from hooks on the walls.

The room itself did not resemble a cave. The walls, floors, and ceilings were all the same material: smooth, hard, and non-porous. Mina tapped it with her foot and found it cold as well. The floor sloped gradually into the center of the room where a metal grid lay.

Beelzebub followed her gaze and flashed a devilish grin. "It's a drain. For cleanup."

Beelzebub chuckled at her wide eyes.

"What are you planning?" Mina asked, second guessing her decision to follow this creature, regardless of how handsome or charming, into a literal pit of Hell.

"Why would I tell you that?"

"I find it comforting when Luci does," Mina offered hopefully.

"That fool."

Beelzebub's appearance flickered a moment as dark claws swept toward her, slashing down the front of her gown so quickly she lost track of them. Her clothing fluttered to the floor around her like falling leaves. She pressed a hand to her breast and glanced down, certain she would see raised abrasions in fresh, pink lines, but her creamy skin remained unmarred.

The demon wasted no time in draping Mina's arm through his and leading her to the center of the room right above the grate. With unexpected gentleness, Beelzebub lifted Mina's arms into the air, running his large hands from her shoulders to her wrists, which he clasped in padded manacles that were secured to a chain on the ceiling.

"Spread your legs," Beelzebub whispered in her ear as he let his fingertips lightly feather over her hips.

As Mina complied, her arms were pulled more tightly above her. She felt like an offering as Beelzebub bent down and clipped her ankles into more manacles attached to a long metal pole. She was spread and locked in place.

A thrill ran through her. She was completely at his mercy.

For the sake of her wrists, she willed her knees to stay strong.

Beelzebub cupped Mina's face in his hands, bringing them eye to eye. His gentle baritone caressed her. "Are you doing all right?"

"Mmhmm."

"I need actual words, human." Although he sounded annoyed, his eyes gave him away. He was concerned. For her.

"I'm good. My knees were feeling a little wobbly there for a minute."

"Wobbly knees?" A finger darted between her legs and nudged apart her folds. "What a minx you are. Already wet for me." Beelzebub tsked as he disappeared behind her.

The urge to squirm was almost too much. She glanced over her shoulder as best she could. He examined the row of impact devices on the wall.

"Turn back around, human."

"How did you know?" Mina asked as she looked at the empty space before her.

"Demon."

She heard his footsteps on the hard floor before his heat greeted her. He didn't touch her, but warmth radiated from him just the same, bathing her back.

Mina gasped when Beelzebub's fingertips brushed her neck as he moved her hair.

"I could gag you, but I'd rather hear your screams." He pressed his lips to the crook of her neck, and Mina shuddered.

He stepped away from her, the gentle caress of leather brushing the small of her back the only evidence that she was still within reach. Then the sound of leather whistled through the air, and the straps slapped across her lower back and upper bottom.

Mina sucked in air from between her teeth. The flogger warmed her long after the initial spark of pain. The next pass came from below, hitting across the bottom of her cheeks. Then again, across her right hip.

He worked his way all over her body. Not a piece of her was left untouched. From her hips, he moved to her thighs, her calves, the tops of her feet. He stepped in front of her and started on her breasts.

He was gentle when he came into contact with bone, but his attacks on fleshy bits became more forceful as he continued. Her breathing was ragged, and when he finally brought the flogger between her legs, a single strap striking her clit, Mina lost control.

His name slurred on her lips, the syllables running together sloppily, as she begged. "Please, more. Please."

He stared at her for a moment, his weapon held limply at his side. He was reading her, she could tell, but for what she didn't know. He flung the flogger to the side and it skittered across the floor. Mina whimpered her distress, craving the feel of it, mourning its loss.

She pressed her eyes shut and tried to focus on her breathing. Her skin tingled against the cold air, aching in anticipation of his next touch or the strike of another implement.

He left her there just long enough for her to question whether he was coming at all. Just long enough for the panic to start and for an ache in her shoulders to set in.

When the palm of his hand caressed her hip, her eyes opened to find his deep blue. He kissed her. It was quick but bruising.

"Are you ready for more, little human?"

"Yes." Mina wiggled against her chains.

He stepped away from her, and she caught a glimpse of the riding crop that he held behind his back. He traced the head of the crop around one breast, running it from top to bottom before snapping it across her nipple. He repeated the maneuver on her other breast before letting the crop kiss her breasts over and over.

She welcomed the warming sting. Pleasure rocked her as Beelzebub circled her, the crop biting sweetly everywhere he brought it down until she was gasping and begging for more.

The crop bit into her clit, and Mina almost toppled over the edge. Almost. But she held herself back, terrified by her own reaction.

"Don't do that again," Beelzebub growled into her ear. His teeth captured her earlobe before flicking his tongue against it.

"Do what?"

"Hold back."

The crop descended upon her calves then her thighs. Beelzebub inched his way closer and closer to Mina's core.

Her breath shuddered as he gently pressed the triangular head against her vulva, rocking it back and forth just shy of her sensitive nub. When he brought the crop down against her there, she crashed and fell.

But he caught her, wrapping her up in his arms as the restraints disappeared. He crushed her to him and brought them to the floor. Mina tried to regain her breath while cradled in Beelzebub's arms, her head propped against his shoulder.

"How do you feel?" Beelzebub asked.

"Bellz, that was amazing. You aren't torturing the others that way, because that was heaven." Despite her words, she was crying—and had been for some time, based on the stiffness of her skin.

"Bellz?" Beelzebub asked, wiping the tears from her face with a black handkerchief

"Uh-huh." Mina let out a congested giggle.

"Lucifer didn't tell me how special you are," Beelzebub said. "Probably wanted me to find out for myself. Quite the gift. I'll have to thank him later."

"Do you think he'll be gone much longer?"

"Who knows, but don't worry. I'll keep you more than occupied until he returns, special one."

"How am I special?" she asked.

"The way you take pleasure from pain. Your responses—they make me want to give you everything you ask for and more. I can't make sense of it. I usually take, but you've convinced me to give without even intending to."

"More?" Mina asked, sitting up to look at him. "Would you give me more now?"

"Are you not sated?" he laughed. "I have to say, I've tortured a lot of humans, and they never ask for more."

"Do you usually hold them afterward?"

"I definitely do not."

"Maybe you should start."

After helping Mina to stand and making sure her legs could hold her, Beelzebub chained her ankles to the same spreader bar, bent her over, and secured her wrists to the bar as well. He brought out a cane and tormented her bottom and thighs until she was writhing and dripping, striped and red, tears staining her face once more.

That's how Lucifer found them. He groaned with longing as he approached.

"You've marked her, Beelzebub," Lucifer said, crouching behind Mina and rubbing his hands along her smarting skin. Soothing her with his concern as much as his touch.

"She loves it," Beelzebub said.

A throaty moan escaped Mina's parted lips. "Don't stop."

Lucifer let out a deep, heartfelt laugh.

Too distracted by the return of the cane, Mina lost track of Lucifer. Her orgasm had been looming before his arrival, just out of reach. When the flogger joined in, leaving gentle thuds along her back, Mina's existence centered only on sensation. It built upon itself, growing to something more.

The explosion started simultaneously in her mind and between her legs. It spread to her breasts and her knees before swooping down to her toes and out to her fingertips. The force of it destroyed her stability and tipped her forward.

Four strong hands stabilized her and lowered her gently to the floor. At some point, someone unlocked her limbs. Lucifer and Beelzebub attempted to pull her into their laps at the same time, resulting in her bottom straddling both of them. She shifted so she could prop her head against Luci's shoulder and dangle her legs over Bellz.

"This place really needs an aftercare space," Lucifer said. "At least a chaise."

Beelzebub rolled his eyes as he gripped Mina's chin and placed a chaste kiss on her lips. He otherwise ignored Lucifer.

"Shall I, then?" Lucifer asked.

"Hell, no. I don't need your crappy style mucking up the ambiance of my room."

"What ambiance?" Lucifer brushed his hand over Mina's hair.

"Leather," Mina said. "Black leather. A couch. And it should be deep enough for three."

"For three? I don't think so," Beelzebub said. "I'm not sharing you."

"You're right. You aren't sharing her." Lucifer's grip tightened around Mina's shoulders. "I'm the one sharing her."

Mina punched Lucifer and then Beelzebub's arms lightly. "Neither of you own me. I'm not property. And I like doing this with both of you. But, Bellz, what Luci and I have, this love that we share, it's something more, something special. He fills me up. He makes me brave enough to love you. I'm not sure I could if I didn't love him first. If he didn't love me."

Beelzebub stared at her for a moment before a smile started at the edges of his mouth and spread to his eyes. For a second the blue seemed to darken to black and sparkle like the night sky before returning to a beautiful dusk blue.

Unceremoniously, Beelzebub pushed Mina's legs away and got up. Lucifer scooped her into his arms and stood as well. Over Lucifer's shoulder, she watched Beelzebub move toward the couch she had described.

The three of them settled onto cushions large enough to swallow them. Lucifer sandwiched Mina between Beelzebub and himself and nudged her toward Bellz, who happily pulled her down until they were both supine. Lucifer braced himself above them. He hovered for a moment, taking in every detail, before leaning down to first kiss Beelzebub and then Mina. He let his arms give out and collapsed on top of them.

"Squished," Mina gasped. "I'm squished."

Beelzebub stiffened his arm around her and pushed Lucifer to the side so Lucifer's weight was no longer on her. Lucifer fell beside them, and she found herself wedged between her two lovers.

Mina giggled as Lucifer's lips danced over her neck. Beelzebub gripped her hip, and she responded by devouring his lips with her own. He slid his hand down to her thigh and yanked it over his side so that she was open to them both. He moved to her ankle and brushed a knuckle across the arch of her foot.

The warm silkiness of two erect members nudged her center. Mina wiggled until their lower halves came into view. Beelzebub and Lucifer had undone the fastenings on their trousers.

"What are you two planning?" Mina asked.

"Don't you dare tell her." Beelzebub scowled at Lucifer.

"Why wouldn't I tell her?"

Mina blinked at Beelzebub and nodded in agreement with the question.

"Because you would rob me of the pleasure of seeing her face when we surprise her," Beelzebub said, dipping to place a gentle kiss on Mina's nose.

"Very well," Lucifer said. He waited a beat before adding, "Do you trust us?"

"Yes." Mina breathed out the word as she realized it was true. She'd come to trust Lucifer weeks ago, but it was a little startling to realize that she also trusted Beelzebub. And in such a short amount of time. He'd taken care of her, brought her to new heights, and been willing to take to heart her opinions.

Lucifer rubbed his length between the lips of Mina's vulva while Beelzebub pressed the head of his cock to her clit. Far faster than she deemed proper, her juices lubricated Lucifer and pooled on her thigh.

Lucifer adjusted behind her, the tip of his steel rod prodding her opening. Desire rocked through her as her tunnel stretched around his length. His glacial pace was torturous, and once fully inserted he stopped all movement. His hand on her waist centered her only a little.

Whimpering, Mina curled her toes and clamped down on the urge to move. Beelzebub tipped her chin up with a finger and pressed a reassuring kiss to her lips.

"Luci, please."

In one swift motion, Luci pulled out of her completely. The loss of him was so devastating that Mina let out an anguished sob. Her demon soulmate brushed her hair aside and tenderly set his mouth to her shoulder.

"This is more agonizing than when Bellz was torturing me."

"Are you okay with this nickname, Beelzebub?" Lucifer asked.

"I love it." A light danced in Beelzebub's eyes. Her lips parted as she felt the head of his erection pressing into her.

Lucifer chuckled deeply, and Beelzebub thrust into her. Unlike Lucifer, he fucked into her deeply before pulling out completely and shoving back in once more. Lucifer's hand tickled its way up to Mina's exposed breast. He kneaded her soft flesh in his large hand and tweaked her nipple between his fingers.

Beelzebub pulled out of her, and Mina cursed. "This is what you had planned? Fuck me just a bit and then deprive me?"

"Is that what you had planned, *Bellz*?"

"Nope. You, *Luci*?"

"Nope." Lucifer thrust into her for a single thrust before retreating. Beelzebub wasted no time in taking Lucifer's spot. A quick in and out and then Lucifer was back. They switched back and forth until Mina was writhing between them.

Each time she thought she might be getting close, the loss of their members prevented her from cresting. When she thought she'd be in sweet limbo for eternity, they both pressed into her at once. She came instantly. Lucifer and Beelzebub had emptied themselves into her as her muscles had clamped around them.

"I seem to fall in love with demons pretty easily," Mina said now as two of Luci's fingers brought her closer to nirvana. He had worked her jeans down to her knees, and she surged against him, shoving her back against her lover's chest.

"Our love is cosmic," Luci whispered into her ear.

"Or preordained. What if we're just—" Mina gasped as Luci ground his palm into her clit, "doing exactly what He wants?"

"Who?"

Luci growled as Mina worked herself against him. He draped a leg over hers in an attempt to restrain her. He already had one arm wrapped around her, clutching her against his hard chest.

"God."

"If our love is the price I have to pay to win my war against Him, it's too high a cost. I would never sacrifice what we have."

"So if we are playing right into His hands?"

"The only hands you are playing into are mine." Luci slipped a third finger into her and grunted possessively.

"And if we bring about the end of the world?" Mina forced the words out, because she knew that this building pleasure would wreck her soon—and her ability to put together a coherent thought.

"God isn't going to give up His favorite play toy." His fingers retreated and Mina whimpered in distress.

"Is that what you are doing now?"

"Playing with my favorite toy?" He brought his wet fingers up to her nub and circled it before giving it a pinch.

"Uh-huh," Mina squeaked.

"You are not a toy. You are so much more to me than that. You're everything." He drove his fingers back into her and her nerve endings erupted into bliss.

Twenty-Eight

MINA STARED AT THE steam rising from her cup of tea, her chest hollowed out. Her townhouse too quiet for comfort. Fleetingly, she considered streaming something mindless to fill the silence, but the thought of that false companionship left her with a weight in her gut.

The aftershocks of her orgasm had just settled down when she had fallen back against the couch in a disoriented heap. Once she had scrambled into a sitting position, panic gripping her, she'd understood that her time with Luci had come to an end. After rushing to her bedroom, Mina discovered that Bellz and Sindy were gone too.

Now she had memories and tea as comfort, and little else. The idea to use a spirit board to summon demons had come so naturally to her, and she had seized upon it rather quickly. So quickly, in fact, that she hadn't stopped to contemplate how else she might go about calling her demons back to her. Now, she found herself back at square one.

Finding another spirit board could solve her problem, she supposed. But something about that didn't feel right, like it would be disrespectful to Oz and his desire to see her safe.

Mina crossed her arms on the table and lay her head down. If only she could coax some tears, she might feel better. But they wouldn't come.

What did come, however, was the nagging glimmer of recollection. She tried to focus on it, and it fluttered away. Flinging herself from the table, Mina screeched in frustration.

"Please," she whispered under her breath.

The force of the memory hit her like a ton of bricks, all at once. An empty farm house which once rang with laughter was now shaken with sobs. Mina recalled sitting at a table not too different from the one in her present and staring at her hands as they rested on the tabletop.

She had traced the veins of her hand with her eyes and wondered at the blood that flowed through them, keeping her alive with no thought of her desire, or lack thereof, to live.

The illness that came and took them all had set in so suddenly that Mina was still trying to convince herself that it had actually happened. That it wasn't just a bad dream from which she had failed to awaken.

Her darling niece had gone first. Tabitha no longer ran around the kitchen asking for her favorite little tea cakes, the expensive kind that they could only afford to make on special occasions.

Mina's father had gone next. And then Dahlia, so soon after that Mina wasn't sure her sister was aware of their father's passing. The broken heart from losing her daughter had surely been the final blow. Then, despite appearing as though she would make a full recovery, Mina's mother succumbed the following night.

After four days, Mina was the sole survivor. Somehow the sickness had skipped her entirely. She hadn't suffered from a single sniffle or stomach tremor. Why fate had decided to spare her, she had no idea. In fact, she wasn't sure that it had spared her.

What was left for her? She couldn't manage the farm alone, and it was unlikely that she could find a buyer.

A knock interrupted her thoughts. The Widow Meyer stood outside the door with a basket full of cheese and freshly baked bread. She had always been a kind woman. Even when Dahlia and Mina had been foolish, young girls gossiping with their neighbor and dear friend, Cassie, that the widow was a witch.

"She is! I swear it," Cassie had defended when Mina raised a questioning brow. "She made a deal with a crossroads demon for wealth and health."

"What's a crossroads demon?" Dahlia asked, mouth gaping.

"Demons who hang out at crossroads, whispering folks' most secret desires. They offer them up in exchange for your soul," Cassie said, leaning in to keep from being overheard.

Mina and Dahlia gasped in unison.

At the time, all three girls had agreed that the widow seemed to know more about the mystical elements of the world than anyone else in their small county. So, by child logic, it made perfect sense that she would be well versed and practiced in the occult.

Mina hadn't thought about that in years, and she blushed to think that she could have at one time thought so poorly of the woman who had become such a good friend.

"Mrs. Meyer," Mina said as she accepted the basket, "you are too kind. Please come in for some tea."

"How are you holding up, dear?" the widow asked as she shooed Mina away from the stove so she could take over the duties of steeping tea. "Let me do that. You sit down."

Mina was unsure of how to answer the question. She didn't feel much of anything. Emptiness. A gnawing sense that there was something she should be doing. Bed linens to change, water to boil, a tincture to prepare. But besides a half dozen animals and a coop full of chickens, there was no one to take care of but herself.

"Lonely," Mina finally answered.

The widow placed a steaming cup in front of Mina and sat down with her own cup of tea. The woman clasped Mina's hand with her own. Her skin felt as thin as a cherished family recipe, folded and unfolded countless times throughout the years until it barely held together.

"Is there anything I can do for you, sweet child?"

Mina didn't think about what she said next, and if she hadn't been so preoccupied with her own grief she would have felt guilty for it for weeks. "Did you really make a deal with a demon for your success?"

The widow laughed. "Now why would you ask me that now when we have been friends for so many years?"

"Maybe I could bring them back, or dull this pain. Or do something. Anything other than just sit here."

"Oh, darling." The Widow Meyer shook her head. "I've never had any dealings with Hell's creatures, much less a crossroads demon, but I do know how one might go about calling one."

"How?"

"Are you absolutely certain this is a path you would like to go down? Once summoned, demons are incredibly hard to banish."

Turning to God had done nothing as she lost one family member after another. Anger simmered, buried beneath layers of emptiness and bitterness. Maybe calling a demon would help. Maybe it wouldn't, but it was certainly better than doing nothing. If all she accomplished was making God angry, she would call it a win.

"I am certain."

"You must create an offering. It doesn't quite matter what is in the offering, but if you have a big ask then you better offer something with a lot of value. Find any old place where two roads meet, and bury the offering in the center of the road."

"I don't have much money," Mina said.

"Not that kind of value." Mrs. Meyer blew delicately on her tea before taking a sip. "Demons crave strong emotions."

"Things like fear, hate, and anger?" Mina asked.

"And lust," the widow added.

"What about love?"

"I'm not sure how a demon would respond to love, but if it's what you are feeling strongly, don't be afraid to use it."

"How will I know if it has worked?"

"The demon will appear in moments. He won't keep you waiting"

The two sat in silence as they finished their tea. When the widow stood to leave, Mina stood also. After they embraced and the widow left, Mina watched the closed door for a solid two minutes.

Then she turned to the kitchen and started to bake those small tea cakes her niece loved so much. As the cakes were cooling and awaiting icing, Mina pulled out a piece of the jerky her father had been so proud of. Fifteen years he had worked to perfect his process, finally declaring it a success the fall before last.

From her pocket she produced a tarnished penny dated the year of her birth. Her sister had given it to her for luck when she turned eighteen. She placed it alongside the jerky on a square of cloth cut from her mother's favorite dress. When it had aged beyond the point of being repaired, Sandra had cut squares out of the salvageable pieces in preparation for a quilt that she would never make.

Once the cakes had cooled, Mina dipped them each in a pink icing and waited for the icing to set before adding two to the heap of memories. Gathering the four corners of the square together, Mina tied it closed with her favorite blue ribbon. The one she'd purchased when she was twelve with the money she had earned from the sale of her prized goat.

Placing a kiss to the top of the bundle, Mina picked it up and headed out the door. She walked to the inside corners of four fields where a path from the house intersected with the path to the barn. The soil was loose and brittle under her bare hands as she dug a hole just big enough to deposit her offering.

After patting the soil back in place, Mina bowed low over the earth. She expected to cry or to be suddenly struck with fear. Instead, she felt nothing. Appropriate, she mused, when after five minutes of waiting no demon appeared.

"Of course," she muttered under her breath before returning to her quiet, lonely home.

The remaining cakes sat untouched on the kitchen table. She thought about eating one but was afraid they would taste of ash, so she boxed them up and put them in the cupboard instead. Maybe she would bring some over to the Widow Meyer tomorrow. If she was feeling up to it.

Although sunset was still a ways off, she headed to the second floor, kicked off her boots, and crawled into bed.

Nothing was going to save her from her misery, she realized just as sleep took her. Not even Hell itself could spare her from this torment.

The chill of the room must have woken her. She hadn't bothered with a fire, and goosebumps covered her arms and legs. But as she opened her eyes, she found a fire blazing in the hearth, and a quilt had been draped over her.

She sat up, clutching the quilt to her chest. Maybe the widow had paid a late night visit just to check in again. Mina had asked for unconventional advice. The woman being concerned followed reason.

Mina's eyes stopped on a dark figure in the corner of the room, obscured in shadow. It managed to avoid the light that the fire cast into the room.

"Who's there?" Mina whispered.

The figure—a man—took a step forwards and placed an arm on the mantle. He was tall, with broad shoulders and a prominent forehead, a straight nose, and a striking jawline. Mina gasped at the handsome lines that the light of the fire defined in shape but not color or detail.

"You called for me," he said in a gravelly voice.

"You—I—What?" Mina asked, tucking her legs in front of her as if they would provide some protection from this stranger.

He tossed something at her. It came to rest on the bed next to her foot: her bundle, covered in a light layer of dirt.

"Oh," she said, eyes widening as she realized just what this creature was. "Oh."

"Don't be frightened." He took another step toward her, and Mina could see that his hair was a dirty blond. "I'm here to grant you your wish. All you've to do is tell me what your heart desires."

"Oh, dear." Mina worried her bottom lip between her teeth. "See, that's part of the trouble. I don't know what to ask for."

"You don't? Well, that's a new one."

"I just can't feel like this anymore."

"Like what?" He advanced once more, stopping at the side of her bed.

Mina swallowed. He towered over her. His suit fit snugly across the muscled plane of his chest. She found herself wondering what he would look like without the black suit, what his bare skin would feel like underneath her palms.

He smirked down at her as if he could read her mind. And maybe he could.

"I lost them all." Any brief respite his presence had brought was snuffed out. "My whole family." The tears were building behind her eyes, but something kept them there. If only she could let them fall, then maybe some of this tension would lessen. But they stubbornly refused.

"Oh, Mina, no." The devil or demon, whatever he was, sat down on the edge of her bed gracelessly, as if she had just told him that his entire family had died and not hers. He scooped her up into his arms and pulled her into his lap so he could rock her, scooting so the headboard supported his back. "I'm so sorry." His breath tousled strands of her hair.

"Do I know you?" she asked, although she couldn't fathom what had possessed her to ask such a thing. Obviously he was a complete stranger and a thing that went bump in the night to boot. It was only that his tone had become so familiar and his embrace so comforting.

He dodged her question, responding with one of his own instead. "Would you like me to help you forget your pain? Even for just a little while?"

That is why she had called. Her plea for help had been answered, and she wouldn't squander it. But she couldn't bring herself to vocalize a response, so she only nodded.

He cupped her face in his hands and placed a kiss to her lips that, despite its chasteness, sent shock waves down her spine. Gradually, he deepened the kiss, exploring and inviting her to do some of her own. As she became more daring, he responded by infusing more passion.

Her hands lifted to the back of his head, and her fingers danced through his hair, massaging his scalp. She gasped when he bit her. Just a small nip to her lower lip and she came undone. Mina had never desired anything like this. She ached for him in her teeth. Her teeth. Good God.

That desire filled her. It became her. There was no longer any bit of her that hadn't succumbed to it. But there were too many layers between them. She shoved her hands under the lapels of his jacket and flipped it down off his shoulders. He helped her tug it off entirely. She wasted no time attacking the buttons on his waistcoat. As he shrugged out of that, she set to work on his shirt.

Once he was naked from the waist up, the demon clutched Mina to him. She braced herself against his bare chest as he undid her gown and corset. Tiny lightning strikes danced under her fingertips as she traced his hard contours. He felt better than she had imagined.

Cool air caressed her bosom. He had exposed her top half. The dashingly handsome demon gathered her skirts in his large hands and lifted her clothing over her head, dumping it on the floor.

He eased her onto her back, his gaze lingering over every exposed inch. "You're so beautiful, Mina."

That sense of familiarity roared back to life, and Mina cocked her head at him, trying to see him from a new angle. When their eyes met, Mina tumbled into green orbs flecked with stars.

"I could live in your eyes," she said.

His chuckle chimed with so much genuine delight that Mina found the corners of her mouth tugging upwards for the first time in days. But then he swallowed her smile with more kisses and distracted her with his hands.

He caressed from her neck to her collarbone before descending to her exposed breasts. As he cupped her, he tantalized her nipples with his lips, teeth, and tongue.

Mina jerked against him as the demon brought his hand to her sex, pressing against her core, bringing her more pleasure and joy than she could possibly handle.

She shattered against him, and he let her ride the orgasmic wave until it fizzled into smaller waves of ecstasy. Immediately, he surrounded her in an all-encompassing embrace that ignited a new spark.

And the memories of a dozen lifetimes flooded into her mind. She remembered the fires of Hell and God's rage as she turned against him. Her love for Lucifer hit her the hardest, like a fist to the gut.

She inhaled deeply, then exhaled in a howl that filled the room.

"Luci?" she whispered into his lips, pushing against his chest so she could seek out his eyes.

"Yes, my love. I'm here."

"You came."

"Mmm." Luci nuzzled against her. "You just came, and I want to watch you come again." He tugged at her hips, grasping them firmly and pushing her up the bed. He spread her legs with his thighs and descended on her core. His lips closed on the center of her pleasure. Sliding his hands under her bottom, he angled her so she was open to him.

Mina gasped as Luci slipped his tongue between her folds, lapping at her clit multiple times before slipping the tip of his tongue into her.

Another orgasm rocked through her. It was accompanied by glimpses from their past. Beelzebub whispering into her ear as she hung from the ceiling. Lilith reaching for her across a bed. Holding hands with Sindy as they stargazed at fake stars. The feeling of Alastor's chest shaking with laughter beneath her head.

Gulping, Mina fought back tears. She had another family, one she had forgotten about completely.

Luci looked up at her from between her legs, tilting his head to the side in an unasked question.

"I remember them all, Luci."

"Who?" He brushed his lips against her inner thigh.

"*Our* family."

"They will be sorry to have missed this," he said, kissing her again. "Are you a virgin, little human?"

"Of course I am," Mina said.

"I thought you might be. You are so easy to play." He dipped back to her center, pulling her clit between his teeth and slipping his middle finger inside of her.

"Again?" she asked.

"I'd like to fuck you before I go back to Hell," Luci said. "You need to be prepared."

"Will you—" Mina cut herself off with a sob. She tried to choke it down, but it refused. Her face remained dry, but the pain was bubbling up. And she needed it out.

"Anything," Luci said, sitting up and tugging her to him so her head was tucked under his chin and against his chest.

"Will you spank me?" she asked, closing her eyes tight.

"You want me to spank you? Why?" He brushed her hair behind her ear.

"There's so much pain, but I can't. I need to feel it."

"Shh," Luci whispered against her brow, pressing a kiss there.

He helped her settle over his lap, running his hands up her legs and over her hips and bottom. He spread her cheeks wide and stopped moving, stopped breathing, for a solid minute as he took her in, as she tried not to squirm under his gaze.

"Tuck your knees under yourself a bit," Luci suggested. "Yes, just like that. I want your ass in the air. I need you open to me." He caressed her again before rubbing warmth into her rear, her thighs.

The first spank came without warning, and Mina jerked with surprise.

"Don't you dare go anywhere," Luci said, placing a hand on her lower back to ground her. "You asked me to spank you, Mina, so that's what I'm going to do. I'm going to keep spanking you until you cry, do you understand?"

Mina nodded.

"If you have changed your mind, please tell me now," Luci said, rubbing her lower back with small circles.

"I haven't."

"If you do at any point, tell me." He leaned down to press a kiss to her hip. "Alright, I'm going to begin."

Mina had hardly registered the words when he started in on her. His slaps fell regularly, but they varied in strength. He peppered her ass and the backs of her thighs, letting the hurt build until Mina could barely stand it.

She felt herself slip to that space between body and mind. The pain was intense, but she could feel her arousal growing.

Luci must have sensed it too, because he slapped her vulva, the tip of his middle finger zinging against her clit. Then followed it up with a round of fierce strikes to her ass and her lower back.

It became almost too much, and she felt tears running down her face. When her sobs filled the room, Luci stopped, flipping her around so she lay on her back on the bed.

He covered her with his body and let her cry. She let his weight sink into her while the catharsis rushed through her.

As she began to come back to herself, she felt Luci nudge his way between her thighs. She bent her knees and spread her legs for him as he slowly entered her. The slight pain when he took her virginity pulled another sob from her, and she buried her face in his shoulder.

He held her for as long as she needed, only moving when she asked him to. They rocked together until she was coming again. Her muscles gripped his hard length, milking him until he had expended each drop of himself.

Afterward, as the sun started to peek its way into her bedroom, they lay spooning on her bed, watching the fire crackle in the fireplace.

"Thank you for coming," Mina said, kissing Luci's arm.

"I could never leave your call unanswered."

She managed a half smile. "I found *you* this time."

"You'll come back with me?" he asked, pulling the hair back from her face and peering down at her.

"You mean live in Hell?" She traced circles along his forearm.

"Yes. With me."

Mina nodded, turning to face him and cupping his face in her hands. "For the rest of this life. Until it's time to start over again." She kissed him.

Twenty-Nine

MINA LEANED ON THE kitchen table for support. "Fuck," she exclaimed, joy returning. And hope. She had hope—a new way to reach out to Luci. "Fuck yes!"

Her family was alive. No, both of her families were alive. And this time she was in a position to change her fate. New determination roared through her. She'd be damned if she allowed anything to keep her from spending her life with everyone who meant something to her—human or demon.

Mina quickly went around her townhouse scooping up anything that would make a worthy sacrifice. It wasn't as profound a grouping as she had managed a few lifetimes ago. But then again, she was living a pretty charmed life. She still had her mother, sister, and niece.

That probably meant she should be offering more. After removing it from its frame on her bedside table, she folded up a picture of the four of them and added it to a small gift bag with the other items.

She remembered the keepsake box in her closet. It was where she should have started. She dumped its contents and the contents of the gift bag over her bed and started sorting through it all.

The picture of the four of them was for sure going into the to-be-sacrificed pile. She was hoping that her connection to it and Luci's connection to her would be enough to get him on the first try.

The heart shaped brooch her grandmother had given her also got added to the sacrificial pile. It was a gaudy thing, a deep red surrounded by rhinestones, but she'd loved it at first sight. The thought of Luci wearing it pinned to his shirt brought a smile to Mina's face.

Mina picked up a small, plastic unicorn that she and her sister had purchased from one of those quarter vending machines when they'd been tasked with turning a bunch of loose change into cash, even though their parents had given them explicit instructions not to spend any of it on one of those "stupid machines." The unicorn had been their secret ever since. She added it to the pile as well. The memory would remain even after the unicorn was gone.

Of the items she had originally put in the gift bag, Mina decided to offer only one of her mother's homemade cookies. It seemed to round out the collection nicely. Something to eat, something to smile at, something to love, and something that connected Mina to her bloodline.

She hoped it would be enough.

There were a series of hiking trails not far from her home where she could easily find a secluded crossroads to bury the items. She just had to wait until dusk when the trails cleared out.

Mina put away the items she'd rejected and tidied up her room and bathroom. It needed it after her love session with Luci, Bellz, and Sindy.

Mina's car was the only one in the parking lot as she set out down the main path. A family was loading up their car when she arrived, but they left before she made it past the line of trees at the edge of the trail.

It didn't take long before she came to the first fork in the road, branching into three diverging paths. She could keep going, but she truly doubted that she'd be interrupted at this point. So she stopped and pulled out a small spade, dug a hole in the middle of the trail, plopped in her little offering, and buried it.

Standing up, she spun around, hoping to find any sign of her paramour. Biting her lip, Mina sighed. No Luci. Maybe it would just take a minute. Finding a tree to settle against, she sat on the soft ground just to the side of the well-manicured path.

As Mina watched the sky turn purple and orange, she wondered if Luci would find her at home if she gave up on waiting. He did it before, but that crossroads was less than a mile from her home at the time. This was within driving distance but was certainly farther away than a field in her own backyard.

Someone sat down next to Mina, their shoulder brushing hers as they leaned back against the tree. Mina glanced over to find blond hair and rugged features.

"It worked."

"It sure did." Luci glanced pointedly at the brooch pinned to his shirt. It was quite possibly the cutest and sexiest thing he had ever worn.

"Sometimes I think you can read my mind."

"Maybe sometimes I can."

"Will you come home with me?"

"Of course, but we could fuck in the woods first."

Mina shook her head. "That's a no-go. A forest ranger is bound to investigate my vehicle being here if it's not gone soon." She stood to leave, reaching out a hand to help him to his feet. He clasped it but didn't budge.

"I'm sorry. Did you forget who's courting you?" He pressed the back of her hand to his lips and deposited a kiss, eyes sparkling as he peered up at her.

"Of course not." Mina tilted her head to the side. "Courting?" She raised an eyebrow at him, but he shrugged it off.

"You clearly need to be reminded of my powers. I have full range of them, being summoned."

"Ok, and?" Mina prodded.

"No one is going to find us if I don't want them to." His smirk proved a perfectly timed distraction as he stood, tugging her to him. She fell against his chest, heart pounding as he spun her and pressed her back against the tree, bracing his hands on either side of her head.

Her tongue flicked out against her bottom lip in anticipation, pulse thumping loudly in her ears, thrilling at being caged in by him.

"Things to never tell a girl on the first date."

"Mmm, you like a little bit of fear, though." Luci nuzzled into the side of her neck, treating her to tickling kisses. She squirmed against him. "How did you get me back here so quickly?" His whisper against her ear just made her wiggle more.

"I remembered this trick from a previous life. You didn't tell me that I have chosen to live with you in the past."

"Those were never ideal. A lifetime with me, yes, but still a lifetime of pain. I would rather have you not remember those times." He pulled back to look at her, sadness coloring his face as the sky shifted from purple to dark, dull blue.

She caressed his cheek with her palm and kissed him, hoping he could taste her love. It was a burden, all the memories that he kept on his own. And it broke her heart to think that she was incapable of fully sharing it.

"I wish I could do more," she whispered against his open mouth.

"Something about you is different this time, Mina."

"How do you mean?"

"You're so brave. You could have summoned anyone."

"No one I couldn't handle. I love you, Luci. I want to be with you. I'm willing to risk the wrath of all of Hell for you."

"That," Luci said, mouth brushing her nose, "is exactly what I mean. You've always been strong willed, but this is on a different level."

"I think I've just been so desperately sick of not getting what I need. I didn't know it, but I've been looking for you my whole life. I'm sure as fuck not going to let you go now."

Luci's growl was possessive. He stepped closer to her, lifting her right leg and wrapping it around his hip. His hardness pressed against her, and she let out an embarrassingly loud moan.

Using the tree for support, he lifted her, bringing his package into contact with her sex.

"I'm going to have you, Mina," Despite the thick denim of his jeans, she could feel every curve and contour of him as he pushed against her. "Right here against this tree."

Mina laced her fingers through his hair. Her bottom lip quivered at the thought of having him inside her. His eyes flicked to her mouth, and he rewarded her with that cocky smile she loved so much, heat blazing in his eyes.

"If you have any objections, you better tell me now."

"Do your worst."

"You might regret it." The glint in his eye sent chills down her spine. He used his body to hold her roughly against the tree, giving him free rein to grab her wrists and hold them above her head.

"I dare you to make me regret it." The consistency of three branches shifted, becoming more pliable as they slid down the trunk to wrap around her wrists and bind her to the tree's trunk.

Luci stepped back, gently placing her back on the ground. Her arms stretched above her as she stood on her toes. He dropped to his knees. The clasp at the front of her jeans proved little challenge for him, and before Mina knew it her pants were at her ankles and being tugged off her feet.

"Remember how I said that no one would find us if I didn't want them to?"

"Yes," Mina said. "That was only about ten minutes ago."

Luci grabbed her chin in a near-bruising grip. "Cheeky minx." He forced her head to the side and licked her cheek menacingly. "What if I want them to find you?"

"You wouldn't."

"The forest ranger is doing her final rounds. She'll be at the parking lot in mere moments. And I think she would find the sight of you highly erotic."

"Have you shared me with another human before?"

"Who said I mean to share you?" Luci pushed her sweater up above her breasts. The chilly night air tightened her nipples into hard points. A small branch worked its way around her top to keep it from sliding back down.

"Maybe I'll just let her watch as a phantom force has its way with you."

"A phantom force?"

"Well, I can't very well have her seeing me now, can I?"

"Why not? You are definitely worth being seen."

"She's not into men." Luci shrugged. "I like that you chose to go braless, by the way." He flicked her stiff nipple then tugged.

Luci once more knelt before her, this time to remove her panties. He spun them around a finger before letting them fly into a nearby bush.

"Hey, I liked those."

"Is that regret?" Luci asked, light in his eyes and excitement in his voice.

"Uh, crap." Mina pursed her lips. "No?"

"Yeah, I don't believe you. I win. What should my prize be?"

Mina wiggled her eyebrows at him.

"No. That won't do. I was already going to have you."

"Are you really going to celebrate such a small victory? Regret over a lost pair of panties that can pretty easily be replaced? I think you can do better."

Mina tugged at the branches in a futile attempt to free herself. She knew that Luci would enjoy watching her squirm, and being trapped gave her a thrill that pooled below her belly. She tugged a little harder. Splinters dug against her wrist, and moisture pooled between her legs.

"So brave, taunting the Prince of Darkness like that. I almost believe that you have no idea what you are getting yourself into. But that can't be right."

He reached for her, and Mina's breath caught as she waited for the contact. But he only brushed the hair from her face. His smirk expanded into a grin as disappointment spread across her face.

Luci traced the outline of her body, coming within millimeters of her skin but oh so carefully not making contact. His fingers hovered before her nipples. They grew harder as if straining for him.

"Truly, Luci, the only thing I will regret is you not touching me." She whimpered with frustration. Sparks danced across her flesh as he moved from her breasts to her hip and across her stomach. There was the heat of him and electric anticipation, but nothing else.

"Is that what you want, gorgeous?" He blew across her neck.

"Of course it is."

Something rough wrapped around her ankles, pulling her legs apart. Mina glanced down to find two more branches spreading her limbs.

"Then I guess you shouldn't have poked the bear." Luci's hand slipped between her legs, hovering below her. He reached his middle finger up toward her clit and stopped short.

Mina bit back her bratty retort. She'd likely already pushed him too far. And she needed his goddamned hands on her.

"This is worse than any torture Bellz has put me through."

"You shouldn't have underestimated me."

Mina couldn't fight her smile. "I didn't."

Luci's hovering hand jerked back as he startled. He straightened his spine and peered at her. Her smile must have been contagious, because he responded with one of his own.

And then he finally touched her—a loving caress to the cheek. He lowered his lips to hers, lingering above her for only a moment before capturing her in a passionate kiss. The fingers of his other hand traced light circles on her hip.

He pressed his knee between her legs. "You are wet, and I've barely touched you."

Mina moaned. *I'm wet because you barely touched me.* She didn't say it aloud, but he smirked at her like he'd heard it all the same.

Luci gathered her hair and tugged her head back. His mouth descended upon her exposed neck and nipped at the vulnerable flesh there.

His finger played with her pussy, teasing her folds before testing her entrance. When Luci finally slid inside, she was thankful for the branches holding her up. Her knees wobbled as his thumb brushed against her clit.

"Please, Luci. I need you."

"You have me." He bent his head to suck on a nipple.

"No. I need that hard cock of yours."

He hummed as he sucked on the other nipple then drew back to assess them. Mina watched helplessly as he pulled a pair of chained nipple clamps from the back pocket of his black jeans.

"Please."

Luci dangled the clamps between his fingers then adeptly attached each clamp behind her nipples with one hand. He had to have used some of his demonic magic for that trick. They were alligator clips and damn near impossible to tighten without being held in place. So what if it was kind of cheating? It was hot as Hell.

"Luci, please. What do you want? More of my soul? I will gladly give you every bit of me."

The pad of his fingers ground against her g-spot as he pressed his thumb more firmly against her clit. "I want you to come."

Mina barely registered what he said. The pleasure was too much, but it continued to build. The cliff she desperately needed to tumble over just out of reach.

He tugged on the chain connecting the nipple clamps, and the pain heightened the pleasure. It cascaded, breaking against her nerve endings, across her spine, through her core.

"That's my girl." Luci closed any remaining space between them, and his bare skin met her chest. When had he had time to remove his clothes? He was relying pretty heavily on those powers of his today. Not that she was complaining.

If she were complaining, it would be to protest her inability to touch him. Her longing to run her fingers, her tongue, over every inch of him was overwhelming. As soon as she was free from this tree, she would worship him properly.

Luci replaced his fingers with the hard length of his cock in one fluid motion. The branches pulled Mina's legs up and out as Luci supported her ass in the palms of his hands. Her legs were forcefully wrapped around Luci's waist, tilting her so that Luci brushed against her g-spot with each thrust.

She arched into him as her mouth parted in a silent moan. Her desire to touch him only increased, and she trembled with it. "Luci, please."

"What do you want now?" he mocked, his rhythm steady and fierce. The bark of the tree bit into Mina's back with each beat.

"To touch you." He was close enough that she could place kisses along his cheek and jaw, but it wasn't enough.

He turned his head and kissed her. Their lips collided and tongues danced.

The branches around her wrists slipped away, and she immediately wrapped her arms around Luci. She caressed the back of his head, her fingers feathering through his hair. She traced his spine with the tips of her fingers.

She flattened her palm against the straining muscles of his back and clutched him to her. Even though she knew she could not keep him here with her forever by her will alone, she'd do everything in her power to let him know that she never wanted to go without him.

His movements became more frantic as he ground her clit beneath his palm and pulled down on the nipple clamp's chain. She knew he was getting close. The thought of him spilling his seed inside her drove her into the clutches of another orgasm, and her inner walls clamped around his dick.

She got her wish then. His face flushed as he cursed, and his eyes rolled back. He came apart inside her.

The branches around her legs and ankles slipped away. Luci caught her and lowered them both to the ground. He brushed her hair back from her face and kissed her gently before tucking her against his chest.

Mina nuzzled against her demon lover, her soulmate. "How long do I get to keep you this time?"

"Shh," Luci said. "Did you mean it before?"

"What?"

"You'll not let me go?"

"Not if I can help it." She squeezed him to emphasize the depth of her feelings.

"There's something I have to do, then." He swallowed, and his intensity alarmed her.

She propped herself up on an elbow, balancing her chin in the palm of her hand to look at him more easily. Her arm still lay draped across his chest. "Something dangerous?"

"Not inherently." He winced a little under her scrutiny.

"But there's a chance."

"Yes," he said, finally making eye contact.

"Can you bring help? I'm sure Bellz—"

He cut her off, "It's really the kind of thing one does alone."

"Oh."

"You shouldn't try to summon me either for a bit."

"For how long?"

"Give me one Earth week."

"Can you at least stay until morning?" The thought of waking up in his arms and sharing breakfast warmed her. The chill of the night had already set in, but she was only just starting to feel it.

"Yes." He pulled her on top of him. "That I can do."

"Good." Mina kissed his chin.

"But can I drive us home? I've never driven before."

She narrowed her eyes at him. "That seems like a terrible idea."

"I promise not to kill you."

"Again, you mean?"

"Again?"

"Yes, you have to promise not to kill me *again*."

"That doesn't count," Luci said, pressing a kiss to her forehead. "It didn't stick."

Thirty

MINA HAD WOKEN UP in Luci's arms the following morning. After a scary drive home that luckily ended without damaging lives or property, they'd stayed up late talking and making love. She had worshiped every square inch of him by the time they had passed out together.

Waking up with him in her townhome had been a dream come true. Even if she experienced it a thousand days in a row, she'd never get used to it or take it for granted.

But their domestic bliss didn't last. He'd left quickly after breakfast, determined to carry out his important tasks. He had not given her any more details.

That had been almost a week ago. A week she'd spent in her art studio trying to capture the likenesses of her demon lovers with varying success. She'd just finished cleaning her brushes for the day when her phone rang.

"Tabitha! How are you?"

"I'm good, Aunt Mina." Tabitha took a steadying breath. "But I need your help with something. Can you pick me up from school?"

"Of course, kiddo." Glancing at the clock, Mina realized that school had ended fifteen minutes ago. "You didn't take the bus home?" Mina plopped down on the couch, struggling to put on her sneakers. She balanced the phone on her shoulder and her ankle on her knee as she fumbled with her laces.

"I stayed after so I could get homework for my classmate, Juliane."

"Alright. I'm leaving now." Mina hopped up from the couch, grabbed her purse and keys from the table in the entryway, and headed for her car.

There was no pickup line by the time Mina arrived at Tabitha's middle school. Just a lonely girl with an extra pile of books in her arms. Mina put the car in park and reached over the console to open the door.

Mina helped Tabitha toss her book bag in the backseat. Her niece sat down on the front seat with her friend's homework in her lap and fastened her seat belt.

"Do you need me to take you by Juliane's house?"

"No." Tabitha shook her head. "She lives on the other end of the block. I'll walk over before dinner."

"Are you two close, or did you get volunteered because it was convenient?"

"Eh, I wouldn't say that we are close, but we are both weird in similar ways. So we often team up for school projects."

Mina hummed, waiting for Tabitha to say more.

"She's pretty cool, I guess, but guarded. At least she has been this year. Last year she was all into witchcraft and Ouija boards—"

"You've been messing with Ouija boards?"

"I'm an American preteen, of course I have."

"You do know that that's dangerous, right?"

"Not when you don't get blood on the board, Aunt Mina," Tabitha said in a pointed tone.

"Please tell me you don't know more about my use of a spirit board than that. Seriously, Tabitha. There is a lot about my time with demons that is not suitable."

"Ewwww," Tabitha said. "Gross. I would never go looking for anything like that!"

"Good," Mina said and then, after a beat, added, "Promise me you'll try and hold onto your innocence for as long as possible."

"I promise," Tabitha said, and Mina could practically hear her rolling her eyes.

"Yeah, that seemed sincere."

"No, really. I do promise. It's just that, well, it's part of why I called you and not Mom."

Mina pulled up outside of her family home where Tabitha lived with Dahlia and Sandra, located in a very nice neighborhood that they could afford, at least in part, because of the life insurance plan that Mina's father had had the foresight to buy.

Mina turned off the car and focused on her niece. "What's going on, kiddo?"

"I'm worried about Juliane. I don't think she's just sick."

"Have you heard something, or is this a gut feeling?"

"A bit of both." Tabitha twisted a strand of hair around her finger nervously. "She owns the Ouija board, and the morning after we used it last, which was months ago," Tabitha held up her hands defensively, "she stopped talking to me or our friends. She's always writing in her journal."

"Okay, well, she could be going through something. You are at the age when hormones might start affecting kids in your class."

Tabitha nodded and then shook her head. "I've seen some of what's in her journal. It's dark. Demonic, maybe, even. And not in the friendly demonic Sindy kind of way, either."

Mina caught sight of her sister in the window and knew that she'd be on her way out to greet them momentarily. "So, what conclusions are you jumping to?"

"I think Juliane might be possessed. That's why she hasn't been at school in the last week."

"Oh, wow." There was no way that Luci would sanction possession. Especially not of a minor. She knew that without a shadow of a doubt. But he had said that there were plenty of demons who didn't follow him anymore. Could a rogue demon have enough juice to possess a little girl?

"I'm going to try and see her when I drop off her homework," Tabitha said.

"Be careful, Tabby." Mina hurried her speech as Dahlia was now closing the front door and making her way toward them. "I know Bellz gave you that protection spell, but there are still plenty of ways to get hurt indirectly."

"I will be," Tabitha said as Dahlia opened Tabitha's car door. "I promise."

"Mina! What a surprise," Dahlia said. She then turned her attention to Tabitha. "I was worried when you didn't get off the bus. You didn't think to text me?"

"I thought I did," Tabitha said, pulling out her phone. "It failed to send." She held the phone out for her mom to see.

"Double check next time, please," Dahlia said, hands on her hips.

Mina came around to the other end of the car to help Tabitha with the extra load and to give her sister a hug.

"You're staying for dinner, aren't you?" Dahlia asked, mid-hug.

"Sure." It would be nice to be with family. "Is Mom here?"

Dahlia nodded. Mina missed their noise. Having her own place was great, and imperative given her most recent hobby, but it could get lonely.

"Tabby, I'll take your backpack inside if you want to head over to Juliane's now and drop off her homework," Mina offered.

Tabitha handed her the bag and nodded. She swallowed as she started off down the street, her posture a bit more rigid than usual.

"What was that about?" Dahlia asked.

"Juliane is sick, so Tabitha offered to bring some of her missing schoolwork home for her. I think she's worried about her friend."

"Hope it's nothing contagious."

"If it is, I'm sure Juliane's family won't let Tabby in." Mina slid her arm through her sister's. "Should we go inside and get dinner going?"

Half an hour later, Mina was setting the table as Dahlia placed large serving bowls of pasta and steamed broccoli in the center. Their mother sat at one end, tapping her fingers irritably.

"Where is that girl?" Sandra asked.

"Mom, she's checking in on her friend," Mina said.

Mina sat down to the left of her mother while Dahlia went back to the kitchen to fetch a drink. Grabbing her mother's plate, Mina loaded it up with a plentiful helping of food and plopped it down in front of her.

"So what's this I hear about you having a boyfriend, and when can I meet him?" Sandra asked as Dahlia walked into the room.

With a guilty expression, Mina's sister turned around to walk back into the kitchen.

"Oh no you don't! Get back in here, Dahlia," Mina said, staring daggers.

Dahlia shrugged as she slinked over to her chair and dropped into it, a sheepish look on her face.

"How does Mom know about my new boyfriend?"

"Your sister was nice enough to tell me. Is he that cute man who saved you on the yacht?" Sandra asked.

"Mom, that was the serial killer that I helped catch. I know I told you about that."

"I thought you were joking."

"It was all over the news."

"I only listen to NPR." Sandra shrugged.

"I got reward money," Mina said. "It's how I was able to quit my job and buy my townhouse."

"I thought you sold some of your art."

"The comic book I illustrated didn't pay enough for that, Mom. Not even close."

How did this conversation go so off the rails? It was infuriating. Her Mom was so good about prying where she wasn't wanted and then conveniently forgetting the things she'd rather not have known. But even as frustrating as it was, she missed this.

If she weren't constantly plotting ways to break her boyfriend out of Hell for a date night, she'd seriously consider moving back home.

"You are deflecting. Tell me about your boyfriend," Sandra said.

"He's tall, blond, and handsome."

"What does he do for a living?"

"He's an, um, administrator for a therapist practice," Mina said, cringing that that was the best she could come up with. It was kind of true. And hopefully would be good enough of an answer, and boring enough, that her mother wouldn't badger her with follow-up questions.

Luckily, Tabitha picked that exact moment to come in through the front door with a half-hearted smile on her face. Mina's stomach sank.

They didn't have a chance to talk at all during dinner, but as Mina got up to start clearing dishes, Tabitha offered to help.

Finally alone in the kitchen, Mina turned to Tabitha. "Well? What did you learn?"

"Not much, unfortunately." Tabitha pushed out her bottom lip. "Her parents wouldn't let me see her."

"Then what took you so long?"

"I might have climbed the tree outside her bedroom window," Tabitha whispered.

"Of course you did."

"I couldn't really see anything, but I thought if I waited late enough for them to turn a light on, I might be able to see inside. But they drew the curtains almost immediately after switching on a light."

"So, no news then?"

"There were some weird sounds, but they could have been coming from a TV."

Mina nodded.

"I'll keep trying."

"Do not break your neck climbing any more trees. Seriously, could you not have just texted her?"

"She's been leaving me on read." Tabitha shrugged. "Maybe I'll just tell them I know someone who can help with demonic possessions. See how that goes over."

"Not well, I'd imagine."

Tabitha shrugged and turned away, her posture slouched more than usual.

"Just be careful, please. You are loved by everyone in this house pretty intensely."

Tabitha smiled at Mina over her shoulder then rolled her eyes.

Thirty-One

MINA LEANED AGAINST HER bathroom counter, her mind reeling with everything Tabitha had told her after dinner that night. A week had passed since she last saw Luci. His special mission could be over. Either way, it was time to drum up intel on a possibly possessed girl.

Besides, seven days was too long. She needed to see him, and it would be worse for him. A human week was about a quarter of a century in Hell.

But after two failed summoning attempts, she was starting to get really worried. She'd even purchased another spirit board, but there hadn't been any answer. None. Not from Oz or any other demon. Complete radio silence.

So she'd put together a second offering and headed to the same hiking trail. But after burying the thing, no one showed up to claim the prize. She'd waited two and a half hours before throwing in the towel.

She studied the dark blue edges of her irises in the reflection of the mirror. Was she really going to go through with this? It was a stupid game kids played at slumber parties, more ghost story than trick for summoning demons.

But she didn't have time to try to scout out a bunch of bars for a potential demon-friendly haven. If Tabitha's friend was possessed, then she needed Mina's help and fast. Besides, there could be serious trouble brewing in Hell right now if such common means of communication were cut off.

"Okay," she said to herself, striking the match against its box. It flared to life, and she quickly bent to light the three candles she'd set out on the counter before blowing out the match and tossing it into the sink.

"You can do this," Mina said, willing herself not to think of Dahlia's eighth birthday party. She'd chickened out then, but she didn't have that luxury tonight.

Her hand reached for the light switch like it had a mind of its own and flicked it off. Only the flickering candles illuminated the small space. They cast creepy shadows in the mirror, and she had to fight the urge to glance behind her.

"Bloody Mary," she said, then paused to swallow. *Don't be silly. Nothing is going to happen. Probably.*

"Bloody Mary."

Although, did she want nothing to happen? What if she couldn't get in touch with Luci? What if Hell had been closed to her indefinitely?

This better fucking work.

"Bloody Mary," she practically growled at the mirror.

As one, the candles snuffed out. A wind whipped around the room. Someone or something had a hold of her upper arms. She was yanked from her feet and pulled forward. Mina braced herself for an impact with the mirror that never came.

Instead, she felt like she was passing through a cold pool. On the other side, she opened her eyes. She was bone dry.

She found herself in a poorly lit room, the floor cold beneath her feet. The arms that gripped hers were covered in blood, and it took Mina a minute to register who they belonged to.

"Don't worry. It's not my blood," Lilith said.

"Lilith!" Mina wrapped the demonic goddess in her arms and squeezed tight. "It's really good to see you."

"Likewise, but your timing is pretty fucking awful."

"Why? What's happening?" Mina took in Lilith's state. Aside from being covered head to toe in blood, she had a sword strapped to one hip and a handgun strapped to the other.

"It's Luci," Lilith said, and then stopped talking as she tilted her head to the side, listening.

Mina held her breath.

After a moment, Lilith relaxed, seemingly satisfied that they were still safe, and Mina exhaled. "He left on a quest, and he's been gone so long that things in Hell have kind of gone tits up."

"A quest? What kind of quest?"

"He's working on reclaiming all the parts of his soul that he's surrendered over his very long lifetime."

"Oh," Mina said. "That must be the potentially dangerous thing he told me he had to do. Bellz isn't holding everyone in line while Luci is gone?"

"He's doing his best. This is just a little skirmish. Shouldn't last much longer. But it would be easier to manage if I wasn't stuck babysitting a human—no offense."

"Where did Luci go to recapture part of his soul?"

"Well, he reclaimed a bit from Bellz and Sindy already, but he hasn't collected from Alastor or me yet."

"And I have some too."

"Yes, you do, but you get to keep yours."

"This is part of some plan to allow us to be together, isn't it?"

Lilith nodded. "I believe so. Without relying on you to give up your mortal life."

"Then this chaos is all my fault."

"That's not a particularly helpful line of thought, Mina," Lilith said, stepping forward and placing a kiss to her crown. "He loves you. The rest of us love both of you. We're happy to handle some chaos if it gets the two of you your much-deserved happily ever after."

"Can I do anything to help?"

"I could use a little extra juice." Lilith bit her bottom lip as she grabbed Mina's ass and pulled them chest to chest.

Lilith was at least six inches taller than Mina, so her breasts nestled atop Mina's. After paying them a slightly-longer-than-proper glance, Mina looked up at the dark seductress.

"Kiss me, Mina." Lilith ran her fingers through Mina's auburn hair. "Please?"

Mina rose up onto her toes and pressed her lips to Lilith's. Although she remembered next to nothing about her relationship with Lilith throughout her lifetimes, she couldn't ignore this pull between them.

Mina ran her fingers down Lilith's arm. She grasped Lilith's hand in her own and twined their fingers together, uncaring of the blood that squelched between them. Lilith's tongue brushed against Mina's mouth, and she opened to her.

Abruptly, Lilith broke the kiss, pushing Mina back with a saucy shrug. "Your tenderness is delightful." Lilith's smirk was as arousing as it was terrifying.

Mina gulped, taking an involuntary step back. She glanced down at her hand and her clothes. Anywhere that had touched Lilith was now stained with a light layer of blood. Demon blood, she assumed.

"Don't look so scared, Mina." Lilith chuckled. "I just can't hold back anymore."

Mina continued to back up with slow, small steps, as if she could convince Lilith that she wasn't retreating. Why was she trying to put more space between them? She wanted Lilith desperately.

Lilith snapped her fingers, and Mina tripped over a soft piece of furniture that had definitely not been there seconds ago. Landing on her back, she propped herself up on one elbow.

"Don't you dare get blood on my favorite chaise," Lilith said. With another snap, not only was the blood gone but so was most of their clothing.

Lilith now stood in only her combat boots, a red thong, and a black push-up bra.

"With a different pair of shoes and a whip, you'd be a bit of a cliché."

Lilith glared. "Would you like me to find a whip?" Her tongue flicked out to moisten her lips, and Mina was rapt.

"I want you to do whatever you want to do."

"Is that what you tell Luci and Bellz?"

Mina nodded, gulping. She hoped Lilith wanted the truth.

Lilith climbed onto the chaise, caging Mina beneath her. She straddled Mina's thighs with her own and ran her hands over Mina's stomach and bra-clad breasts.

Mina shuddered beneath her, reaching up to place her hands on Lilith's hips. She could feel Lilith's breath on her cheek.

They made eye contact. The brown of Lilith's eyes contained every shade of the rainbow, clustered so closely together that they blended to the deep, rich brown they appeared from afar. Like the rest of her, they were breathtaking.

"You're gorgeous, Mina," Lilith said as her hand caressed Mina's cheek. "I wish Luci would just let us keep you."

Mina didn't know what to say. She could complain that she wasn't an object, or that Luci's say in it wasn't the final word. But, honestly, she didn't want to bring any of those harsh realities into this moment. So she kissed her instead.

Lilith buried her fingers in Mina's hair and pulled her in. Mina unsnapped Lilith's bra and worked the straps down her shoulders. The bra hung from her arms, but Lilith, preoccupied with massaging Mina's scalp and keeping her in close quarters, left it.

Mina couldn't get a look at Lilith's breasts, but they felt amazing in her hands, nipples hardening beneath her palms.

"Does Luci let you use your hands?"

"Sometimes."

Lilith sat back on her haunches and tossed her bra to the side. "Hands above your head, please."

As Mina raised her arms over her head and let them drape off the back of the chaise, her breath caught at the sight of Lilith's naked breasts. They were plump and high, tipped with dark-brown nipples that pointed outwards. Her abs and arms were sculpted. Her shoulders strong. And even in just combat boots and a thong, she looked ready for battle.

Of all the demons whom Mina had met, Lilith was the most like a human. Yet Mina had never once met a human as beautiful. If it weren't for the desire to feel Lilith's hands all over her, she could happily stare for hours.

"Wrists together," Lilith said, her eyes devouring the sight before her, seemingly unaware of the rundown Mina had just given her. She wrapped her arms around Mina's torso and unclasped her bra, pulled it up past Mina's head, and threw it to join her own in the corner of the room.

With a silk rope, Lilith bound Mina's wrists together. Lilith then looped the other end of the rope to a hook on the back of the chaise.

"Mmm." Lilith let her head fall back in her bliss. "There's something addictive about having you at my mercy." She tickled her fingers down Mina's side to her hips. Hooking her finger around the waistband of Mina's panties, Lilith worked them down her legs and off her feet.

Lilith knelt between Mina's legs, nudging them lightly, prompting Mina to open them. With her hands on each of Mina's thighs, Lilith surveyed the territory before her before placing a kiss on Mina's labia and twirling her tongue against her clitoris.

"Keep your legs open," Lilith said as she removed her hands from Mina's thighs. With a recently freed hand, Lilith held Mina's folds open, giving her better access to lick Mina's center.

Mina flexed her toes as Lilith slipped a finger inside her. Lilith thrust the finger in and out, and Mina arched her back. Lilith sucked on Mina's pleasure nub as she added a second finger, then quickly a third.

Lilith fucked her human toy with her fingers. Pleasure built along the base of Mina's spine, and she fought to keep herself from thrusting upward, knowing what was expected of her.

Lilith sensed her struggle and placed a hand right above her pelvic bone and pressed her into the cushion. Lilith bared her teeth at Mina in warning, and Mina grew wetter around Lilith's thrusting digits.

"You're mine, Mina," Lilith said. "And I want you completely still for me."

"Okay," Mina said, shocked at how small her voice sounded.

"I want to have you the way he does," Lilith said while her fingers continued to piston.

"He's not here to stop you." Mina's voice did not tremble as she said it, but her body did, ever so slightly.

"Indeed, he is not." Lilith removed her fingers from Mina's passage. "Open your mouth." As Mina complied, Lilith slipped her fingers past Mina's lips and against her tongue. "For the first time since he left, I'm glad he's gone."

Lilith fucked Mina's face with her fingers, and Mina convulsed with each thrust. Lilith's fingers weren't long enough to slip into her throat, but the angle caused Mina to gag regardless. By the time Lilith pulled her hand free, Mina was drenched in drool and gasping for air.

She was also much, much wetter.

"You little human slut, you liked that." Lilith grinned ear to ear. "He claims to share you, but there's so much I haven't done to you. So much I still want to do."

"Like what?" Mina bit her bottom lip. She couldn't help but ask, even though she knew it would only encourage Lilith. Or perhaps that's exactly why she did ask.

Lilith brought her hand to her own mouth, covering it with saliva. She pressed her first four fingers into a cone, and slid them into Mina's well-lubricated vagina. Twisting her hand, Lilith spread her fingers wide.

Mina gasped as she realized that Lilith was trying to stretch her. And with that realization came the knowledge of what Lilith wanted to do to her.

Pulling her fingers back into a tight cone formation, Lilith tucked in her thumb and pressed forward. Mina's eyes rolled back in her head as the pain of the intrusion enhanced her desire. It took everything she had not to thrust her hips, but she managed to stay still.

The pain had almost become too much when it was surpassed by a wave of pleasure. Lilith's fist was inside her. Mina glanced down, in awe at the sight of Lilith's hand disappearing into her. Her muscles clamped down on Lilith's wrist as she came.

"Lilith," Mina gasped as she started to come down from her peak.

"I know," Lilith said. "Give me another." She closed her teeth around Mina's clit and bit down gently.

Mina crested again in an explosive orgasm that hit hard and fast.

Lilith breathed in Mina's moan. Her skin glowed and she cackled. "That was a rush." Gently, she pulled her hand free, rubbing against Mina's soaking vulva before giving the human's clit a sharp smack and triggering an aftershock. Lilith's eyes sparkled with purpose as she brought her glistening hand to her own mouth.

"I'm glad I could help," Mina said, entranced by the beauty of the warrior before her. "I'd love to help in other orgasmic ways."

Lilith shook her head. "Another time, when I don't have a war to get back to." Lilith slid her body over Mina's, nuzzling against her neck before she licked the sweat from Mina's brow.

"Will you tell me about our time together?" Mina asked as Lilith untied her hands. "During our first lifetime together, I mean."

Mina sat up, snuggling into the corner of the chaise, and Lilith settled beside her.

"Let's see, Luci brought you by my torture chamber in hopes that you could reform me."

Mina draped an arm around Lilith's shoulders, tugging her close. "Did it work?"

Lilith's feminine chuckle vibrated against Mina's shoulder. "I was desperate for a solution. As you and Luci were falling in love, I was falling head over heels for Alastor."

"You and Alastor? I mean, I know you love each other. But romantically?" Mina drew lazy circles on Lilith's shoulder.

Lilith nodded, blushing a bit. "You're the only one who knows how I feel about him. Although I guess you only know what you remember."

"And does he feel the same way?" Mina kissed the upper swell of Lilith's breast. Hells, those breasts. Mina couldn't get over them. She cupped one lightly in her hand, and whimpered at its softness.

Lilith shrugged, her breath hitching slightly in response to Mina's fondling. "He's so hard to read. But when Luci brought you to me, I was in the middle of rendering punishment to his many muscular body parts."

"You were punishing him?" It was hard to imagine sweet, gentle Alastor doing anything worthy of punishment. "For what? Giving someone a hug?"

"He had been acting out in my section of Hell. Which was weird because he had his own section. Technically, we are in the same tier of the hierarchy." Lilith took strands of Mina's hair and started braiding them.

"Right below Luci?"

"Right below Bellz. Bellz has always been Luci's right hand man."

"But you're all still demonic royalty."

"That's for sure."

"So why was Alastor causing trouble in your sector?"

"I think because he wanted me to be in a position to punish him."

"Oh," Mina said, laughing. "Okay, I also need to know what he was doing to cause trouble."

"Moving people around to different torments unsanctioned, absconding with some altogether." Lilith shook her head. "Really whatever he could do that was so obvious it would catch my attention."

"It sounds like he has pretty strong feelings for you too, Lilith. Whatever they are."

"I don't know for sure, though. I'm assuming a lot about his motivations. Maybe I was just an inconvenience he was willing to suffer through for whatever his actual goal was."

"Why don't you ask him?"

"What? I can't do that!" Lilith sat up, eyes wide. She looked frightened.

"Of course you can. You have plenty of options. Sit him down and say, 'Alastor, do you love me?' Or write him a note and pass it to him in sixth period, 'Do you love me? Yes, No, Maybe?' Complete with little squares."

"What? That last bit felt nauseatingly human."

"It definitely is and is definitely adolescent. What's the worst that can happen if you ask him?"

"I'll be humiliated."

"Okay, but any more so than Alastor repeatedly and purposefully putting himself in situations where you strip him down, tie him up, and torment him?"

"I guess not." Lilith leaned back against Mina once more.

"So, how did I solve your dilemma?"

"Alastor and I started fucking, and then he stopped acting up."

"Yeah, you guys seriously just need to have 'the talk.'"

"'The talk?'"

"Yeah, the 'where are we going what do we mean to each other' talk."

"That's another human thing."

"That's a relationship thing, Lilith. Just talk to him."

Lilith bobbed her head then bit her bottom lip. "I'm worried about Luci, Mina."

Mina swallowed and nodded, but Lilith's words hit her like a gut punch.

"Will you keep trying to summon him?"

"If he's not here, I don't see how it can work."

"Maybe if I give you the piece of his soul that I carry. I'll ask Alastor if he'd be willing as well." Lilith stood up, dressing herself and Mina with a flick of a wrist. "I'll go get him. Stay here."

Lilith disappeared in a puff of smoke that billowed throughout the room. Mina was still coughing when Lilith and Alastor came through a door at the far end of the wall together. Mina hadn't noticed the door before, and as soon as they were through it, it ceased to exist.

"Couldn't have used a magical door to leave, huh?" Mina asked through teary eyes.

"Sorry," Lilith said. "I forgot that you don't *choose* to breathe."

"Yep." Mina stood up and awkwardly crossed her arms. "Oxygen, definitely a necessity." Mina tiptoed over to Alastor and held her arms out to him.

He scooped her up in a hug, lifting her feet from the ground and swinging her around. "It's good to see you."

Back on her feet, Mina smiled up at the gentle giant.

"Lilith tells me I owe you my bit of Luci's soul."

"Are you sure? I feel bad taking a piece of him from both of you. He loves you both so much."

"And we love you," Alastor said. Was he blushing? "But we need you to save our prince. I know he got himself into more than he was planning."

"Why do you say that, Alastor?" Lilith said, hand on her hip, eyes rolling. "Could it be that he isn't back, and he said he would be?"

Alastor tried to hide his smile, but he couldn't quite manage it. Lilith turned to face him, sighed heavily, and rolled her eyes again.

Mina sighed. They so clearly needed to have that conversation, but now was hardly the time. They had battles to win, and Mina needed to focus on figuring out how she could locate Luci and set about saving him.

"Can we get this over with?" Lilith tapped her foot impatiently, gesturing to Alastor to hurry up.

He placed his hand over Mina's heart. His palm warmed until it was glowing a bright white. Removing his hand from her chest, he held it palm up where a small orb formed. He lowered his hand, and the orb hovered in place. He flicked it with two large, green fingers.

Mina gasped as the orb flew at her. A warming sensation overtook her, and then the orb was gone. Or, not gone, but part of her. She could almost feel Luci's arms around her. Almost, but the sensation was fleeting.

"Thank you, Alastor," Mina said. Alastor promptly wiped away the tear that slid down her face with his thumb. Mina briefly wondered if they had a competition going to see who could collect the most of her tears.

"My turn," Lilith said, embracing Mina and pulling her in for a kiss. Lilith teased Mina's lips apart with her tongue. The glow started where their mouths met. When Lilith nudged into Mina's mouth, she felt the orb tingle down her spine. An unexpected orgasm set her nerves on fire, and her legs turned to jelly.

Lilith did her best to hold her up, but all she managed to do was slow their descent to the ground. Alastor stepped in, slipping an arm around each of them to hold them up.

Mina placed her head against Alastor's chest. "It was like he was here for a moment."

Lilith shushed Mina, smoothing down her hair.

"I'll keep trying to summon him as soon as I'm home," Mina said. Then she remembered part of the reason why she had been so eager to get in contact with Hell. "You haven't heard any chatter about the possession of a twelve-year-old, have you?"

"No," Alastor said.

"Why?" Lilith asked, her tone sharp.

"My niece has a classmate she suspects is possessed. Don't worry about it. I'll deal with it when I get home."

"Before or after summoning Luci?"

Mina shrugged. "Hopefully after, but, honestly, if a little girl needs my help, I'm going to prioritize that."

"You would put the safety of some yes-maybe-no note sender over that of our lord and corrupter?" Lilith asked.

"Luci isn't defenseless. This girl is, and for all we know her possession is a direct result of Luci not being here. He wouldn't want me to abandon her, and you'll just have to believe me on that given that I currently have more of his soul than either of you."

"That's already coming back to bite us?" Alastor asked.

Mina stood on her tiptoes and managed to peck the underside of Alastor's jaw.

The room shook as something exploded outside their little sanctuary.

"It's probably time we get you back home," Lilith said. "You have a lot on your plate."

"As do the two of you." Mina gave Lilith a pointed glance. *Talk to him.*

"Before you go," Lilith snatched a piece of paper out of midair as it materialized between them. "You can use this to summon him directly. But it is seriously risky."

"How risky?"

"It could kill you."

"Really, Lilith?" Alastor asked. "Luci is going to skin you alive when he finds out you gave that to her."

Mina folded the paper and clutched it to her chest. "I'll only use it if absolutely necessary. Now hug me and send me home."

Thirty-Two

MINA MANAGED TO TAKE a shower and put on pajamas before her phone started ringing.

"Tabitha, it's late. What's up?"

"I'm sorry, Aunt Mina. I just had one of my nightmares."

"A premonition-masquerading-as-a-nightmare nightmare?"

"Yeah," Tabitha said, her voice so reserved that Mina barely heard her.

"Was it about Juliane?"

"Yeah."

"I'll put on some real clothes and head over."

When Mina arrived she found Tabitha waiting by the door. She opened it quickly, ushering her aunt inside. The lights of the household were out. The streets on the way over had been empty and quiet. It seemed like their whole suburb was asleep. All except for a house on the other end of the block that was lit up like a stadium on game day.

Mina jerked her head toward it. "Juliane's house?"

"Yes." Tabitha removed her sneakers from the shoe trolley and sat down on the entryway bench to put them on. She was wearing jeans and a t-shirt.

"You don't need to go with me." Mina crossed her arms. She had expected to find her niece in pajamas.

"Of course I do." Tabitha stood up and tucked a piece of hair behind her ear. "They don't know you."

"I don't want you involved in this kind of thing. What if the demon jumps to you?"

"They can't. I'm protected, remember?"

Mina grimaced. It was true. She had even helped place the protection. But her stomach dropped at the thought of letting Tabby anywhere near this part of her life.

"You can go over with me and introduce me to her parents, but then I want you to come straight home and get some sleep."

"I won't be able to sleep not knowing if everything is all right."

Mina braced her hands on Tabitha's shoulders. "You're going to have to try, kiddo."

Tabitha nodded.

"You ready? Let's go."

They were quiet on the walk over, only the sound of their shoes scuffing across the concrete accompanying them, but their steps were hurried. Mina grasped her niece's hand in her own, and they glanced at each other. She saw her own determination reflected in Tabitha's eyes, the set of her jaw.

Mina knocked on the door as Tabitha rang the doorbell. A woman in a wrinkled pantsuit answered. The strong scent of coffee reached Mina's nose, emanating from the mug clutched in the woman's hand. From the bags under her eyes and the slowness in which she took them in, it was clear she hadn't been sleeping lately.

"Hi," Tabitha said. "This is my Aunt Mina. Mina, this is Juliane's mom, Bianca."

"It's nice to meet you, Bianca."

"What are you doing here, Tabitha?" Bianca sounded less than amused.

"My aunt is here to help Juliane."

"Juliane has pneumonia." Bianca crossed her arms across her chest. "Go home." Her inability to hold eye contact and the hitch in her voice made it obvious that her posturing was just that.

Bianca used her foot to kick the door shut, but Mina stopped it with the palm of her hand. "Bianca, with all due respect, we know you're lying."

A priest appeared at the top of the stairs behind Bianca. "Is Father Stevens finally here?" Even from the doorway, Mina could see that he was flushed.

"No, Father Nadir. Just some concerned neighbors." Bianca stepped backwards, allowing Mina entrance into her home with a shrug.

Mina shot a look at her niece. People don't call multiple priests for pneumonia. Mina poked Tabitha in the side to remind her of their agreement. Peering up to the landing, Mina nodded to Father Nadir in greeting. "You need some backup?"

"Desperately," he said.

Mina took a step into the foyer, motioning Tabitha to leave. Tabitha didn't waste a moment before turning on her heel and heading away.

"Can I please see your daughter?" Mina asked. "I think I can help with the exorcism. I—" she shook her head, "I at least have to try."

Bianca nodded and closed the door behind her. "I'm honestly willing to try anything. I'm not even Catholic. This is all my husband's doing."

Father Nadir gestured for her to come upstairs. When Mina reached the top of the stairs, the priest narrowed his eyes at her. "What, exactly, qualifies you to participate in an exorcism?"

Mina glanced at his collar, the sweat beading at his brow. "What qualifies you?" She cocked her head at him.

"I'm a priest." He blinked back at her.

"I guess you could say that I'm kind of a demon whisperer." Mina held back the bile that formed in her throat at the description. It was a gross understatement and perversion of what she shared with Luci, the others, or even Oz. But she hoped it was a concept that he could grasp quickly.

"Honestly, at this point, and with Father Stevens still a no-show, I would try just about anything." Father Nadir led Mina to a door down the hall. He sat down on an armchair to the left of Juliane's bedroom door. "I'm not sure how much longer that girl can survive." He gestured to the closed doorway.

Mina tightened her core and flexed her fingers before grasping and turning the doorknob. She noticed the smell first, like earth, sulfur, and human waste. Oh, this poor girl. She was tethered to the bed, asleep by all appearances, but as soon as Mina stepped into the room, her eyes opened. They snapped to Mina with predatory swiftness.

"Hello," Mina said. "Who's in there?"

"Who is this, Nadir?" the thing inside Juliane said, using the twelve-year old's voice. "Are you trying to tempt me with a mature body? Did you bring me someone else to corrupt?"

Mina laughed aloud. "That's the best you got? Oh, honey, you are completely out of your depth."

Father Nadir stood in the doorway, half leaning against the door frame in his exhaustion, his eyes plastered to the ground as if afraid to witness any more of the atrocity before him.

"Although I think you probably figured that out pretty quickly, which is why you are still poking at the priest instead of me." Mina moved to the bedside and smiled down at Juliane and the thing inside her.

"What's your name, mortal?" The voice changed. It was gravely, deep, and if Mina wasn't friends with multiple demons who sounded nothing like it, she would have described it as demonic. It exemplified what common culture assumed a demon would sound like and would easily fit in any number of horror movies.

"What are you willing to give me in exchange for my name, demon?"

"A name for a name, human."

"Deal." Mina grinned. "I'm Mina."

"Mina." The demon's voice shifted again, and Mina knew she'd shocked him.

"You sound like an adult human," Mina said, sitting down on the edge of the bed.

"Lucifer's Mina?" The glare on Juliane was frightening. To see that much rage in one so young was shocking. But Mina knew that the demon was trying to scare her, so she propped herself up on one arm and leaned back in a more relaxed position.

"What do you think?"

"Hmm." The creature squinted its eyes at her, assessing her anew.

"Your name, please."

The being inside Juliane chuckled. "In a bit."

The girl's skin was paler and dotted with sweat. Her hair looked hopelessly knotted while her breaths came in wheezing fits through very chapped lips.

Whoever this demon was, he was sucking Juliane dry. This had to end.

"Get out." Mina stood up. "Get out of her now." Mina poured every ounce of her frustration and anger into her command. That Luci was missing. That they were stuck in this ridiculous situation to begin with. That God was such a fucking asshole. That this little girl was just a pawn in a war she knew nothing about. Mina left no room for argument.

The demon shrugged as best it could before a blinding light filled the room. Mina brought the back of her hand up to guard her eyes. The light dimmed but did not completely diminish.

Lowering her hand, Mina was surprised to find a tall, bleach-blond man standing before her. His wings and flowing robes were bright white. A halo sat perfectly above his head.

Mina took a step back. "I'm sorry, what?"

The thud of Father Nadir hitting the floor distracted them briefly. Mina checked to make sure his chest rose and fell steadily before turning her attention back to the glowing being before her.

"God's not going to be happy about that. Hopefully apprehending you will be enough to make up for it."

"You're a goddamned, motherfucking angel?" Mina asked. "How could you possess an innocent middle schooler like a fucking parasite?"

The angel smiled more wickedly than even her Prince of Darkness. There was not a hint of playful mischief in it. No twinkle of amusement in his eye. It contained only pure, demented hate.

And for the first time, Mina felt fear. "You promised me your name." She fought the urge to retreat another step.

"All in due time."

"No, now."

The angel stepped toward her and swooped his arm around her waist. Mina braced herself against him, his chiseled chest so hard it could be made of stone except for the warmth radiating through his robes.

"What are you doing?" Mina failed to push him away, his grip on her too strong.

He snapped his fingers and the room filled with light. Wind whipped through Mina's hair as the angel tucked her against him, wrapping his other arm around her.

The light dissipated, and the wind calmed. They were in a penthouse suite overlooking the San Francisco skyline. They stood in a large family room filled with a couch, a loveseat, and an oversized chair. She could see the edge of the kitchen around one corner. Two steps led up to a large entryway and the front door.

The angel stepped back, his arms falling to his sides again. He gave Mina a funny look, like he was just now seeing her completely, and tilted his head to the side for a moment. A lock of hair dipped over his eye as he shook his head, his arms crossed.

"Name." Mina put a hand on her hip. "Now!"

"Michael." He pursed his lips and glared down at her.

"An Archangel to boot? You cannot be serious." She started pacing in front of the long row of windows. "How could you do that? She's just a girl."

Michael shrugged. "Her suffering guaranteed her a spot in Heaven."

"What? That's pure evil."

"She agreed to it."

"Did you use scare tactics? Tell her that Hell is some awful place where she will burn for eternity? That's not how it works anymore." Mina found herself standing toe to toe with the Archangel, her finger pressed into his pec.

His hand closed around Mina's finger. "It's your fault. You upset the balance, little human. You made Hell better, and God retaliated by demanding we pick up the slack."

"He did what?" Mina tried to pull her finger back, but Michael held tight.

"Of course you wouldn't understand." He lowered his face until it was inches away from hers. "There has to be balance."

"Not like this," Mina said softly.

With his free hand, Michael clutched Mina's throat. He worked her back until she stumbled onto the couch and held her down, her legs awkwardly angled off to the side. Although he finally released her finger, he used his free hand to hold her down at the hip.

"You saved Hell, but you can't do anything to save all of us. You doomed us." His eyes were wild as his grip tightened on her.

"Please," she croaked as her vision narrowed. It was like being in that serial killer's bed all over again. But this time, Luci wasn't in a position to save her. She clutched at Michael's wrists, his shoulders, neck, back, anywhere she could reach.

Her vision narrowed further, and she could feel her heartbeat in her temple. Abruptly, Michael let go, stumbling back. As Mina sputtered for air, her knees connected with the floor. She braced herself against the front of the couch. Struggling for breath, for control, for calm.

Michael tugged at his robes until they lay in a puddle on the floor.

"He gave me this rod," Michael said, and Mina glanced over her shoulder to peer at him. He was gesturing at the rigid length of his penis. Every bit of him toned, he looked less like an angel and more like a Greek god. Except for that proud cock, standing up and out, hovering many inches from his groin.

"What am I supposed to do with this, Mina? Why do I feel this desire all the time? Only when I find an innocent to possess and can abandon this form do I get any reprieve." He crumpled to the expensive rug, head on his knees, arms wrapped around his legs.

Even as a cough erupted from her ravaged throat, Mina's heart broke for him. He wasn't any different than all those demons she had saved centuries ago. They shared a creator; only their choices differentiated them. And he had been changed in ways he didn't have the capability of understanding. At least not on his own.

Mina crawled across the carpet and sat next to him. Tentatively, she placed her hand on his back, rubbing the smooth skin there in small, soothing circles. "I know you don't think I can help, Michael, but please let me try."

He moved fractionally closer to her, and Mina draped her arm across his back, nudging him closer until he fell into her lap. She wrapped her arms around his still-hunched form and rocked him.

"He never gave me any choice," Michael sobbed. "I didn't fall! I didn't fall!"

"Shh." Mina pet his head, her fingers slicking back his silky hair.

"Why is He punishing me?" Michael turned in her arms, and when she held his head to her breast, he sighed into her.

"He's not, Michael." She placed a kiss to his brow as he wrapped his arms around her. "He's just so self-involved that he doesn't think about the way things impact others. And he's so convinced that his vision for the universe is right that he has closed himself off to any critique."

"I feel like I've failed Him."

"Of course you haven't. If anything, he's failed you."

Michael turned against her skin and sobbed. She held him as tremor after tremor rocked through him. After a time, the angel calmed. Well, mostly. Mina glanced down and couldn't help noticing that his penis was still rock hard.

"Michael?"

"Hmm?" He peered up at her, his eyes clear. The hate she had seen there earlier was gone completely.

"Are you always erect?"

"Not always." He looked down, pink rising on his cheeks. "Only most of the time. I don't know how to make it go away."

"Would you like my help with that?"

He sat up straight and recoiled a bit. "That's what you do with Lucifer."

"Yes," Mina said, "among other things."

"I don't think I can go back to Heaven after meeting you. Suddenly my whole existence feels like a sham."

"Okay," Mina said, struggling to follow his train of thought.

"If Lucifer finds out that we lay together, surely he won't welcome me in Hell. And I'm not sure that I can live out eternity on Earth."

Mina smiled. "Luci, sorry, Lucifer, doesn't own me, and he won't mind if we, um, lie together."

"He won't?"

"No." She bit her bottom lip and Michael's eyes darted to her mouth like a magnet. "Although I should warn you that he might want to join us in the future."

Michael thought it over for a moment before nodding. "That is acceptable."

She laughed as he pivoted them so that she lay on the rug beneath him. Desire burned in his amber eyes. As he gazed at her, glancing down to take in the breasts pressed against his chest, Mina noticed the blush returning to his pale cheeks.

Other than his roaming eyes, Michael was stiff as granite. Mina ran her hands over his rigid back, hoping to ease some of his tension, but it had the opposite effect. His eyes froze up, too.

"Are you all right?" Mina asked, brushing a rogue lock of hair from his forehead.

"I don't know what to do," he whispered.

"Let me." Mina used her hip and shoulder to nudge Michael onto his back.

He was tall enough that Mina had to scoot down so her head was level with his nipples to have his cock easily in reach. She brushed the palm of her hand against him there.

He gasped, eyes wide.

"What do you feel?"

"Bliss, carnal bliss."

"Do you want me to do it again?"

He nodded meekly, biting his bottom lip in a way that was as adorable as it was sexy. Mina wondered what that lip would feel like between hers.

She caressed him again, and his eyes shuttered. Starting with her pinky finger, she slowly wrapped her fingers around his length, keeping her eyes on him all the while.

Mina pumped her hand around him, and he tilted his head back, letting out a deep moan that she felt rumble through the floor. He was purring.

"You still doing okay, handsome?"

"Don't stop." Michael thrust his hips into the air.

Mina moved farther down Michael's body and flicked her tongue out against the head of his penis. When she enveloped his length in the warmth of her mouth, Michael grew harder.

While continuing to stroke him with her hand, she took him into her mouth as far as she could. Which proved to be all the stimulation he could handle.

"Mina!" Michael grunted as he came.

She waited for the salty taste of him to fill her mouth, but nothing happened. After a lick, Mina released him.

"Humans can feel that whenever they want?" Michael asked, lifting himself up on his elbows.

"Not all the time. We have jobs and obligations. Hobbies. Other things that bring us different kinds of joy." She couldn't help the chuckle that erupted. From terrifying to adorable in the span of maybe an hour.

"But if you didn't?"

"We'd probably be endlessly trying to orgasm."

"And why wouldn't you? God really gamed the system in Hell's favor all along."

"Yes, but we're gonna fix that."

"Who?"

"All of us," Mina laid down next to him, pressing a quick, tender kiss to his lips. "Together."

"Can I touch you now?" Michael asked between gasps for air. "I need to touch you."

"I'd like that." Mina sat up on her knees and stripped off her sweater and tank top. She hadn't bothered to put on a bra when she left the house. Her nipples puckered in the cool air of the condo.

Sitting knee to knee with Mina, Michael cupped her breasts. His mouth hung open in shock. "These feel amazing. I would call them heavenly, but that would vastly underrate their perfection." He let their weight settle into his palms then jiggled them lightly.

Mina pulled her lips between her teeth to hold back her amusement at his enthusiasm.

Michael took on a faraway look. Mina tracked his eye line over her shoulder and found nothing of interest. She poked his forehead to get his attention. "What is it?"

"I need to tell you something."

"What's wrong?"

His reply took the breath from her lungs. "Lucifer is a prisoner in Heaven. He approached Gabriel about recovering the piece of his soul he gave them. They were in love, or at least they thought they were, before the fall. Before it pulled them apart."

"He's in Heaven for me." She clutched Michael's shoulder for support.

"Who else would he go to the mouth of the beast for?" Michael shook his head. "I'm an idiot."

"How so?"

"If I had fallen, I could have been the one to win your heart instead of God's chosen one, Lucifer."

"I don't think it works that way, Michael." She smiled at him sadly and brushed that misbehaving lock of hair from his forehead again before staring at the view outside his condo. "How do I fix this?"

"Why do you think it's on you to fix anything, human?" he asked, affection ringing in his voice.

"He's only there because of me." Mina thought about every story she'd ever heard about humans trying to reach Heaven. None of them ended well. Falling to Hell was a lot easier than climbing to Heaven.

"How do I even get there?"

"I can help with that, but I won't go with you. I'm never going back. Never."

"A second fall?" Mina asked.

"I think I'll stay on Earth, slum it with you humans for a bit."

"We aren't all so bad."

"That you are not." He gripped Mina by her hips and pulled her into his lap. "I'm going to give you my ability to move between Heaven and Earth." He leaned forward until his mouth met hers. His lips brushed hers in a sweet caress that made her heart clench.

Mina swept her tongue against his lower lip, urging him to open to her. His tongue timorously explored her mouth after she demonstrated with her own.

She felt a pinch in her back that turned into a deep burn. She arched into Michael, but he wouldn't let her break the kiss. She clung to it, to him, as the pain became more intense. It zapped up her spine to the base of her skull.

Michael held her as the pain became too much and she broke the kiss. "Hold on to me, Mina. You're almost through it."

Mina rested her head on his shoulder, the pain receding. She took in a deep, calming breath.

"Mina?" Michael rubbed her back.

"I'm okay. What did you do?"

"I have given you my metaphysical wings."

Mina sat up straight, turning to glance at her back, thinking she would find a pair of wings to rival Luci's. But there was nothing there. Just her normal, human back.

"Metaphysical, Mina." A set of gold wings unfolded behind Michael. "I still have my physical wings."

"How do I activate it?"

Michael shrugged. "Just think about it."

Mina thought about going to Heaven, and she could feel the glow growing within her. It hurt a bit.

"Whoa!" Michael grasped her hips to break her chain of thought. "You can't go to Heaven without a shirt."

"Who says?" Mina reached for her tank top and toppled off of Michael's lap. "A surprise attack."

"That would be a new one, but you'd encounter a bunch of angels who wouldn't know what to do with you. Except for the ones who were gifted with these bits." Michael gestured to his semi-erect penis. "You might short circuit their brains."

"Short circuit? Keeping up with human technology, eh?" She tugged her tank top back over her head.

"I think I'm only a few decades out of date."

"Can I take Luci back with me using this power? Bring him back to Earth?"

"You should be able to."

Mina kissed him one last time. "Wish me luck." She stood up.

"Good luck!" Michael chuckled. "That's the first time I've ever said that."

"Should I look you up when I get back in town?"

"Bring that man of yours around."

Mina nodded then closed her eyes and thought of Heaven.

Thirty-Three

MINA WOULD NEVER IN a million years have hoped to be so lucky as to transport herself right to Luci on her very first try. Maybe it was easier to locate him now that she possessed more shards of his soul. Or maybe it was just blind, dumb luck. Or maybe an angel wishing her good luck had granted it in spades.

Mina's heart broke as she took in Luci's state. He was chained—torn shirt, bloodied lip, and all—to the far wall of a cell. A cell Mina now found herself locked in. A cell from which she prayed, to whatever higher power wasn't God, that she could break them free.

His head listed to the side, supported by his raised upper arm, one leg crossed over the other, jeans ripped, feet bare.

She had never seen him bleed before. He looked dirty, disheveled. Mina's heart broke at the same time that a deep rage sparked in her belly.

"Luci?" she whispered, and his bloodshot eyes rolled toward her.

A pitiful chuckle emanated from his chest. "I'm finally hallucinating. Gabriel will be so pleased."

"No, baby." Mina took two steps before falling to her knees and cupping Luci's face. "It's really me."

"It can't be you. I might be losing it, but I'm sane enough to know that I'm in Heaven. Only place my magic doesn't work."

She'd never heard him refer to it as magic before. They were his powers, a part of him. That worried her. How long had he been here? She had no idea how time passed in Heaven relative to Earth or Hell.

Another problem presented itself. If he had no magic, how was she going to get him out of those manacles? It's not like she had anything she could pick the lock with. If she'd worn a bra, maybe she could have used the underwire, but she hadn't bothered to put one on.

She traced the chains with her eyes to where they were anchored to the wall. The ancient screws looked rusted and loose. Perhaps he could yank himself free from the wall. Or maybe if she tried to teleport them back to Earth, he would just leave the chains and manacles behind.

"You're thinking very hard about something, mirage Mina." Luci tilted his head to the side and smirked at her with one of his knee-weakening, panty-dampening smirks.

"Can you yank the chains from the walls?" she asked, pressing a kiss to his temple.

"I felt that." Luci nuzzled against her. "You are a very believable Mina. Before you disappear, wanna fuck?"

Mina looked at him with disbelief. They could worry about tupping when they were safe and sound in her town-house. Then she would happily fuck him for days.

"Gabriel just left. They won't be back for several hours. We have time," Luci said, reaching for her. He growled in frustration when he came up short. She stood, stooping over him so that he could run his fingers through her hair and then along her breast.

She inhaled deeply at the contact. His touch was a starry sky to a lost sailor, and just being with him after being so frightened for him was a strong aphrodisiac.

"I'd give anything to be inside you right now, Mina."

Well, that was that. No way she was giving up on that opportunity.

"Anything?" She traced a finger down his neck and chest as she squatted, her legs to either side of him.

"Hells yes."

She leaned forward to whisper into his ear, "You do realize that you are chained, don't you? You won't be able to touch me, Luci. I'll have all the control."

His eyes blazed as he trembled beneath her.

She smiled down at him as she stood up, swaying her hips as she did, kicking off her sneakers. Her fingers danced at the closure of her jeans, unbuttoning and unzipping. She wiggled out of them. All the while watching Luci watch her.

His desire for her was palpable. It filled the air, and she could taste it.

"What would you like me to remove next?" She was only wearing her tank top, a pair of lace panties, and ankle socks.

"Are those pineapples on your socks?" he asked.

"They sure are."

"Ugh. Those. Please take those off. That's entirely too cute." The twinkle in his eyes as he peered up at her betrayed the false annoyance in his voice.

She peeled off the socks, abandoning them to the disgusting floor. They would definitely be showering immediately upon returning home.

"What next?"

"Just take it all off and get over here," he growled.

Mina laughed, shimmying out of her panties and peeling off her tank top. She piled both articles of clothing neatly atop her jeans to hopefully help keep them clean.

"That's the last order I'll be taking," Mina warned as she undid his jeans and tugged them down past his hips. She didn't remove them completely, enjoying how they constricted his lower half a bit.

"Are you sure you want to play that game, mirage Mina? I'm liable to take it out on you later."

"Silly demon. You can't punish a hallucination."

Luci gasped as Mina wrapped her hand around his semi-erect penis. She worked it in her hand a bit until he hardened and grew to his full length. Hovering over him, she lined him up with her slit and then rocked against him, enjoying the pressure of the head of his cock bumping against her clit.

"Put me in, Mina." Luci's voice was full of gravely need.

"I will when I'm good and ready." She devoured his mouth as she continued teasing him with her vulva but pulled back abruptly when Luci bit her. "Ouch!"

"You are driving me to madness, woman."

"Coming from the guy who thinks I'm not real." Mina smiled mischievously at him as she tweaked her nipples. She waited for that spark of desire in his eyes to boil over.

Only then did she lower herself on his length, taking him completely. And something in her settled. She hadn't realized just how much she had itched for the sense of completeness only he could provide. She had to fight the intense urge to ride him hard until completion. Her need for him was intense. But she was determined to remain in control. He deserved a little taste of his own medicine.

And the punishment that would follow was destined to be divine.

Mina let go just a little, riding him hard right to the edge of an orgasm and then stopping all movement completely until his pleasure receded just enough. Then Mina rode him with abandon again.

She could feel her climax creeping up on her, and soon she was over the edge. She knew that her muscles gripped Luci's dick and drove him to his own release. So she rose onto her knees and pulled off of him.

"Mina, dammit." His eyes caressed her where his hands couldn't. He was enjoying himself. Enjoying her in this dominant role, if only for a little while.

Mina cackled in response but filled herself with him once more. She rolled and twisted her hips, working to keep him inside her as she did. His cock bumped against her g-spot with each movement.

This time when Mina came, they came together. Their bliss rolled on until they were both left breathless. Mina collapsed against Luci's chest, his cock still firmly wedged inside her.

If only she could be in his arms, back in his mercy.

She looked at him with pleading eyes. "Can you get out of those chains, Luci?"

"I'm not sure," Luci said. "Even if I could, what good would it do?"

"Well, for one thing, you could touch me."

"Good point." Luci studied the chains with appraising eyes.

"More importantly, I can get us out of here," Mina said. "But I'm not sure if the chains will be a hindrance, and I'm not willing to risk it."

"No one is going anywhere," a voice came from behind them, beyond the bars of the cell.

Mina watched Luci's eyes widen as he struggled futilely against his bonds.

Thirty-Four

MINA TURNED TO SEE the intruder. The figure with wide shoulders, small breasts, a tapered waist, and muscular limbs wore their pantsuit and fuchsia pixie haircut with perfect posture and confidence. Their stoic face showed no emotion as they stood on the other side of the bars.

Mina sighed. "Gabriel, I presume?"

"You know, I thought that I was going to find Michael trying to abscond with my prize for some devious plot or another." Gabriel crossed their brown arms and propped the heel of their foot against one ankle. "I'm surprised to find you here. Did he leave you as an apology gift?"

"An apology for what?" Mina asked, although why she didn't know. It's not like she cared overly much about the politics of angels. Her one and only priority was getting Luci out of this Heavenhole and back to safety.

"He's been undermining me since the very beginning. But I captured Heaven's number one fugitive. He must have realized, finally, that I'm superior."

At Luci's chuckle, a little bit of Mina relaxed. He'd seemed so freaked out a few moments ago. But if he could find humor, even sardonically, she knew that he held out hope.

"To say that you captured me, Gabriel, is a vast exaggeration. You didn't capture me. I came to you for closure."

"Oh, shut up, Luci." Gabriel rolled their eyes. "Did you honestly believe that I would do anything to help you and your traitorous lover?"

"I'm sorry," Mina said, placing a hand to her chest. "I'm traitorous? Seriously? God left me in Hell. He abandoned me for having an opinion."

"Your opinion was treason, human." Gabriel's glare tried to cut right through Mina. Instead it only made her angry.

"Fuck. You," she said, standing up and placing her hands on her hips. Gabriel blushed at the sight of her nakedness, but that only made her feel more powerful. More resolved to set the record straight. She wanted to see the look of shock on Gabriel's face when she told them the truth. And perhaps the news would be enough to preoccupy Gabriel long enough for her to gain the upper hand.

"Michael's not on your side anymore."

"What?" Gabriel asked.

At the same time, Luci said, "The fuck he isn't."

"I guess you could say that I recruited him." Mina eyed Gabriel until she located the small keychain they had looped around their right thumb. It was dangling precariously, just begging to be taken.

"You recruited him?" they asked. All right, it was a bit of an exaggeration, but Mina needed Gabriel distracted if her plan was going to work.

Luci chuckled. "Of course she did." He grinned at Mina, adding for her only, "Of course you did." He beamed.

"And in return, well, Michael gave me a gift," Mina said. She had to work quickly if this was going to work.

Mina closed her eyes, focusing on the space just to Gabriel's right. She hoped that this new teleportation gift worked within Heaven. With the possibility for time fluctuations, Mina didn't dare risk popping down to Earth and then back to Heaven. She really should have asked Michael a few more questions before running off.

In a bright flash of light, Mina found herself where she hoped to be. Right at Gabriel's side. She relieved Gabriel of their keychain with a quick dart of her hand and in another flash ended up back in the cell with Luci.

If he hadn't been chained to a wall, Luci would have been rolling around on the floor laughing. As it was, his eyes brimmed with tears.

Mina didn't dare glance back at Gabriel as she started trying keys.

Mina's heart sped faster with each key that didn't fit the lock. The seventh key slid easily into place. She turned it and heard the latch give.

She was just helping to steady him when Gabriel teleported into the cell.

"Shit," Mina said, tugging Luci in tight. He kicked off his jeans to keep from tripping over them.

Mina knew there had been a good chance Gabriel could copy her trick. But the angel looked queasy.

Gabriel took one step toward the couple, bent over, and dry heaved. So maybe angel equilibriums were a bit more delicate than her own. Thank Hell for that.

"You're not a hallucination, are you?" Luci stared down at her, and Mina had to crank her neck back to meet his gaze. "You're a real Mina."

"Did you get what you needed from Gabriel? Can we go?"

Luci shook his head. "They tricked me into thinking that they were going to give it back to me, but it was all a ruse to trap me."

Mina sighed, propping Luci against the wall. It seemed like he was regaining his strength quite rapidly, especially after understanding that Mina was in danger.

"Are you okay?" Mina asked Gabriel, who was straightening and wiping the back of their hand across their mouth. Gabriel looked pale, eyes wide and bloodshot.

"How did you do that?" Gabriel asked. After another failed attempt at movement, Gabriel ended up ass firmly on the ground. "I'm dizzy."

Mina crouched down to bring herself to eye level with Gabriel. "Are you going to give my love what you promised him? He gave you a part of his soul, so I assume at some point you had feelings for him."

Gabriel shrugged but averted their gaze.

"I know you have your differences now, but surely you can do a favor for an old love," Mina said.

"Differences? Is that what you think?" Gabriel's eyes snapped to Mina's. "We are at war. We have been at war for millennia."

"Do you know what Luci said he saw in me when we first met?" Mina asked.

Gabriel shook their head.

"Hope. For the first time in a long time, he found hope—in me."

"I don't understand."

Luci crouched down next to Mina. He wrapped an arm around her shoulders. "How does this war end, Gabriel?"

"You know the prophecy. The end of the war can only be brought about by the reconstruction of everything—reunification into His light."

"I think you are misreading that prophecy," Luci said. "I believe it says the war, when driven to its final conclusion, can only end in destruction. Mina offers us a different path, though."

"No more eternal damnation," Mina said. "No more rigid definitions of who is deserving of everlasting love."

"But all the evils of Hell have only spilled out into the other realms. You abandoned your responsibilities and left us to pick them up."

"That was God's doing, not ours," Luci said.

"Hell has been reformed, Gabriel. Now Heaven must be, too," Mina said. "I think God put a lot of his philosophy on how His grand design should be enforced, conscripting you into roles you didn't wish to inhabit. He had previously done the same to the demons, the angels who fell. Your brethren who fell. Even in their rebellion, they fit his grand design.

"I've said no more. Lucifer said no more. Michael just said no more. You can too."

Gabriel looked to Luci at that, a hint of sadness in their eyes.

"You have all just been pieces on His chess board. I'm asking if you want to be more, and find a way out of this mess together," Mina said.

Gabriel shook their head. "I can't abandon God. I won't." They took a deep breath before adding, "but I can give Luci that sliver of soul I carry." At that, Gabriel struggled to stand, and Mina reached out a stabilizing hand.

The three of them stood in a triangle as Gabriel said, "Lucifer, I will have to hug you as I did before."

"Really?" Mina asked. "Alastor generated the soul in the palm of his hand, and Lilith passed it to me through a kiss."

"We each have our own ways," Gabriel said.

Luci turned to face Mina fully. "Alastor and Lilith gave you their pieces of my soul."

Mina nodded, hoping he wasn't angry. "They knew I would come after you, and they wanted to make sure I was strong enough."

Luci's smile melted Mina's heart. But they didn't have long to gaze lovingly at one another, because Gabriel wrapped Luci into a bear hug. A glowy orange surrounded them before splitting. Yellow light poured into Luci while a red glow slipped into Gabriel.

The two simultaneously took a step back.

"I've long treasured whatever it was that we had, Gabriel," Luci said, grabbing Gabriel's hand in his own. "If you ever change your mind, know you'll be welcome with open arms."

Luci took a step away from Gabriel and moved toward Mina. He wrapped her up in his arms and held her tightly. His hand came up to cup the back of her head as she placed her head against his chest.

"You ready?" Mina asked.

"Let's get the Hell out of here."

She closed her eyes, thought of her nice, warm bed waiting for her at home, and succeeded in transporting them there.

Thirty-Five

L UCI CURSED AS HIS head connected with the carved edge of the canopy. He tore off his ruined shirt and flopped onto the bed, tugging Mina with him. She lay flat on her back, her head propped up on a stack of pillows. Luci rolled, resting his head against her breast and draping an arm over her abdomen.

"I can't believe you saved me," Luci murmured into her bosom.

"I can't believe you risked yourself for me," Mina retorted, stroking his blond locks, enjoying their silky texture.

"I had to get it all back, Mina." Luci said.

"What exactly are you hoping to do now that you have all the pieces? Or, at least, together we do."

"I want to bond our souls completely. Mix it all up into a homogeneous glow and then divide it equally between us."

Mina's core warmed at the thought of it. "That sounds rather permanent."

Luci propped himself up on an arm. "It is, but it's the only way I can think of that God can't separate us anymore. You can live on Earth, and I can rule Hell, but all either of us will need to do is think of the other to summon one another."

A wave of emotions crashed into her. Hope tinged with a pinch of fear that it wouldn't work, of what consequences it could bring. But love drowned out all the rest. She could be his. Really, truly his. Not just at night. Not just when she briefly died.

All. The. Time.

"If you don't want to do it, I'll understand." He tucked a piece of her hair behind her ear. He had mistaken her stunned silence for trepidation.

"No more scrambling to see you, and I get to live out my life with my family. But what happens after I die?"

"You'll be stuck with me forever. I don't think you'll even age anymore." He paused for a moment, letting that tidbit soak in before he continued. "One more lifetime with your family, Mina. Then you would no longer be part of their cycle."

"But we'd have a lifetime to figure a way around that." Mina sat up, her mind already working at the possibilities. Maybe there was a way for her family to leave the cycle as well, and they could spend eternity in their own little paradise in Hell.

"I can't promise that we'll succeed. But we'll do everything in our power."

"Including telling them."

"You want to tell your religious mother and Type A sister that you are in love with Satan?"

"If this is possibly our last lifetime together, they deserve to know why."

"Okay, so what do you propose?" Luci sat up, finding ways as she moved around to keep them constantly in contact. It was nice to feel so cherished.

"Do you want to bind our souls now?" Mina asked. "We can invite our families to dinner. Break the news then."

"Let's do it."

"Can we shower first? I kind of regret thinking of our bed instead of thinking of the shower when I teleported us home. I'm going to need to wash this duvet cover."

Luci gasped as he looked down at himself and took in his state. "Absolutely."

After they showered and shared a simple meal consisting of whatever Mina had around the kitchen, they collapsed on the couch in front of the TV. A long nap wouldn't be out of the question.

"So how do we do this?"

"You're going to surrender your soul to me, along with your body." The thrill of his predatory gaze zinged down to the marrow of her bones. He pulled her from the couch and ushered her over to the dining room table, a refurbished piece that she had purchased during her week waiting to summon Luci. He stripped her of her pajama shorts and t-shirt then gripped her by her hips and flung her onto the sturdy table.

Silken ropes tied her spread eagle, and Mina's breath caught at the way that Luci stared at her exposed core. "I love the way your lips fall, and the way your clit peeks out of your hood at the tiniest persuasion. You are already so wet for me."

Mina was overcome with her love for him in that moment. She'd happily give him her soul and every last atom of her being. He'd clearly do the same, his touch so full of reverence and love.

His palms trailed along her inner thighs, rising until they came to rest right below her wetness. Because of course she was already dripping for him. Just being the subject of his longing was enough to undo her.

"Luci, I'm yours. I've always been yours, and I will always be yours."

He crawled onto the table, hovering over her body, his weight supported by his knees between her spread legs. "Prove it."

His hands found their way under her ass, and he tilted her hips to his face before descending upon her and devouring her. He slipped a finger, drenched already with her juices, into her back passage as his tongue danced around her clit.

"Luci." Mina strained against her bonds. The feel of his tongue flicking against her again and again brought her to the brink. "Please."

She wanted to cry when he stopped licking her.

"Will you give me your world, your soul, your life," he asked, stopping mid question to blow against her engorged clit, "for an orgasm?"

"For an orgasm, for a life and eternity with you."

"That's not the deal." Luci smirked at her. "The deal is your soul for an orgasm."

Mina bit her bottom lip, briefly wondering if this had all just been a long con. The fear heightened her arousal, and then she tossed it aside. He had had plenty of opportunities to destroy her in the past. She knew without a doubt that he loved her. Maybe she even felt it in the bits of his soul she kept.

"Deal."

Luci's groan was deep and long as he fell on her, slipping a finger inside of her cunt, and bringing her clit between his lips.

Her orgasm and her soul were ripped from her in the same instance. She gasped as all she was left with were the few scraps of Luci's soul.

Her soul, a beautiful cyan blue, hovered between them. Luci sat up, pulling her soul into him. His head tipped back and he was coming, his ejaculation landing on her thigh.

The flecks in his green eyes sparkled as he gazed at her. "How about a kiss for those pieces of my soul?"

She nodded.

"I need verbal consent, my love." He said, smoothing her hair back from the perspiration that had gathered at her brow.

"Yes. A kiss for the rest of it."

His lips met hers in a conflagration made of his love. His hard length penetrated her, and even in her almost soulless state, she felt full up. Taking advantage of her gasp, Luci slipped his tongue into her mouth, filling her up there as well.

Tears fell from her eyes as she lost each piece of Luci's soul one by one, and she cried out. The only thing left in her was his hard length, his soft tongue.

It hurt to breathe, and for a time, Mina thought she was back in the ocean, struggling to pull air into her lungs with a body that wouldn't cooperate.

This was death. This was final.

The ropes holding her disappeared as Luci sat up and pulled her into his lap so that she straddled him while he remained within her. He held her tight and rocked her, cupping the back of her head as she rested against his shoulder.

"I know, my love," he whispered soothingly. "I know it hurts, but it's only for a moment." He kissed the top of her head. "Let me distract you."

Mina nodded as she ran her fingertips up his back, reminding herself that he was here with her. That she wasn't dying. He wouldn't let her.

Luci tilted her backwards until she was arched away from him and brought his mouth to her breast. He rocked inside her, making sure to knock against the delicate bundle of nerves just past her entrance. As he held her up with one hand, he brought the other between them to apply pressure to her pleasure nub.

It didn't take long before she detonated again. He followed suit, exploding into her. They were both awash in a green light. His yellow soul and her blue combined.

The large orb their souls created split down the middle. One half for each of them. They hovered over the lovers for a moment before descending and settling back inside them.

What she felt before was nothing. This was fullness—physically, emotionally, spiritually.

"You're my everything," she whispered as he lay her down on the table and curled around her. His wings spread out behind him before curling forward to cup around her and pull her closer.

Luci sighed deeply, his contentment covering her like a warm blanket. He was her home, and they could survive whatever God or life threw at them. The chaos that was sure to follow. Without a doubt it would all be worth it.

Epilogue

MINA STOOD IN FRONT of her full length mirror and admired her gown. The off-white satin bodice met a full skirt of the same material covered in red lace. Her auburn hair was half pulled up and out of her face but still caressed her back in loose curls.

Lucifer came up behind her, wearing a black suit with a red waistcoat that matched the red of her lace. He placed his hands on her waist as they made eye contact through the mirror.

"You look beautiful, my bride." He placed a kiss on her bare shoulder.

"My family will be here any minute," Mina said, turning around to face him.

"The Indian food is on order. And Bellz and the others are waiting in your studio."

Once Mina and Luci had melded souls, it had been easy for both of them to return to Hell. Luci hadn't completely managed to regain control there, but the progress he had made was promising.

Finding ways to summon the rest of her demons had been easy enough. In fact, she thought she was getting to be quite good at it and had already started plotting ways she could use that ability to help Luci rebuild his empire to what it had been before.

"You let them into my studio?" Mina asked, eyes wide.

"Sindy was upset that she hadn't gotten to see it the last time we were here." Luci shrugged. "They are all very flattered."

"I haven't been able to get any of you out of my head since we met. It's all I've been painting during my spare time." Mina groaned. "They aren't very good."

"Of course they're good. The comic book art is, too," Luci said.

"Ugh, you guys slipped into that work as well. Background characters mostly. I suppose you've noticed. That's where this compliment is coming from, right?"

Luci only grinned at her.

"Mmhmm," Mina said, "thought so."

The doorbell rang and Mina's stomach tightened, equal parts anticipation and dread. What if her mother disowned her? Her sister was going to freak out. At least she had Tabitha. Her niece would be on her side and could help smooth the way to acceptance for the other two.

Mina emerged from her bedroom and answered the door.

"Wow," Dahlia said, her jaw practically on the entryway floor as she took in her sister. "I am underdressed. Why didn't you tell me this family dinner was a black tie event?" Dahlia gestured to her normal weekend attire—a UC Berkeley sweater and yoga pants, her hair pulled into a ponytail.

Mina backed up, allowing space for Tabitha and Sandra to enter her townhome.

Tabitha kicked the door shut behind them. "Damn, Aunt Mina, you look hot."

"Language," Sandra admonished.

"Sorry, but she does." Tabitha shrugged.

"That she does," Sandra said. She was in a simple dress nice enough to wear to church, which Mina knew her mother had attended that morning. "What's the occasion, Mina? You look like you're about to get married."

"About that," Mina said as she led everyone into the living room. "Mom, there's someone I would like you to meet."

Having heard his cue, Lucifer stepped into the crowded entryway. He stopped before Sandra, and took her hand, bowing over it.

"Mom, this is Luci. Luci, this is my mother, Sandra."

"It's nice to meet you," Luci said as he straightened.

"We invited you over to celebrate. Luci and I just got married."

They could never get married in a church or in the eyes of the law. But a soul bonding was surely enough of a marriage rite to qualify them for calling one another husband and wife.

"You what?" Sandra asked, eyes round. She balled her hands into fists and placed them on her hips. "You married a man you hadn't even introduced me to?"

Oh, boy. This was off to a bad start.

"Your sister says she's never getting married. This was my one opportunity to help plan a wedding, and you cheated me out of it!"

Yep, this was going as poorly as could be expected. On the bright side, maybe her mother would be so upset about their elopement that she'd be too distracted to process the bombshell that her daughter had in fact married The Devil. And they could just dance around it for the rest of her life, deluding themselves that she really knew on some level. Just perfect. Or Mina could make this right somehow.

Tabitha waved at Luci, and he stepped toward her, pulling her into a brief hug. He whispered something to her, and Tabitha skipped off toward the stairs leading to Mina's studio. She narrowed her eyes at him before turning her attention back on her mother.

"I'm sorry, Mom," Mina said. "We can do a large reception, if you want, and you can help me plan it."

"Oh," Sandra said, then nodded. "Yes, that is exactly what we will do."

"Mom, Dahlia, there's more." She guided them to the couch and bid them sit. After they were both comfortable and Luci had joined Mina at her side, his hand in hers, she told them everything.

Silence descended afterward, stretching onwards until Mina grew so uncomfortable that her knees gave out, and she sat down on the coffee table.

Dahlia broke the silence, "You've lost your mind."

"Did you join a cult?" Sandra asked. "Is this man some cult leader?"

"Of course not," Mina said.

"Eh, I guess you could probably have made the argument that I was a cult leader back in the day."

Mina couldn't believe he had just said that, and she gave him a look that telegraphed her indignation.

He shrugged and then amended, "A reformed cult leader now!" And threw up his hands in defense.

An unwanted laugh bubbled out of Mina.

"He's not the devil, Mina," Sandra said. "That's ridiculous."

"You have. You have absolutely lost your mind," Dahlia said. She began to get up but realized that she'd have to come into too close proximity with Luci and sat back down.

"Maybe a demonstration would help," Luci offered. "You said you were feeling underdressed. I can fix that." He snapped his fingers, and Dahlia looked down to find herself in a beautiful green dress that complemented the red undertones of her brown hair.

This time Dahlia did stand up, pushing Luci away from her and crossing to the other side of the room. The dress was long and sleek, flattering her plentiful curves. Dahlia stared down at it before crossing her arms. Although Dahlia looked more than a little freaked out, Mina blinked back a tear.

"Dahlia, you're gorgeous," Mina said, taking two tentative steps toward her sister.

"I—this can't be real," Dahlia said.

"Why did you send my one ally away, Luci?" Mina stage whispered, whipping her head around to locate her husband.

"I thought she would like to be reunited with Bellz and Sindy."

"There are more of you?" Sandra asked, rising to her feet.

"Mom, it's okay. Luci and I are in love." Mina said. "The Indian food will be here any minute. I ordered all your favorites. Let's just enjoy it and get to know each other a little better."

Tabitha decided that was the perfect moment to rejoin the group, but with five demons and a recently fallen angel in tow. Her attire had changed as well. She now wore a pink dress and a beautiful crown fashioned from flowers.

Mina noticed that Tabitha and Michael were holding hands. Did she know that Michael was the entity that had possessed her friend, Juliane? Sindy stood on Tabitha's other side. They were followed by Bellz, Lilith, Alastor, and, surprisingly, Oz. When had they tracked him down? Mina had added him to the guest list, but she hadn't actually expected Bellz to find him and deliver the invitation.

He looked good in a cowboy hat and boots, a big smile plastered on his face as he flirted with Lilith. Alastor, who stood on Lilith's other side, scowled in their direction.

Sandra, Mina, and Dahlia all congregated in the center of the room to greet the new group.

"He's green," Sandra said. "Mina, your friend is green." She clasped Mina's arm in a firm grip.

"Mom, this is Alastor. He's as large as he is friendly."

Alastor's scowl transformed into a warm smile as he looked down at Mina and her mother, and Sandra's fear melted completely.

After too much food and a lot of conversation, Mina's family members began to relax. Laughter filled the air. So much laughter that Mina knew things would work out this time.

"Let's dance," exclaimed Tabitha.

They had just started to push back the furniture in the living room when a flash of memory struck Mina, taking over her senses completely.

She was in Hell, and Luci stood before her, his hands clasped around hers and a brightness shining in his eyes. He looked so happy.

"I've figured it out, my love," he said before kissing her hard.

"What have you figured out?" she asked, feeling weak kneed from the imprint of his lips.

"I think, maybe, I can get you home."

"What? How?"

"I didn't think it would work, and maybe it won't, but it's at least something to try."

"Can you please tell me what?"

"If I give you a piece of my soul, I think it will allow me to take you to Earth with me."

"Oh." Mina's heart lightened at the thought of carrying a piece of him with her. No notion had ever made her happier. Even if nothing came of it and she didn't find a way home, she would never regret saying yes to this plan.

So she had said yes.

And it had worked.

A different memory commanded her attention, and she swayed on her feet.

Mina walked hand in hand with Lucifer. His other hand held a flaming sword as they crested the hill above her family's home. Her small cottage stood intact, nestled in a corner of the valley.

They stopped to look down at it and smiled at one another. Beelzebub, Lilith, Alastor, and Sindy joined them on the hill.

"Have we found it?" Lilith asked.

"Yes," Mina said. "We're here."

She could see a figure working in the garden. Her mother, perhaps. When they stood, their posture stooped with age. Luci estimated that at least five earth years had passed since she had been left in Hell. Five years, and not much had changed except that her mother had aged.

A small girl ran out of the hovel, Dahlia tight on her heels. The girl looked no older than four.

"Who's that?" Sindy asked.

"I don't know," Mina said.

Dahlia noticed them standing on the hill then. She shaded her face with her hand and peered up at them. Mina waved and started down the hill.

The earth shook beneath her feet, and a hand, Bellz', caught her elbow to steady her. A crevice too wide to jump opened up between Mina and her family, cutting off her path home.

Gabriel, Michael, and other angels Mina had not met or could not yet remember descended from the heavens.

"Halt!" Michael demanded. "You have violated God's orders. The human should not be here."

He unsheathed the sword at his hip and held it to Mina's chest. Luci knocked it away with his own sword. Chaos erupted as the demons and angels came to blows. Mina felt Sindy's arm around her waist leading her to safety.

And then she found herself once more in her living room. She laid on her back, her head in Oz's lap. He looked down at her with concern.

"What happened?" she asked.

"You tell me," Oz said. "One moment we were moving furniture, and the next everyone just kind of fell over."

"Mina!" Sandra said, crawling over to her daughter. "Oh, Mina. I remember."

Dahlia clutched Tabitha to her chest. "How many lifetimes have we lived?"

"Somewhere around ten, at least once every century for a thousand years," Luci provided as he stood and dusted off his nice pants. He held a hand out to Mina and helped her stand.

"That battle. What happened?" Mina asked him.

"Let's not worry about that now. Let's celebrate being together."

"Okay, but tell me in the morning."

"I will, I promise. But first I want to dance with my wife."

Acknowledgements

A giant thank you to my readers. I hope that you love Luci and Mina as much as I do.

Thank you to my family and dear friends. Your support made this possible. You put up with all the word count texts and the overly excited updates at family dinners or over video call.

To my beta readers, Judy, Robby, Lily, Ben, and Amy, who gave me so much needed feedback and helped me meld this into something readable.

Thank you, Jenny, for all the great edits and for making my first experience with an editor such a positive one.

To the FFXIV mount farm crew, thank you for giving me an outlet to beat up a big, scary boss almost every week. The community we have created together means the world to me.

I started writing this book in the last quarter of 2019. When inspiration struck, it was like being hit by lightning. This was the book that my entire life had led to. From the podcasts I was listening to at the time (Box of Oddities, A Funny Feeling, and Astonishing Legends) to the frustration I felt as a kid in Sunday school because we never learned about the Greek gods, or any pagan gods, for that matter. I grew up Unitarian Universalist, so I did not believe this was beyond the scope of my spiritual education at the time. Thank you to all the friends and enemies who are no longer a part of my life yet nonetheless inspired me one way or another. You still live in my heart.

Thank you to the teachers who inspired me, especially my junior and senior year high school English teacher, who finally taught me those Greek myths and advised me that romance sells.

Thanks, Mom, for never growing tired when the words "what if" passed my lips for the millionth time, and Dad for always telling me to give 'em hell.

And a big thank you to the authors whose work has left a lasting impression on me: Katee Robert, Rebekah Weatherspoon, Kimberly Lemming, D.N. Bryn, Brooklyn Ann, Olivia Dade, Celestine Martin, Farah Rochon, Tessa Dare, and so many others.

Lastly, a big thank you to my husband for encouraging me to quit my job so I could write full time and then empowering me to find the time and space to still write when our two beautiful children came along.